Charles R Edwards

A story of Niagara

To which Are Appended Reminiscences of a Custom House Officer

Charles R Edwards

A story of Niagara
To which Are Appended Reminiscences of a Custom House Officer

ISBN/EAN: 9783743444027

Manufactured in Europe, USA, Canada, Australia, Japa

Cover: Foto ©Andreas Hilbeck / pixelio.de

Manufactured and distributed by brebook publishing software (www.brebook.com)

Charles R Edwards

A story of Niagara

A

STORY OF NIAGARA.

TO WHICH ARE APPENDED

REMINISCENCES OF A CUSTOM HOUSE OFFICER.

BY C. R. EDWARDS.

BUFFALO:

BREED, LENT & CO.

No. 240 Main Street.

1870.

WARREN, JOHNSON & CO.
Stereotypers, Printers and Binders,
BUFFALO, N. Y.

CONTENTS.

CHAPTER VII.

CHAPTER VIII.

CHAPTER IX.

CHAPTER X.

CHAPTER XI.

CHAPTER XII.

CHAPTER XIII.

CHAPTER XIV.

PART II.

INTRODUCTION.

——◦◆◦——

AMONG the incidents at Niagara Falls, and in life on the Niagara frontier, may be found the material for many an interesting volume that has never been written,—facts that are stranger than fiction; and events, which, however exciting in themselves, possess additional interest from their association with one of the most romantic and most famous localities in the world.

The traveler from every country who journeys to any foreign clime, is as sure to wend his way to Niagara as the Arab to make his pilgrimage to Mecca. Here have come some of the most renowned personages; among whom have been Presidents and Princes, and the Queen of the Sandwich Islands. The Europeans, the South Americans, and the Japanese, have paid their respects to Niagara. So have ambassadors from China, with their gaudy costumes, and long braided hair dangling from their heads in Oriental style. And then a score of Indians, chiefs on their way to Washington from the region of the Rocky Mountains, have paused to look

1*

upon the work of the Great Spirit, and upon the white man's bridges over the chasm! And while viewing the scene, with the serious gravity of the red man, have they sat in groups upon the banks of the river and passed round the pipe of peace, each taking a few puffs of tobacco smoke after their peculiar custom. Occasionally an Indian trafficker from some small tribe, not far away, can tell of the once renowned war-chief, Brandt.

And some of the Senecas here remember their celebrated chief, Red Jacket, who died near Buffalo, N. Y., not many years ago, at the age of one hundred years. It was Red Jacket who said to the missionary, that the white man's religion was not necessary for Indians, else the Great Spirit would have sent it to their fathers!

Nine miles north-east of the Falls is an Indian village of Tuscaroras, a tribe numbering about three hundred. Several interesting accounts of real life among this tribe are related by the white inhabitants near them, one of which is the true story of the British officer, who, many years ago, married an Indian girl of the tribe; a descendant of whom is now a well known Captain in the United States army. Known to many also, was the white missionary girl, who married a pious Indian of the tribe. Frequently has the visitor at the Falls gone to the Indian village and heard her Indian husband interpret the sermons of the white preacher. The wife of the present Tuscarora chief is a well educated Indian woman, and her brother is known to the people of the United

States as a gentleman of fine accomplishments, and who served with distinguished ability upon the staff of Gen. Grant.

The small remnant of Indians now found in this locality, seem, however, like some ancient relic of a mysterious race which soon will take their last look at Niagara.

Upon this frontier, time has witnessed the important movements of armies, Indian massacres, and the abortive attempts of Canadian rebellions. Here the political fugitives of one country have crossed for safety into the other; and criminals have left their own country—for their country's good! And still continue the expert and daring operations of smugglers, and the attempts of government officials to detect and capture them; the secret history of which will furnish all varieties of incidents from the amusing to the tragical, and from plans of successful strategy to plans of ridiculous failure.

Across this river the so-called underground-railroads once had several of their terminations; where fugitive slaves were landed from the United States into Canada, a work once secretly carried on by the anti-slavery men. Subsequently, during the great rebellion, the tables were turned, and the original owner in many cases became the fugitive, crossing the same frontier for safety where his former slaves had once fled before *him!* but could now return to the States for their year of jubilee!

The Niagara River is thirty-six miles in length; its course northward, and the center of the stream part of the boundary line between the United States and Canada. It is the outlet of Lake Erie, carrying the waters of the great upper lakes into Lake Ontario on their way to the River St. Lawrence and the Atlantic Ocean. On the shore of Lake Erie, at the head of the Niagara, stands the city of Buffalo, containing a population of one hundred and twenty thousand inhabitants, which are principally of English and German descent.

From Lake Erie to the Falls the distance is twenty-two miles; the river in no place less than three-fourths of a mile in width; the banks low, and the surrounding country comparatively level.

Five miles before reaching the Falls the little village of La Salle stands upon the American shore. At this place was constructed the first vessel that ever navigated Lake Erie or the upper lakes. It was sixty tons burden, and built in 1679, by Robert La Salle, a Frenchman, who, a little before this time, had established trading posts here and at the mouth of the river. *A little below this once stood Fort Schlosser. Upon the opposite shore, three miles from the Falls, is the Canadian village of Chippewa, near which the Niagara receives the waters of Welland River, also known as Chippewa Creek. To these places the Niagara River is navigable. And between these landings and among the islands of the river the smugglers make their midnight trips by sail and oar, at the risk of accidents that would send them into the merciless rapids below, as well as at the risk of meeting custom-house officers on shore and river, armed with as deadly weapons as themselves.

For a distance of one mile before reaching the Falls, the river—a mile in width—becomes grand and terrible in its swift descent; and finally, being divided. at the edge of the fall by a wild, romantic island, the parted waters plunge on either side in a perpendicular descent over the end and side of a chasm one hundred and sixty feet in depth.

The gorge of Niagara with its varied and picturesque scenery, and increasing in depth by the descent of its rapids, and being about one-third the width of the Falls, winds its way for seven miles, when there is a sudden descent of several hundred feet in the face of the country, forming a one-sided mountain, which stretches far away on either side, to the east and to the west. At the top of this mountain-side, near the gorge, and upon Canadian ground, stands Brock's Monument, erected in memory of the British General who was killed about half-way down the mountain in the battle of Queenston Heights, fought on the 11th of October, 1812, between the British and Americans. At the foot of the mountain is a small Canadian village known as Queenston. Upon the American side of the river, directly opposite, is the ancient looking village of Lewiston, once the scene of an Indian massacre, and famous in the history of this frontier.

From these two places the river flows in a smooth current to Lake Ontario, a distance of seven miles. At the mouth of the river, upon the American shore, is the old Fort Niagara. Directly opposite stands guard the Canadian Fort Massasauga. From Lake Ontario steamboats bring their passengers up the river as far as Lewiston and Queenston.

No boat has ever attempted to ascend the rapids in the gorge. Only one instance of safe descent has been known, which was that of J. R. Robinson, an old resident at the Falls, whose daring and skill, among other good deeds of the kind, rescued Chapin in 1839, from an island in the rapids near the brink of the Falls, below Goat Island bridge, and near the spot where in 1853, citizens and strangers witnessed for eight hours the vain attempts to rescue Avery.

The village of Niagara Falls is upon the American side and has a population of four thousand inhabitants, besides the strangers who in summer throng its extensive hotels near the great cataract. It is estimated that more than one hundred thousand people visit this place annually. One peculiar feature of busy life near the large hotels and at interesting points upon the banks of the river, are the bazaars of Indian curiosities and geological specimens, and whatever the visitor could desire to take home as appropriate mementos of Niagara.

Goat Island, which divides the Falls, contains sixty-one acres, and is reached from the American side by an iron bridge over the rapids. Immediately below the Falls the river in the deep chasm, is for a short distance, safely crossed in small ferry boats, which the visitor may reach by descending a stairway of 291 steps. At the top of the banks the chasm is crossed by footmen and carriages, upon one of the longest suspension bridges in the world ; where, upon the Canada side is one of the best and most extensive hotels in the country, built in this rural and romantic location to afford its guests a front view of the whole Falls. A still better view, however, is obtained by approaching near where the famous Table Rock once was. Large portions of this rock, which projected for a great distance over the chasm, fell in 1818, 1828 and 1850. Here, descending by a stairway into the chasm, the visitor may be safely guided into a cave behind the great sheet of water. The large number of visitors to this locality, upon the Canada side, led a gentleman of wealth and scientific taste, some years ago, to conceive the idea of building an extensive museum for the exhibition of natural and artificial objects of interest. For this purpose a fine and imposing stone structure was erected near Table Rock, where one of the most interesting and scientific collections is visited by the traveler. Another elegant stone building with a large observatory at its top, is built close upon the bank of the Canadian Fall. From this observatory the traveler obtains one of the grandest views of the Falls, the chasm, the rapids and the surrounding scenery.

One mile west is the battle ground of Lundy's Lane, a point of historic interest, where that terrible midnight contest was fought between the United States forces under Gen. Scott, and the British under Gen. Drummond, July 25th, 1814, twenty days after the battle of Chippewa.

Among points of interest along the gorge of Niagara are Buttery's Rapids, the Whirlpool and the Devil's Hole. At the latter place, three and a half miles below the Falls, and upon the American side, a detachment of one hundred British soldiers, in 1763, were surprised by a party of Seneca Indians, and all but two men, Steadman and Mathews, were massacred or driven to destruction over the precipice. Near Brantford in Canada, sixty-five miles west of the scene of this massacre, is the grave of Brandt, the Indian chief who led on this terrible slaughter.

Across the chasm, two miles below the Falls, is the great railroad suspension bridge, completed in 1855, and the first of the kind ever constructed. Its magnificent and substantial appearance, with long trains of cars moving on its deck or upper floor, its net work sides, and footmen and carriages crossing on its lower floor, excite the wonder and admiration of every beholder. This bridge unites, in social intercourse, the American village of Niagara City with the Canadian village of Clifton. As railroad stations both places are more commonly known as Suspension Bridge. The New York Central Railroad being connected by this bridge to the Great Western, running through Canada and connecting with the Michigan

Central, makes one of the most direct and desirable routes from New York city to Chicago and the West.

And now, dear reader, having given a somewhat lengthy historical introduction to the locality, we offer only a word about the story:

Its plot will illustrate how strangely and how secretly fortune and misfortune, happiness and sorrow, do sometimes come upon the realities of life, and how varied are the characters and the scenes in which God's designs are controlling human plans; from the pious contentment of Black Tom and the fisherman to the troubles of the dis sipated Figsley; from the hypocrisy of the aristocratic Jared Bailey to the unsuspicious family of Deacon Sommers; from the anxieties of Miss Sommers and her rival lovers to the desponding Adeline and the mirthful Dinah.

It is well, too, if many a reader shall receive a few hints through some of the characters in this book, before meeting them elsewhere.

The interest and value of the story are greatly increased in the fact that some of the characters, especially the custom-house officers, and one of the rival lovers, bring to light much of the secret history of life and doings at Niagara. That this task might be correctly performed, the writer took occasion to become personally acquainted in the locality. And hence, reader, the manuscript for this book was written within sight of the great cataract.

Respectfully,

THE AUTHOR.

A STORY OF NIAGARA.

CHAPTER I.

THE locality, a picturesque and fertile valley—the neighborhood, a farming community; and here, a mile distant from the pleasant little village of Fallington, N. Y., stood the farm-house where Mrs. Bailey had resided since the death of her husband. She had grown feeble with age; and a nervousness from which she had long suffered, had become much aggravated by her anxieties occasioned by the war. The intended husband of her daughter Matilda had been killed at the battle of Fair Oaks, and it was only by Mrs. Bailey's almost frantic exertions and certain influences with the examining surgeon, that her son Benjamin had been prevented, three years before this, from entering the army.

Widow Bailey was patriotic, but she had a holy horror of war; and when her son told her that both the Fallington ministers urged the young men to enlist, she replied:

"Mercy on me! Benjamin; they had better read the Scriptures where it says, 'Thou shalt not kill!'"

When told that the South were fighting for a freedom to enslave, but the North for the Union and freedom for all, without distinction of creed, or birth, or color, she said:

"I know it, Benjamin; but mercy on me! the rest of the politicians, and the ministers too,—if they can't settle it peaceably,—can go to the war as well as I can spare you! Mercy on me! they are no better to be shot at, Benjamin, than you are!"

At last, the war had reached the summer of 1864, and although its actual presence was almost wholly confined to the slaveholding States, yet, in many ways, its effects had been felt in every home in the North.

Of late, or rather since the fall elections, Mrs. Bailey had surmised a new source of trouble: Benjamin—although he had been rejected by the examining surgeon, as McLiner had contrived it for Mrs. Bailey—was becoming an active politician, and had made several speeches favoring the war. She was not so anxious now that politicians should do the fighting. She feared her son's increasing influence in his political party might lead him to obtain a captain's commission in the army; and she thought—poor, innocent soul!—that captains always rushed into battle in front of their companies.

Possibly widow Bailey may have been musing upon these things, when, one afternoon about the middle of July, in the year above mentioned, her thoughts were interrupted by somebody rapping on the front door of her dwelling. Her fingers stopped on a half taken stitch of her knitting-work, and, eager to know who was the caller, she hastened to the door herself.

"Here's a telegraph dispatch for Mr. Benjamin Bailey," said a voice, which began uttering the announcement an instant before Mrs. Bailey had fairly observed who was the caller; for the message-boy had just begun the duties of his new employment, and had been instructed by the operator that "telegraphic dispatches must be dispatched with the utmost dispatch;" which tautology the operator explained by adding, "or, in other words, boy, take these messages quick as you can;" from all of which the idea of *haste* had been certainly and effectually conveyed to the boy's mind and practice, whatever the real practice of the operator.

"What! a telegraph for us? Why, mercy on me! Why, where is Benjamin? I wonder if anything has happened—or if anybody is hurt—or what's the matter! I told him so—ever since that awful dream!" said Mrs. Bailey, addressing her remarks to nobody, and in a very nervous and abstracted manner; at the same time, having taken the sealed message, she had turned, in search of somebody, back toward the sitting room. The hasty utterance of the boy at the door had, no doubt, enhanced her idea of the importance and seriousness of a telegraphic dispatch.

There was something so peculiar in her manner, and in the expression of her features, whenever Mrs. Bailey manifested her fears, or her astonishment, that it was often difficult for strangers to avoid a smile. But on this occasion the message-boy simply opened his eyes and his mouth with intense curiosity, till her entire disappearance produced in his mind a vivid recollection that he had only half finished his errand. So he rapped again on the half open door for the return of the peculiar old lady who had taken off the telegram without paying for it, or even expressing her intentions to do so.

On hearing the knocking repeated, Mrs. Bailey immediately reappeared, saying, in a confused way:

"Why, mercy on me! have you got another?"

"No, ma'am," replied the boy, in a state of increased wonderment, waiting for the old lady to approach him. At the same time it was not very certain, from Mrs. Bailey's movements, which way she was going; for, almost in the same breath, she said—as if to whomsoever it might concern—looking this way and that—

"I wonder where Benjamin *is!* Matilda," said she to some one who was not in sight, "see if Benjamin is in the library—or, it may be he is in the old shop fixin' up some liniment. Deacon Soloman was here this morning after some for his rheumatis. I don't see where he went to—Benjamin seems to be somewhere *always!*"

Finally, Mrs. Bailey, coming to the door, inquired what else the boy wanted.

"Please ma'am, shall I wait for a reply to the telegraph?"

"I don't know anything about it," replied Mrs. Bailey.

"There is a dollar and forty-five cents to pay for the telegraph," said the boy.

"What! a dollar and forty-five cents to pay on a letter? Mercy on me! I wonder where *is* Benjamin!"

Again she disappeared, and had been gone only a moment, when both Mrs. Bailey and the message-boy were frightened nearly out of their senses by a sudden noise, occasioned, evidently, by an explosion, and instantly after the report, a scream from Matilda; who, in searching for Benjamin, had just reached the door of the old laboratory—a kind of liniment shop, in a small, dilapidated building, at the end of the wood shed, and which, in its better days, before Mrs. Bailey became a widow, had been used for the office of her husband, Dr. Bailey. The instant after the explosion, Matilda opened the door, when she beheld the object of her search standing with his hands to his eyes, exclaiming:

"THUN-DER-A-TION!"

The room was nearly filled with smoke. Matilda feared fire—smelt gunpowder—and seizing a pail partially filled with water, which was standing near her, the next instant its contents were dashed against the bewildered Bailey and some chemicals his ingenuity had led him to experiment with.

"Hold on there!" said he to Matilda, "it is only that thundering anvil that has *waked* up here all at once for a little extra powder that got near it—and," he continued, still rubbing his eyes, "a little witch-fire that I've blundered into somehow with an infernal mixture!"

"But your eyes, Ben!—are they injured much?"

"O no; they will be all right in a few minutes—the flash came a little too near them; but it seems to me you are as careless of water as if the house were on fire?"

Matilda, seeing that no harm was done, went back to

the sitting room to report to her mother, whom she found almost speechless from alarm.

The message-boy, too, from fright, had run away from the house, nearly down to the front gate, where he had stopped, turned around, and stood gazing at the house, every instant expecting the mystery to develop itself!

When Benjamin reached the sitting room he found his mother recovered from her fright enough to exclaim:

"Mercy on me!   Where was Benjamin?"

"Why, mother, it was nothing but the old anvil," explained Benjamin, "loaded the same as it was on the Fourth!   You know we used to call it the old black-smith's cannon, mother!"

"Mercy on me! and here 'tis the middle of July!"

"Yes, mother," interrupted Matilda, "how could we think Ben was celebrating the Fourth again, so quick!"

"Mercy on me! how came you so wet, Benjamin? Just look at your coat!"

Matilda was now quite unsuccessful in attempting to subdue a hearty laugh, while she humorously suggested to her brother:

"How lucky it was there was no more water in that pail!"

"Why, what do you mean?" said Mrs. Bailey, omitting her usual utterance.   "How was it—what is it?   I can't see how the old anvil should throw water like a steamboat explosion!"

"Why, mother, Matilda means that she performed a very expert performance without the slightest rehearsal, by tipping over a pail of water; and that I am the humble recipient of the contents of said pail—be the same more or less."

"You see, mother," added Matilda, "I was trying to put out the explosion!"

"Trying to put out the explosion! Mercy on me! What *do* you mean? I do believe you are always going to be children if you live a hundred years!"

Benjamin then explained how the explosion occurred; which was substantially as follows: By one of those unaccountable blunders, which even the most careful people sometimes make, the old anvil, which had been used on the Fourth as a substitute for a cannon, was left loaded, and had been set on the floor near an old marble table in the room where Benjamin kept a few drugs and chemicals, where he occasionally mixed up a liniment or other preparation. Mrs. Bailey was troubled with "corns on her feet," and Benjamin had lately heard an old corn doctor, or chiropodist, tell of a mixture that was a "sure cure." As near as he could remember the recipe, he had obtained the ingredients and was mixing them on the old marble tablet.

"Let me see," said he to himself, "I think they were equal parts of potash, lime, and sulphur—and, it seems to me, gunpowder."

So he took down from a shelf, a flask of powder, and turned out a little upon the tablet. As he put up the flask the thought occurred to him that he had got the idea of powder from another recipe, for a different purpose. Brushing the powder aside, he then mixed about a thimbleful, each, of potash, sulphur, and quick-lime;

2

when, to his utter astonishment, this mixture produced fire, resembling a live coal of fire mashed into fine fragments. He had barely noticed the mystery when the explosion took place.

"It must be," said Bailey, manifesting a kind of scientific curiosity, "that the dampness of the potash made the lime become so hot as to set fire to the sulphur, and a spark of it somehow got to the powder which I had brushed aside, and through that communicated to the load in the anvil! At any rate," continued Bailey, "I can swear, or affirm, to the way I created that fire on that marble; and as for the old anvil—why, that—very evidently and very positively—has spoken for itself!"

Matilda smiled, and so did Benjamin; but Mrs. Bailey did not smile—she only noticed the danger; and when her son closed his explanation, she repeated her usual exclamation, "Mercy on me!" And then she added:

"How venturesome!—and after all I have told you! It seems as if some folks just courted danger. You would have been killed a dozen times, Benjamin, before this, if you had had your own way about it! Mercy—only think of it! You would have gone to the war if it had not been for the doctor who examined you, and if I had not given one of his friends fifty dollars, so he would tell the truth and say you were not strong enough to endure being a soldier! You didn't thank me for it at the time, Benjamin; but when half the boys in the neighborhood never come home again, and the rest of them come home cripples for life! you'll thank your poor old mother for looking ahead a little, then! I'm as patriotic as anybody, but I don't believe in wars; and I shall always be glad that McLiner took the money which made the doctor tell the honest truth! for I know you never could have stood it."

"Ben," said Matilda, "it seems to me these are awful times, when you have to pay some men so much to keep them honest, while poor private soldiers get so little for being killed. Of course you can say it is glorious to die for one's country; but the Northern States would be large enough for my country, without having my head blown off, or whining as Alexander did, for the privilege of controlling more. And the newspapers say Horace Greeley thought so himself at first."

"Perhaps he did," said Benjamin, "for it was terrible to think of war. But, at last, he and almost everybody, saw that the principles of men who believe in slavery are dangerous, and that two such opposites as slavery and freedom would not and could not live together in peace, and freedom must conquer while it could. Mr. Seward, years before this war, said no more than a simple truth in reference to such antagonistic principles and interests, when he foretold the people that such a conflict was 'irrepressible;' and, Matilda, do you not see that freedom and slavery are natural enemies?"

Just at this moment a loud knock was again heard at the front door.

Benjamin, having already changed his coat for a dry one, proceeded to attend the call.

"Mercy on me," said Mrs. Bailey, "there is that telegraph boy again! Here, Benjamin! There, Matilda! what have I done with that telegraph letter?"

"Why, what is that in your hand?" asked Matilda.

"Yes, there it is now! Well, I'm getting *so* nervous and so forgetful."

Benjamin, having directed the message-boy to wait a moment, returned to the sitting-room, when Mrs. Bailey handed him the message, saying:

"Mercy on me! Benjamin, here is a telegraph letter! I wonder what has happened for a telegraph to be sent here to us!"

Benjamin took the message, opened it and read aloud as follows:

"WASHINGTON, D. C., *July* 16, 1864.
"To BENJAMIN BAILEY, ESQ.,
      "Near Fallington, N. Y.
   "The appointment is made. Particulars by mail.
                    "LYMAN BALDWIN."

"What appointment does that mean?" inquired widow Bailey, who, no doubt, apprehended some appointment in the army.

"Wait a moment, mother," said her son, "till I settle with the boy at the door."

"Yes," joined in Matilda, "for goodness' sakes! This is the third time that poor boy has rapped on that door! and say, Ben, not only *pay* him, but convince him there has been no earthquake, or any other accident worth his while to alarm the villagers with!"

At last, the boy who had brought the telegram was settled with, his wonderment put in a state of moderation, and he departed. Benjamin returned again to the sitting-room, where the inquiry was repeated, as to what appointment the dispatch referred to.

"It is no appointment in the army," he replied. "It is a secret office to aid in catching smugglers, which our friend Mr. Baldwin urged me to take, though I told him I should know as little of my duty at first, as half the brigadier generals do of theirs!"

"Where will you have to go?" asked Matilda.

"Smugglers!" said Mrs. Bailey at the same time. "Mercy on me, where?"

"I shall have to go to Niagara Falls, and all along the Niagara river, from Lake Erie to Lake Ontario, and wherever else I should see a prospect of detecting smugglers on that frontier. It is a secret office, and you must be cautious even here, only to say I went west on business. You can avoid giving any direct answer as to the *kind* of business.

"But, suppose," suggested Mrs. Bailey, "that they ask us to tell *what* kind of business?"

"Then, tell them I said it was private business."

"That," replied Matilda, "would make them quiz all the harder!"

"No matter—keep giving the same answer—private, private business! That reply is short and true; and, mother, it is easy for you to remember—private business—private."

"Why, mercy! how it would look to keep giving the same answer, perhaps a half dozen times to the same person. Wouldn't they get offended?"

"No—such folks would not—at least they should not," said Benjamin.

"That's a queer kind of office, though," said Maltilda. "For goodness sakes! you would have to go right among the smugglers themselves. And from what little I have read about them, I should think some of them were just as desperate as robbers! They cross rivers in little boats, in stormy nights, and they try to shoot everybody that attempts to catch them!"

To this Benjamin was about to reply, when his mother, who had raised both her hands in astonishment, exclaimed:

"Mercy! mercy on me!"

And widow Bailey turned her face away as from some foreseen danger, her complexion as white as the neat lace fringe of the cap which bordered her face.

"I wouldn't think," continued Matilda, "there was any honor in such an office as that!"

"My son," added Mrs. Bailey, "have you got to be such a politician as that? after being brought up to go to Sunday school and to meeting, and always to choose good company or none at all? Only think of it, Benjamin! being among robbers as Matilda says—and being out nights in little boats—and getting drowned, perhaps!"

"Mother, I think Matilda has given you too bad a picture. The office is one which Judge Bailey would be glad to secure for his son David. And Mr. Baldwin himself told me it is a good office; that I would be my own master, mostly; and he thought it would be a very pleasant way of making acquaintance with the people and the country in Canada and on the frontier. The pay, too, is four dollars per day, and my expenses paid by the gov-

ernment, and I would get one-quarter of the seizures and
fines which I would be the means of bringing about."

"Among robbers and such folks! Mercy on me! Benjamin!"

"About all I would have to do, mother, would be to
detect smugglers privately and report information to the
Collector of Customs. That is about all!"

"Goodness sakes, mother, how is he going to find out
about such folks without associating with them? just as
I have read of police detectives going among all kinds
of rough people!"

Ah! Mr. Benjamin Bailey, while you have been flattered by the bright side, the quick perceptions of a
female have glanced at the other, where you will find
more trouble than even your sister anticipates for you.

CHAPTER II.

To Matilda's last suggestion, that Benjamin's office "would compel him to associate with all kinds of rough people," widow Bailey said her usual exclamation, and Benjamin made further explanations. He had been told that smuggling was done by all classes of people, and with little, if any, compunctions of conscience, nobody seeming to consider it disgraceful to smuggle what they wanted for their own use, and speculators of course smuggling as a *matter of principle*, believing professedly in the "principles of free trade."

"Only yesterday," said Benjamin, "I had a talk with a man right from Niagara Falls, and he says that a hundred thousand persons visit the Falls there every season, and that it is almost a private fashion among themselves for the very finest ladies to smuggle the very nicest things out of Canada, and that even the Judges of the United States Courts generally let off a smuggler with a light fine; so, you see," he added, "there is no reason why these novel stories need make Matilda imagine that I must be among robbers and such desperate fellows all the while."

"All the while!" repeated Matilda, with more of regret than rebuke in her manner; "it is a bad place, Ben,
to be with such fellows any of the time."

"But Mr. Baldwin is the Special Agent of the Treasury, you know, and he told me the older detectives might
do the rough work, and, if I did not like the position, he
could secure me some better office after a while."

Widow Bailey must have been somewhat satisfied by
these explanations; for, dropping that part of her objections, she told him that "it would be unpleasant to have
him so far from home, in such strange business, when he
had never been fifty miles from home in his life."

"Yes, mother, the business will seem strange to me;
but you know people give me the credit of being easy to
learn, and of having a little tact at management—don't
they, mother?"

Of course, Mrs. Bailey was proud to admit that fact.
But Matilda hoped that Ben would be *hard to learn* of
such fellows as she believed some smugglers were.

"Mercy on me! Benjamin, I don't see what business
you can try next! Do you ever think of the old saying:
'A rolling stone gathers no moss?'"

"O, say, mother, I wish you would remind him of another old saying: 'It takes a rogue to catch a rogue!'
Then how can he be successful in such business without
becoming a rogue himself, as well as being with them?"

Matilda said this in such an amusing way that Benjamin only smiled—made no reply.

"And now, brother Ben," continued Matilda, "if you
won't think me too bad—although I think you just as
2*

firm as anybody—I must say that this going into a business where you must become acquainted with everything bad, makes me think of the verse that the minister quoted last Sunday:

> " ' Vice is a monster of such frightful mien,
>   As, to be hated, needs but to be seen.' "

"So far," interrupted Benjamin, "that is what *I* think; and that is why I shall be safe—shall hate vice by seeing it!"

And he laughed with an evident feeling of triumph at turning her quotation to his advantage. But so soon as he was ready to listen, Matilda deliberately added:

> " ' *Yet seen too oft, familiar with her face,*
>   *We first endure, then pity, then embrace!*' "

"My dear sister," said Benjamin, taking her by the hand, "the kind and earnest manner in which you have quoted the last couplet, shall make me remember the caution that you have so kindly intended." And here, taking the hand of his good old mother, also, he continued: "And wherever my duty as a secret detective shall call me, though I may be obliged to practice deception against the guilty, as must be sometimes done to detect and punish crime, or to defend one's country and sustain the laws which protect the innocent, I do most solemnly pledge to each of you, my mother and my sister, that you shall have no cause in any act of mine— though every act were known to you—for any anxiety for aught else than my personal safety, and of that I will also take as good care as may be consistent with duty and honor."

During this unexpected and impromptu reference to a parting, and while Benjamin Bailey held in earnest grasp the hand of mother and sister, Mrs. Bailey was overcome with tears, whilst the eyes of both sister and brother were glistening with the same affectionate tokens.

Their hearts were too full for utterance, and not another word was spoken, as Benjamin silently turned away, and repaired to the old laboratory.

As he stood again by the marble tablet, where he had mixed up such a singular chemical fire, he instinctively examined to see if all was safe; though he had, before leaving, carefully put out every spark which Matilda's pretty well directed dash from the water-pail had not extinguished.

While Bailey was here setting things in order, his thoughts were occupied about his new office. He must detect smugglers without being detected himself. He might not meet expectations before he would be removed from the office, as he would have to learn the whole business. "It is some as Matilda says," thought he. "In order to learn much, I shall have to assume the character of a smuggler when among smugglers, and try to have them post me up in their operations. But if anybody expects me to associate with a drinking, carousing, low set of rowdies, thieves or cut-throats very much—considerably, constantly, &c.—they are hereby notified that I, Benjamin Bailey, of Bailey's Corners, am not that kind of a politician, and shall not degrade the office, nor the country Baileys, to any such extent!"

"But stop; instead of talking to this old anvil, I had better go and arrange my papers a little." Then, as he turned away from the marble table, he said to himself: "I rather guess that corn medicine was a humbug—an *all-fired* humbug," he added, as he thought of the singular combustibles.

Bailey was soon engaged in looking over some old letters in his library. He came to one addressed in a neat hand, which he looked at a moment with a sad expression in his countenance; then slowly unfolding the letter, he said to himself: "Yes; Laura Sommers was the best girl I ever knew."

There was a mystery about this letter which Benjamin Bailey had never yet solved, although one year had passed away since he received it.

The letter read as follows:

"FALLINGTON, N. Y., *July* 6, 1863.

"BENJAMIN BAILEY, ESQ.:

"*Dear Sir*—You can never know how it pains my feelings to be obliged to write this letter to break off our correspondence. I thought you so manly, so good, and generous; and I enjoyed so much your intelligent and original thoughts.

"But my parents have been made to believe many things against you, and that you have very recently treated one young lady in the most dishonorable and heartless manner.

"Father has just written me to discontinue our correspondence. I will, however, take the liberty to say, that
this unpleasant termination has made me very unhappy.
I shall not, therefore, make my visit here, at Judge
Bailey's, so long as I intended; but, having finished my
visits at other places here, I will go home to Niagara
Falls, in a day or two.

"O, how I wish I might *know* if all I have been told,
and all that has been written to my father, is true! and
yet they pretend it is told as a Christian duty. But I
think queer, that I must be pledged not to tell what it is,
nor who told me. Benjamin, I cannot believe what they
say of you, and yet I don't see how I can doubt their
word. When I go home, I shall ask father to give you
an opportunity to prove it is *not true*, or to show, at least,
what *motive* they may have to speak ill and falsely of
you. Perhaps you have told some *truth* against them,
and they are telling falsehoods secretly against you, to
injure you, so that what you say may not be believed!
I know a family of Vromans who always take that course
to injure innocent ones whom they fear may tell some
truth against them!

"But, Benjamin, I cannot disobey my parents, and
hence our correspondence must cease until they are satisfied to have it renewed; yet, I am willing to wait years
to see if time will explain for you, or defend you. And
I remain your friend,

"LAURA SOMMERS."

As Benjamin Bailey looked upon this letter, which, at

times during the past year, had given him so much
unhappiness, he fell into a thoughtful and melancholy
mood; and, seating himself in a chair by the side of his
open secretary, he again read Laura's last letter.

But, ere he had finished reading it, he had paused
several times, as if in deep study with his own thoughts.
It was plain to him that Miss Sommers had been made to
believe the most cruel falsehoods against him; but how
the same unprincipled inventors of slander could so far
influence Deacon Sommers, that he would decline to consider any defense from him, (which he had offered,) or, so
far as he knew, to investigate in any way, was a mystery
he could not account for.

The insinuation that he had treated some one in a dishonorable and heartless manner, had not the slightest
foundation in fact! Where could such base falsehood
originate? thought he; and what could be the motive to
tempt any one thus to deceive Miss Sommers and her
parents? It must be, of course, some one who has their
confidence. It must be a consummate hypocrite, too,
whose depravity could secretly contrive such falsehoods,
and still retain a respectable hearing from Laura and her
parents. It was evident, too, to Benjamin, from Laura's
letter, that the guilty parties had disregarded her happiness as well as his own; and, could they be detected,
would be despised by Mr. Sommers. But they had been
only too successful in their hypocrisy.

Many had been the queries which Benjamin Bailey had
revolved in his mind since receiving that letter. Sometimes he had wondered if the secret slander which cut off

communication between himself and the Sommers family had turned any advantage to its wicked authors.

As Benjamin folded up Laura's letter and proceeded to arrange his papers in the secretary, he had some vague impression that chance might, somehow, bring him to an acquaintance with Mr. Sommers under favorable circumstances, should he remain long at Niagara; but as matters now stood, he felt that he could not compromise his dignity by further directly seeking to communicate with Mr. Sommers.

CHAPTER III.

The Country Baileys—And the Village Baileys—The Country Cousin becomes a Politician—The Mistake—Social Inconsistency.

AT the time of his appointment to this office of secret detective, Benjamin Bailey had reached the age of twenty-four years; and the almanacs of that year, which were given away as vehicles for the circulation of various advertisements, declared it to be the year of our Lord one thousand eight hundred and sixty-four, or, according to a more ancient order of reckoning, as handed down by King Solomon, and others further back, it was denominated the year of the world five thousand eight hundred and sixty-four.

At this time if any one had inquired of the farmers in the neighborhood, as to what business Benjamin Bailey followed, they would, probably, have said, if they undertook to decide so puzzling a question at all, that he was about as much farmer as anything else; though they would have come to this conclusion, principally, because the farm he had fallen heir to, by the death of his father, had a more visible and a more permanent existence than anything else he had amused himself with.

There was hardly any kind of business requiring tact and head-work, which had fallen under Benjamin Bailey's observation, that he had not thought over, and almost dreamed over, at one time or other, to make up his mind what he had better do—what business he had better follow.

The farm, which had been left by his father, who died when Benjamin was only three years of age, produced an income sufficiently large to support the heirs in a plain way of living. This, though convenient in some respects, may have been in other respects, a misfortune. For, before he had acquired experience in any particular branch of business, so as to excel in it, as he evidently had the natural abilities to do, he felt that he could *afford* to change to something else, which he fancied he would like to try. What he was losing in this way, he did not realize till gradually the time and best opportunity for learning some profession, or acquiring a practical knowledge of the details of some business, had passed away.

If Ben Bailey had been a little more pinched for means, so that he could not have *afforded* to make so many beginnings, but had felt compelled to drive through in some one direction, or, if in his earlier youth his friends had been thoughtful enough to have urged him to make choice of something which he felt was best adapted to his capacities, and he had given that his steady attention, his natural abilities might have placed him in a position where, at a later period, the secret work of unprincipled enemies could not have been successful in deceiving the parents of Laura Sommers.

When Benjamin was sixteen years old he left the district school of his neighborhood and went to the village academy two terms, where he was awarded at the close

of the last term, the highest prize in his classes for pro-
ficiency in mathematics and composition.

For several years afterwards he divided his time between
various mechanical employments and farming, occupying
most of his evenings, however, in his library.   When he
worked at any mechanical art he seemed to do so more
to practice skill in handiwork, as did Louis XIV. at the
smith's forge, or to acquire knowledge as did Peter the
Great at ship-building, than with a purpose to follow any
trade as a business.   Even the old laboratory, once used
by Benjamin's father, had been of late the scene of some
queer chemical experiments; one of which was noticed
in our first chapter, and several of which, I have no
doubt, would have been interesting even to the wise professor of Fallington Academy.

In the winter season, at Bailey's Corners, as well as in
the village of Fallington, lyceums had been sustained for
years back, and at both of which places Benjamin was
at one time acknowledged to be the most pleasing and
accomplished speaker.

In this way time and Benjamin went on till the fall of
1863, or just after his short love experience with Miss
Laura Sommers.   Feeling at this time keenly the unpleasant termination of his correspondence with Miss Sommers,
he determined upon a course which he hoped would give
himself a more positive influence in the community.
He must be better known in society, so that slander
would not so easily injure him.   He thought he had been
active, public spirited, and liberal; and so he had been.
But he began to see that he needed influential friends to

favor him. What new course could he take to gain these?

At last he thought that the secret had come to him. He must seek every opportunity, politically and otherwise, to favor persons of influence who could and would do *him* favors in return. He could suggest their names for nominations to places of profit or power. In this and other ways he thought that he might gain a position which would aid him to obtain a successful hearing from Laura's father. Indeed, what do *not* lovers think of?

Impelled by a sense of justice, Benjamin Bailey had believed in anti-slavery principles ever since he had first been told the meaning of the word *slave!* And when the war to perpetuate slavery was begun by the slave-holders in 1861, he was the first in the town of Fallington who offered to enlist as a soldier; and had he been accepted by the examining surgeon, he would probably never have been in the secret service on the Niagara frontier.

When, therefore, President Lincoln made the call for three hundred thousand more volunteers, in October, 1863, war meetings were held all over the Northern States to encourage enlistments; some of these meetings were held at Bailey's Corners, and there Benjamin Bailey, the rejected volunteer, made the first speech, which brought him into political notice.

Before the fall elections were over, Ben Bailey had become a favorite political speaker at Bailey's Corners, and by invitation had spoken at several meetings of his party elsewhere in his county, where he always modestly claimed

to speak only as a farmer. His success began to turn the
notice of the villagers, socially as well as politically, in
his favor. Mr. Benjamin Bailey and his sister Matilda
began to be invited into village society. And occasionally some far-seeing, prominent politicians of Ben's politics, ventured to be so democratic as to invite Ben's
brother, and even his mother, nervous as she was, to
"come and spend an evening with them."

But until within the last year the country Baileys,
though members of one of the largest churches in the
village of Fallington, had never received an invitation to
any of the evening parties, or even to visit among the
"leading families" of the village.

Jared Bailey—or Judge Bailey, as he had been called
for a number of years—was supposed to be an uncle of
Benjamin Bailey—or rather a half-brother of Benjamin's
father. It was said, and I have never learned the contrary, that the title, "Judge," came to Jared Bailey
through the persistence of a wag, who, in derision of Mr.
Bailey's private character, frequently called him "*Judge*"
for mock dignity, instead of "Jed," a nick-name for
Jared. For many years Jared Bailey had resided in the
village of Fallington. He was wealthy, and he wielded
considerable influence over a certain class of politicians,
whose smaller influence he was able to buy up at a cheap
rate. His family had styled Benjamin their "odd country cousin," and had slighted him and his sister Matilda,
as persons too plain to be invited into their society.
And yet, this same Matilda was the best scholar of the
village academy. Then, too, of course it would not be

consistent to invite Matilda and not Benjamin; and as for
the older brother, "Why! he had married a woman
who," they said, "would be sure to mortify the whole
family by wearing something ridiculous, that had been
out of fashion three months!"

In short, widow Bailey's family, though highly respected
for their integrity and intelligence, had been so treated
by Judge Bailey and his family, or at times so signifi-
cantly let alone, that the other wealthy portion of the
villagers did as the village Baileys did—treated them at
church, or at any place of accidental or perhaps unavoid-
able meeting, with outward, Christian civility; but to notice them on grand occasions, or as if a meeting were
sought, or to invite them where equality might be infer-
red—why, that was another matter! a duty among many
Christian relatives not expected to be performed.

But Mr. Benjamin Bailey becomes a politician among
farmers, has a political influence, makes political speeches
in favor of this candidate and against that one! This
has given Ben Bailey influence—this has introduced Ben
Bailey and the rest of the country Baileys into a brotherly
fellowship, even among the aristocratic members of *their
own church*, as well as other villagers of Fallington.

It is true the villagers still notice Ben Bailey's oddity;
but, apparently unmindful of any change in their programme, they unite in flattering opinions *now*, of his
"originality of thought!"

The village cousins, and the old Judge in particular,
see their mistake, but fear it is too late to be corrected.
He wonders now why he did not advise his family to

speak well, and not ill, of their country cousins. He considers now how little their friendship would have cost! "And who knows but Benjamin may rise to influence in spite of us? Their friendship would not have harmed us," ponders the Judge, as a few things in his secret history come back to his memory, and he fears that sometime he may have friends too few or enemies one too many!

CHAPTER IV.

Deacon Sommers of Niagara—Too slight an acquaintance with Jared Bailey—How Benjamin and the Deacon's Daughter became Lovers.

WILLIAM SOMMERS, or Deacon Sommers, as he was generally called in the town of Niagara, was one of the wealthiest men on the frontier; a plain, good, kind-hearted man; and, without making half the usual allowances for human frailties, we may say he was in a fair sense of the term, a Christian. He undoubtedly had errors of the head, but his heart was generally right. He was a man of positive character. There was very little of the half-way or undecided in his faith or in his practice. He loved right so well that he hated even the appearance of wrong. He loved justice and freedom so much that he had a pious abhorrence of slavery or oppression in any form. And yet he loved his country so well that, like the noble Lincoln, he would have saved it with all her faults, rather than risk her ruin in attempting to abolish her greatest evil. But when it was known that the evil itself, unless abolished, would ruin the country by the terrible war, Deacon Sommers was ready to sacrifice all in efforts to maintain the Republic, and was almost glad of the terrible opportunity to strike down a national crime which he had always hated.

Deacon Sommers, therefore, was a politician, but he

was a politician whose present policy was consistent with
great moral principles which he had always advocated.
Add to this, his wealth placed him above that temptation
which comes sometimes successfully to others; for no
corrupt politician was emboldened to approach him with
bribery for any *need he had of money!*

At times politics reached so high a standard in his
election district that Deacon Sommers, in spite of enemies
envious of his good fortune, was chosen a delegate to
conventions for nominating important officers. At some
of these conventions he had met with Judge Bailey, so
that a sort of acquaintance had been kept up ever since
his removal to Fallington from Niagara, many years
before. For Mr. Bailey had once lived a short time
within a few miles of Deacon Sommers, and both had
belonged to the same church. During their summer
visits to Niagara, Judge Bailey and his wife had made
calls upon Deacon Sommers and his family; and hence
the latter thought they were acquainted with the former—
that is, with their outward character—but there was a private character known to a few, of which Deacon Sommers
and his family knew nothing.

Laura Sommers was the only daughter of Mr. and Mrs.
William Sommers. At the time she wrote the letter
breaking off her correspondence with Benjamin Bailey,
she was in her nineteenth year.

It seems that in the early part of May, 1863, which, it
will be remembered from the date, was one year prior to
young Bailey's appointment to go to Niagara—it had
been arranged for Laura and her mother to make a visit

to some of their acquaintances in Fallington; and Deacon
Sommers insisted that they should, while there, make
Judge Bailey's family a visit also.

Whether Deacon Sommers, like many other fathers
having marriageable daughters, was thinking it good
policy for his daughter to make the acquaintance of
wealthy families, and whether it occurred to him that
possibly Judge Bailey's son David might be a suitable
young man to reciprocate such acquaintance, I am not
able positively to say; but I can say most positively, that
Deacon Sommers should have known more of David
Bailey before taking any special pains to favor a matter
of such moment.

Of their visit in Fallington, and how it happened that
Benjamin Bailey, of Bailey's Corners, and Laura Sommers became acquainted, and how they at first were mu-
tually interested in each other, and why it was that Laura's mother was also pleased with Benjamin, and why she
returned home to Niagara Falls, leaving Laura to make a
longer visit, were circumstances which, though very interesting at the time to the parties themselves, were matters which most of my readers no doubt can imagine
more vividly than I can picture, on account of little personal experiences of their own!

I will, however, say that the primary cause of it all
seemed to be as in "oft repeated tales"—"love at first
sight!" And then, was it not perfectly natural that the
mother should be pleased that somebody loved her
daughter?

As a further apology, however, for Benjamin Bailey's
3

very human weakness of "falling in love at first sight,"
we might say that there was nobody but what said (if
they said anything about it) that Laura Sommers was a
beautiful girl; and that her face bore an intelligent and
amiable expression; while there were those besides young
Bailey who thought her charming and lovely. She was
cheerful and lively, without appearing rude; modest, but
not bashful; frank and plain spoken, and yet careful not
to wound the feelings of others. But as to her disposi-
tion or temper under great provocation, and whether she
may not have sometimes exhibited human failings—we
dare not say that in all this she was perfection. She
seemed, however, to secure the good will of all who knew
her. Her manner and conversation were easy and entertaining, never haughty or affected. Her stature was a
little above the average height, and her form perfect.
Her *own* dark brown hair hung in natural ringlets to her
shoulders, leaving her intelligently formed head free from
artificial disfigurement; while her animated thoughts gave
expression to her deep blue eyes, and furnished a natural
rose tint to the whiteness of her complexion.

It was at church, the next Sabbath after Laura Sommers' arrival in Fallington, that Benjamin Bailey first saw
her. Twice on that Sabbath day their eyes met—probably a mere chance occurrence, and no doubt each regarded
it as such, or at least, like two well-bred strangers, they
had the manners to make it *appear* so; though I should
not like to say positively that it was as accidental as it
appeared to be! for the next Sabbath a like occurrence
took place. And then, too. a letter which he wrote to

Miss Laura Sommers, just after he had seen her one day in Mr. Baldwin's store, was dated within less than two weeks of the first Sabbath referred to. In the letter he expressed a desire to make her acquaintance, and asked the pleasure of an interview with her at the house of her friend, Mrs. Cummings, where she and her mother were then visiting.

The interview was granted, the reply being made in a very neat and proper letter. Benjamin called upon Laura, introduced himself, Mrs. Sommers was present, the visit closed, and the mother and daughter were favorably impressed with Mr. Benjamin Bailey. Other visits were made, and before two months Benjamin and Laura were lovers, betrothed on conditions that her father would give his approval.

And was it anything so very strange that he loved her? I think not!

But how I shall apologize for Laura Sommers taking such a liking, as she did from the very first, to Benjamin Bailey, is not an easy task to do; for it has always been a wonder to me how such pretty, little, sensitive creatures as the ladies all are, could ever really love anything so ridiculous as a great stout man, with such awkward, large hands and feet, and such a coarse, harsh voice that always sounds like grumbling, and never as if he had any feelings that could make him cry or scream! No, I never could understand it; and even my own little wife's explanation doesn't seem reasonable about it! Only think of it! Ladies, what taste! What inconsistency for you to put tender, lace covered arms on a plain, heavy, everyday coat sleeve—and perhaps around *his* neck; and your tender faces against great, huge whiskers, or rough, stubbed beard!

All I can possibly say in explanation is that it must be because God, in his good providence, has so ordered it for the good of *man* kind. Then as to Benjamin Bailey, he was not a great, huge fellow, and he was a man of as fine feelings and good sense as I ever became acquainted with on the frontier or elsewhere.

Was it strange, then, after all, that Laura Sommers should be interested in being loved till she loved Benjamin in return? Perhaps not.

CHAPTER V.

" The course of true love never did run smooth."

SHAKESPEARE, no doubt, intended when he wrote the above line, to make it express a general truth. If Mr. Shakespeare was correct in this, a large number of mankind, since Adam and Eve had their first falling out, have had their little difficulties, as well as Benjamin Bailey, when "the course of love did not run smooth."

The correspondence between Benjamin Bailey and Miss Sommers had begun, no doubt, upon too short an acquaintance. However worthy they were, their good opinion of each other was liable to be changed by unjust remarks from envious persons. Had it been young Bailey's good fortune to have seen some way of making his character and circumstances known to Mr. Sommers—and *certainly* known—before any person with sinister motives could have discovered any object to cut off his communications with the Sommers family, the shortness of the acquaintance would have been less dangerous to his success, and perhaps to the happiness of both. But the beginning of a first courtship, like all other first beginnings, is of course without the advantage of previous experience! and to make the matter still worse, it is said that "love is blind!"

When Judge Bailey knew that his country nephew was paying some attentions to Miss Sommers, he set his wits to work. He had more than one wicked reason for doing so! He had thought that his own son might possibly succeed in winning the affections of Miss Sommers, whose father he knew was wealthy. David Bailey had already been told that he must not marry the daughter of widow Smith. But there was another reason why Judge Bailey did not wish to have Benjamin Bailey become too intimate with people in the town of Niagara—a reason which he has not explained to his son David. No; and he never will. There was an old crime which lay at the foundation of Judge Jared Bailey's property. That crime was known to two or three living witnesses residing in the vicinity of Niagara Falls. John Vroman was a bribed witness of the crime; Jerusha, his daughter, an artful, beautiful and ungovernable maiden, had discovered traces of the crime, but, under promises of gain, and by kind attention from Judge Bailey and his wife, Jerusha had consented to conceal what she knew. And to make the matter still more secure, Judge Bailey had won her affections by offering her a home in his family, which she had accepted, and where at last she became equally interested in concealing wrong.

The old crime related to property of which Benjamin Bailey was one of the rightful heirs. The crime had taken place in Jared Bailey's younger days, but it had been done in the town of Niagara, and, in his guilty fears, he preferred that Benjamin should not go there!

Thus influenced, Judge Bailey planned a wicked and cruel slander against Benjamin, which he cautiously wrote to Deacon Sommers, and which Mrs. Bailey, urged by her husband and by Jerusha, endorsed by writing another letter to Mrs. Sommers. Poor woman, no matter what Jared Bailey had done, Mrs. Bailey loved him. She feared he was in danger, and she almost loved Jerusha for advising wrong upon wrong to save him.

The plan succeeded in causing Miss Sommers, through the commands of her father, to write the unhappy letter referred to.

Judge Bailey regretted, however, that his plan had also caused Laura's immediate departure home to Niagara.

When Benjamin received the letter he was nearly bewildered by its mysterious contents. But he did not rest without attempting to find out the source of this trouble. The same day, after receiving the letter, he called at Judge Bailey's to see Laura Sommers, and was told by Mrs. Judge Bailey that Miss Sommers was not in. He was too disheartened and disappointed to trust himself to ask any further questions concerning her, and he turned away, wondering what course he had better take.

When he reached home he went immediately to his library, and read the letter over and over again. Finally he wrote a short note, simply asking Laura Sommers if he might have the privilege to see her, and offering, so soon as he could find out what dishonorable thing had been told against him, to satisfy her and her friends of his innocence. He went back to Fallington the same afternoon, and put the letter in the post-office.

Toward evening of the next day he went again to the post-office, but found no letter there from Laura Sommers. He went again the second day—no letter; the third day, and the same unfavorable result. He then went to the residence of Judge Bailey, where he knew Laura had been visiting a week or more, and had intended to stay a week or two longer.

At Judge Bailey's he saw no one but the servant girl and his aunt Ellen. The latter informed him that Miss Sommers had that day started on her return home to Niagara Falls.

"May I inquire," said Benjamin, "if you know whether she went to the post-office to-day or yesterday, to get any letters that may have been there for her?"

"Yes; she went to the post-office just before starting for home," replied Mrs. Judge Bailey.

"Did she go herself?" inquired Benjamin, a little disconcerted.

"Of course she went *herself*, if she went at all; and I believe she got a letter, though I do not know who it was from; perhaps it was from you, Benjamin?"

Benjamin was now still more embarrassed; he had made the inquiry without forethought, and instantly regretted that he had done so. He knew too little of his aunt Ellen to know whether she was disposed to injure him by words, or simply to let him alone with an aristocratic neglect. He feared, however, he had trusted an inquiry to one who might color it up as an impertinent question. True, he was in a confused and anxious state of mind, but sometimes one's best friends refuse to be satisfied with such an apology.

After a moment's hesitation he replied, evasively, that he hoped he had not conveyed an impression that Miss Sommers was expecting letters from him; and, said he, "I will say, to do justice to Miss Sommers, I presume she does not—or rather would not, desire to receive letters from me; hence, will you be kind enough not to construe my inquiry in such a direction?"

After waiting a few weeks, and getting no clue to the slander, nor any further information from Laura Sommers, he wrote to her father as follows:

"FALLINGTON, N. Y., *Aug.* 10, 1863.
"WILLIAM SOMMERS, ESQ.,
"Niagara Falls, N. Y.:

"*Respected Sir*—May I beg so great a favor as to ask if you will inform me in what respect any of your family have heard that I ever treated any young lady 'dishonorably,' or in a 'heartless manner?' The assertion, which, it appears your family have heard made against me, is so cruelly false, it seems to me I can satisfy you that it has been told for some base purpose. If even your informers believe it, which I do not believe they do, even then it seems to me that their foundation for so false a report against me, cannot be such that they ought not to allow me the privilege of a defense by reference to respectable persons—if the allegations are what could be well known against me, or by investigation if otherwise.

3*

If I cannot be heard in my defense, will you do me the favor to show this letter to your daughter Laura, or at least say to her that I believe time will develop the truth sooner or later to your family? Either with your informers, or beyond them, there must be a wickedness concealed; and I make this vow, to live single and wait patiently till time shall reveal the truth; and I will remain,

"Yours, respectfully,

"BENJ. BAILEY."

To this letter Benjamin Bailey received the following answer:

"NIAGARA FALLS, N. Y., Aug. 18, 1863.

"MR. BENJAMIN BAILEY,

"Fallington, N. Y.:

"*Dear Sir*—In reply to your letter of the 10th inst., I can only say, that our information is such that it is beyond our power to doubt it. We are also under a promise to a friend in whom I have the utmost confidence, to not speak of the matter for reasons which seem honorably intended toward your family; and in short, to avoid associating the names of innocent parties with unpleasant gossip. You will, therefore, let the matter drop where it is; and especially not seek to continue an acquaintance with my daughter. I understand that my daughter has already written to you that under the circumstances, all correspondence had better cease.

"Yours, etc.,

"WM. SOMMERS."

By this letter Benjamin Bailey saw that his slanderers had been so expert that it was most likely they were old hands in their game of meanness.

Although he could suspect no one but Jared Bailey's family of being the source of the slanderous talk to injure him with the Sommers family, yet he knew no reason why the village Baileys could have any motive that could induce any of them to invent falsehoods to injure him. He knew that David had for a long time back, been paying attentions to the daughter of a poor widow in the village, and he supposed therefore that there could be no motive of rivalry. Neither had Laura Sommers or her father any reason yet to suspect any such motive. No, the plan was a shrewd one; David was to show no such intention till two things were accomplished; first, his country cousin, as an obstacle, was to be removed; then he must get rid of the widow's daughter gradually, or in some way, so the matter should make him as little trouble as possible, and not turn publicly to his discredit. This was a matter for David to bring about, but the other obstacle was what Judge Bailey himself had undertaken to remove.

David had at first loved the widow's daughter as much as a selfish, unprincipled libertine could be expected to love any beautiful and virtuous, high-minded and accomplished young lady. It was owing to the strict propriety, however, of her own deportment that the widow's daughter in their courtship had even partly changed David Bailey's sensual, sordid, selfish love toward an honorable love, based on respect, esteem, friendship, sympathy and

honorable intention.   The widow's daughter knew nothing of David Bailey's private character.   Whatever had
been said truthfully against Judge Bailey or his son,
there had been just enough interested in the Judge's
family to deny the truth of it; and even to retaliate by
falsehood for its having been spoken!

Investigation into some late matters against Judge
Bailey had been threatened, but was dropped from the
delicacy of witnesses, from intimidation, and from his
private settlements, or bribery!

When Judge Bailey first suggested to his son that after
two or three months he had better pay no more attention
to the widow's daughter, neither the son nor his father
for one moment considered the feelings of the young lady.
The Judge summed up the case; the son thought he
could agree to it.   The conclusion was, that the widow's
daughter was poor, and that Miss Sommers was rich!
To the widow's daughter this heartless conversation and
conclusion was no doubt, to be to her, a blessing in disguise.

It was for want of knowing a motive for Judge Bailey's
family to interfere, that Benjamin Bailey did not form a
more positive opinion as to whence came the slander
against him.   It was not because he had too good an
opinion of Jared Bailey to suspect him; for, besides many
things which passed as mere rumor against him, there
were some late matters whispered of among the relatives,
not known to the public; and Benjamin knew more of
some of these than the Judge was aware of.   It was
Benjamin's private opinion that the old Judge would
stoop to almost any wickedness which he could conceal.

As Benjamin read and re-read Mr. Sommers' letter, the thought would come to him that the originator of the slander might be Jared Bailey; but if it were so, how could he convince Mr. Sommers against his assertions, without first showing that he was an unprincipled man, and prompted by selfish motives? And how could he do this while he was refused even a hearing? It was a delicate matter, too, for Mr. Sommers' family as well as for himself.

And then Benjamin called to mind several disreputable things, positively known, against Judge Bailey's character, which, for the sake of the family name, the relatives had concealed among themselves.

There was a *belief*, too, among some of the relatives, that Judge Bailey, many years before this, had obtained fraudulently the signature of his father to a will just before his father's death, and by fraud or bribery had also obtained the signatures of the subscribing witnesses to the will.

The circumstances which led to the suspicion that Jared Bailey had, somehow, obtained more than his rightful share from Benjamin's grandfather, Mortimer Bailey, were as follows: his last will and testament gave property to the amount of seventy-five thousand dollars to Jared Bailey, and only about twenty thousand dollars worth of land, near Fallington, to John, Benjamin and Matilda Bailey, heirs of Dr. Luke Bailey, deceased.

Mortimer Bailey, at the time this will was made, was on a visit to Jared Bailey's, where, by an accident, he met with injuries which, though not at first thought

serious, did at the end of three weeks prove fatal. After
his death a will was produced, making the above unequal
division of property. The will was dated two weeks after
the injuries had been received. The friends of Mrs. Dr.
Luke Bailey's family inquired into the matter, but found
that the signatures of Mortimer Bailey, and the witnesses
John Vroman, James Figsley and Adeline Wilderman,
were genuine. And Mrs. Jared Bailey, with great seriousness, and having the reputation of a pious woman, declared that she was present and heard the testator express
his wishes and dictate the writing of the will, and saw
him read and sign it. The doctor who attended him,
affirmed that he was in his right mind up to the day and
hour of his death. A circumstance, however, took place
afterwards, which created a suspicion that a fraud had
been committed; but the legal evidence was wanting! or
rather it was not to be obtained at the time it was wanted
or sought for!

An innocent girl, by name of Eleanor Grace, was living in the family of Jared Bailey at the time the will was
made. She, not long afterward, stated some facts in
answer to inquiries, which created suspicion and contradicted important declarations that had been made by
Mr. and Mrs. Jared Bailey, who had become frightened,
and, in order to throw discredit upon Eleanor's statements,
had represented her to be a girl of so bad a character,
that they had been compelled to refuse her a home with
them any longer than till she could find some other place
to live. For reasons that could only be surmised, the
witnesses to the will, and parties interested in it, sided

with Jared Bailey's family against Eleanor's character, till some of Eleanor's friends for whom she most cared, including a young man to whom she was expecting soon to be married, could not doubt so many witnesses, and turned against her also—without considering that they were, perhaps, all interested in securing a portion of the property. Heart-broken and desperate for the injustice done her, she was too impulsive to wait for time to defend her, and she suddenly disappeared—no one knowing whither she went.

A brief letter sent to Benjamin's mother, from Eleanor, read as follows:

"*Dear Mrs. Bailey*—I saw and heard enough to know there was another will. I heard the sick man read it; it divided the property equally, giving no more to Jared Bailey than to you and each of your children. The next day after that will was made and signed, they pretended there was a mistake and they would write it over. They then let the old man read a copy which was written as he wanted it should be, and while he was raising up to prepare to write his name they exchanged for a different will than what he had read. This I saw with my own eyes as the door stood ajar! Mrs. Bailey was in the room and aided the deception. Adeline knows the truth, but is afraid to tell it.

"But my evidence could do you no good, for they would swear me into prison for telling the truth. They have robbed me of all that was dear on earth to me, and

now—but no matter. Vindication and vengeance will
yet be mine.

"Yours truly,

"ELEANOR GRACE.

"P. S.—As heaven is my witness, all I have stated
above is true.　　　　　　　　　　　　　　　　E. G."

And the letter *was true*, but it took twenty years for
time to develope the evidence; but when it did so, it
brought to light the accumulations of other wrongs.

At the time her letter was written, however, the statements of Eleanor Grace were thrown into discredit; and
when at last she did not appear, John Vroman started a
report that Eleanor had been seen in a dance house in
New York city, in a pitiful state of intoxication. *Under
the circumstances*, it was for Mrs. Jared Bailey's *interest*,
to believe the story; and so she reported, as she touched
with feigned regret the corner of her handkerchief to her
eyes, that she supposed the story was true!

Nearly twenty years was now passed, and nothing more
had been heard of Eleanor Grace, and no further light
about the will; so that at this time Benjamin detests
Jared Bailey less for any suspicions about the will, than
for the mean, heartless and relentless falsehoods he was
known by a few of the relatives to have reported, to screen
himself from blame, by attempting to misrepresent certain respectable females, who had exposed his peculiar
style of abuse, and sometimes his criminal assaults upon
them. Benjamin himself had a partial knowledge of one
instance, which happened an evening a few weeks before

Laura Sommers came to Fallington. The circumstance confirmed him in the opinion, that the aristocratic old man was a criminal at heart. He did not, however, deem it best to report the matter, since it would be embarrassing to innocent parties, and truth might have to battle with so many falsehoods that the *innocent* would be injured!

What he knew of the affair was this:

Benjamin had been requested by Mr. Baldwin, on the evening referred to, to leave a letter at Judge Bailey's, as he passed that way.

"A fine residence this," thought Benjamin, as he opened Judge Bailey's front gate, and walked toward his house, through an alley bordered with box wood; "and it hardly seems possible that it covers so much sin as some of the family relatives hint of among ourselves! 'Charity hideth a multitude of wickedness!' as black Jim quotes it," said Benjamin to himself, " but riches and hypocrisy," added Benjamin, "a great deal more!"

When about to ring the door bell, he was startled by a sudden jam against the door from the inside, as if a person had run or been pushed against it, which of course led Benjamin to pause a moment before ringing an interruption to the inmates of the residence of the dignified Judge Bailey.

The disturbance was repeated, during which time our accidental listener overheard a female voice saying, " You old hypocrite! if your wife would slander me to screen you, I shall expose you just the same, as a heartless wretch! or, if you like it any better, I will give you till to-morrow noon to settle this matter. This is your last insult! you old brute!"

"For heaven's sake, stop your noise and I'll settle it," said a voice which Benjamin was certain he recognized as that of the old Judge! though the voice was in a subdued tone.

As soon as this mysterious little quarrel had seemed to cease, Benjamin rang the door bell; but no one came to the door till he was obliged to ring a second time. Then old Bailey himself came to the door, and received the letter as if nothing had happened; except that Benjamin thought the old man's attempt to smile looked as if it was composed of equal parts of hypocrisy, depravity, selfishness and confusion.

As Benjamin put away the letter from Mr. Sommers in his secretary, and thought of the circumstance just related, he said to himself, "As I live, if I had much grounds to suppose that he is the one who has separated Laura Sommers from me, by some wicked plan, I would have that front-door mystery investigated! I would find out what female voice that was, and how crime can be settled! It was undoubtedly an assault with criminal intent."

Then he reflected, that, in case of his exposing the Judge, it would be no credit to himself to have it said that Judge Bailey was any *relation* of his; "and yet," thought Ben, by way of apology, "everybody is related to *somebody* whose organism has been unduly affected by the law of total depravity.

But, finally, Benjamin concluded that he must drop the slander matter; at least so far as to wait further developments.

Up to the time when Benjamin Bailey received the appointment to go to Niagara, which was, as we have before
intimated, about one year after the occurrences above
related, nothing took place to give Benjamin any light on
the subject of the slander. Though he sometimes con-
soled himself with the old adage, that "Truth and right
will prevail," or that "It is a long road that has no turn."

And it is, indeed, true, that the guilty have as much
reason to fear as the innocent have to hope. For they
who follow a course of deception and depravity, or do
any acts disregardful of the rights and feelings of others,
O, do they not find at last, that events connect themselves
together on the map of time, so that they trace each other
out!

CHAPTER VI.

JUDGE BAILEY was a shrewd politician, and had managed to keep in office, first in one party and then in the
other, for a number of years; and, since his son David's
last failure in the dry goods business, he had been talking
with some of his confidential, political friends on the
prospect of securing an appointment for his son, to some
good government office. These friends had all promised
to do what they could. This meant much, or little.
With some it meant all they could do "consistently;"
with others, all they could do "under existing circumstances;" with some it simply meant that what they
could do was nothing; for the delicate reason that they
had more particular friends whom it was more to their
own interest to prefer; besides, there were many others
whose friendship they would be glad to purchase by the
same favor; or, perhaps because they had alike promised
their influence to a dozen others for the same place; or,
perhaps it meant they could do nothing, simply because—
as they secretly knew—they had no influence in the direction they were giving encouragement!

There are, however, some men in politics as in other

matters, who can be relied on. Judge Bailey understood
all this. He understood, too, the influences which would
be most effectual in making his professed friends serve
him, whether they were real friends or not. So long as
he could make them believe that it was to their *interest*
to serve him, so long he told himself they would serve
him. He understood all the shades of political promises,
and had made them; promises with mental reservations;
promises with various conditions; and no doubt many
for various "considerations." Some of these promises
Mr. Jared Bailey intended to keep faithfully. When he
thought it was for his interest to remember a political
"understanding" he never forgot how it was understood.
When he did not accomplish for others, all that political
advantage which he had led them to expect, he either
made ingenious explanations, or declared that he had
found it, at that juncture of affairs, impossible. Then he
made new promises.

The day before the scenes at widow Bailey's—the nota-
ble explosion and the telegraphic announcement of Benjamin's appointment—some of Judge Bailey's friends and
political subalterns, whom he could rely on, were invited
to a consultation at his office, where it was talked over
who would be good men for such and such offices. Some
who were not present were talked over at first; but
finally they took up each other's "claims" on the "party,"
and the result of their little private caucus showed that
under the head of "claims," and "availability," and the
self-sacrificing spirit which each and all had shown in
attending war-meetings, and in urging men to enlist in the

army, each one there present at Judge Bailey's caucus, was marked down on the political slate, for nomination or appointment, and chances were canvassed for three or four years ahead.

"There are," said Judge Bailey, "certain persons who have influence in every neighborhood, and, as a matter of policy essential to success, we must secure their friendship; but if we find that we cannot control their influence—if they are too selfish, and try to gobble up offices that naturally belong to some of us, why, then, we must *put them down*, and put forward some others in their places whom we *can* control! And right here," added the Judge, "while I think of it, we must all be sure to advise our friends in each election district of the county, to get their friends to be seen at every caucus and preliminary meeting; for, don't you see," said the Judge, with a significant smile and a cunning sparkle in his small red eyes, "there is where the ball is started—where the twig is bent, and where the secret lies—where they make the delegates that set up either our friends or our enemies!"

Finally, Judge Bailey got things ready where he could modestly say, that seeing they were all together he wished they would get up a letter and all sign it, so that his friend, Mr. Lyman Baldwin, who was now in Washington, could see (said Judge Bailey, watching closely the effect of his artful words) that "we are all acting together as his friends, and that we can support him in recommending David to the appointment as custom-house detective on the Niagara frontier. Mr. Baldwin," he continued, "is the special agent, you know, and there is a vacancy, so that he can make one selection to fill an office there. He wants David to have the appointment, but if the pressure of influence is too strongly in favor of some other candidate, on account of our *neglecting* the matter, of course he would have to go for whoever that other candidate might be."

Of course Judge Bailey don't want these friends of his to suspect that David can fail of getting the appointment by any lack of *his influence;* for their *belief* in his influence is his power over them!

"Let me make a suggestion here," said one of the shrewdest of the number present. "You know, Judge, that Lyman Baldwin is under great obligation to some others besides our friends. Now, there is Ben Bailey, I've been told this very day has more influence with Baldwin's friends than any other man among all the farmers in the county, and if you could get his name to our paper it would show that we have the farming community represented with us, which none of our names you know will show."

" Well, that is so, Judge," said another, "and of course you being a relative can easily get his name.

" The worst of it is," said the Judge, after a moment's hesitation, " our families have never been intimate enough."

" No," said David, " I don't suppose we could ask or expect Ben to favor me in such a way as this, and I don't think father and I need his help."

" I think we can find some better man to represent that class," said the Judge.

"Get *him*, though, if you can," said the man who had made the suggestion.

David Bailey's letter of recommendation was then made out, and as they walked up to the table, one after another, and signed their names, the Judge said he presumed that Ben Bailey would sign it, too, as he had always treated him very kindly himself; at any rate he would see him the next day.

Finally, they had all signed except the village lawyer, who had not appeared well satisfied with the prospects allotted to his share of the political future.

"If there be nothing more to do here," said the little lawyer, with a mysterious expression, "I claim the privilege to propose ——"

Here the little lawyer paused and looked slowly around as if to inspect the number present. The Judge was afraid something was going wrong. All turned attention to the little lawyer, who, knowing the tricks of a public speaker, had lengthened his pause on the word propose, just enough for their impatience to intensify their curiosity to know what it was he wanted to propose, when they had supposed everything agreed upon.

"To propose," repeated the little lawyer, "that as soon as we shall have completed the signing of this document, we proceed *en masse* to the American Hotel or to Dutch Henry's lager beer saloon, and that the Judge and David individually, and at two several times successively, stand treat for all that shall be then and there present."

"Certainly, a perfect *sine qui non !*" said one.

"Bravo! bravo!" said another.

"So mote it .be," acquiesced the Judge, in a merry mood.

At the same moment all the rest manifested in some way that they favored the little lawyer's proposition—as exactly the thing.

"Oh, one thing more," said the little lawyer, as he stepped forward and took up his pen, "the Judge is to go for me for Member of Assembly next year."

"Yes," said the Judge in his most winning way, while he took care to qualify his promise, "we will all go for you just as long as there is a possible chance for your nomination."

And as the little lawyer turned his eyes with an inquiring look, he thought the rest of them gave a very cordial sanction to the aforesaid political promise. The little lawyer signed the paper. The Judge thanked his friends. And the little lawyer said: "Now which, the hotel or the saloon?"

"The nearest one first, and the other afterwards," promptly responded one whose face had acquired a permanent blush.

They went accordingly.

4

CHAPTER VII.

An Unusual Visit—Mysterious Matters Referred to—Most Angry towards whom he
has most Injured—How a bold, bad man tries to stand upon his dignity.

THE next day after the private caucus held in the office
of Judge Bailey, he drove into the country to see his
nephew. He has the paper in his pocket, which was
signed by his political friends, in favor of his son's appointment. Judge Bailey wants Benjamin's name to that
paper! We shall see if he gets it. This day was full of
events at the farm house—even the old anvil had to ex-
plode, as you remember. And the boy, who had brought
the telegram announcing Benjamin Bailey's appointment
to the very office the Judge is seeking for his son,—had
been gone from the door of the old farm house less than
half an hour, when the aristocratic relative rapped on the
same door. Matilda proceeded to answer the call; and
her mother, in a suppressed tone of voice, exclaimed:

"Mercy on me! Matilda, I hope that telegraph boy is
not back here again!"

Matilda met her uncle at the door, and invited him
into the parlor so politely and kindly, that the Judge
was now willing to forget that he or his family had ever
wronged or proudly neglected his country relatives.
And he hoped, in his selfishness, that he might find

Widow Bailey equally forgetful of the old suspicions against him, and willing to "let by-gones be by-gones." The Judge had the vanity, too, to think his call was an honor to the widow's family; for he had a habit of forgetting, or seeming to forget, any mean thing he had done against his poorer relatives. No matter how great that injury, any reference to it, or any satisfaction demanded, he considered an insult, and thought himself meanly used if not immediately forgiven, in consideration of what he intended to do for them—after his death—in his will!

When Mrs. Bailey entered the parlor, and shook hands with Jared Bailey, she exclaimed:

"Mercy on me! Mr. Bailey, what brought you here! Why, how is your family? Why don't they never come to see us?"

Mr. Bailey was very agreeable; he had *often intended* to come, but he did not go anywhere!

After a few moments, he inquired for Benjamin.

Benjamin was sent for—came into the parlor. The uncle and nephew met! The uncle was never so cordial in his greeting; the nephew was polite, but formal. They talked of the weather, and of matters of general interest. At last, the Judge was glad to hear that Benjamin was quite a politician; and if he ever wanted an office, he, the Judge, could help him, and should be glad to do so. "The way it is with politicians," said Judge Bailey, attempting a very pleasant smile, "they must help each other; and I thought, perhaps, you would like to put your name down with some of the most influential ones of our party, who are friendly together, and are always willing to help each other. It is for an office Mr. Baldwin's friends are asking for your cousin David."

"Cousin David! Very doubtful compliment!" thought Benjamin; but he checked himself, and asked:

"What is the office which he desires?"

"Well," said the Judge, "Mr. Baldwin is a special agent of the Treasury; and, as he is a particular friend of mine, he is anxious to give David an office, which will require him, I suppose, to go to the Niagara District on some private matters connected with the customs department!"

Without replying to this last remark, Benjamin invited his uncle into his library.

The Judge entered the library with Benjamin, and seated himself with all the confidence of a bold and selfish hypocrite. He had, no doubt, long ago settled into the conviction, that his wealth, his duplicity, and the standing of his friends, were sufficient to conceal his meanness from very much *notice*, even if not from belief. Though it was true a few of his acts had sometimes been the gossip of his neighbors; but they had been hushed up by presents to those who cared little for their truth, or smothered by other influences, so that the status of the village Baileys in society remained not perceptibly changed. In fact, there were many who claimed that Judge Bailey and his wife were both very benevolent people—very kind, very obliging. But there were a few, and Benjamin among them, who knew that what appeared to be generosity was generally prompted by motives extremely selfish—a sort of bribe thrown upon "society."

to work up its good will; or, in special cases, a bid for
the attention of friends and flatterers; or a stingy amount
of something, as a mixture of conscience money and
hush money, given for wrongs they had brought upon
others!

O, if Benjamin only knew positively—if he had the
evidence of the secret history of this man, how much it
might have availed him towards making Judge Bailey set
him right with Deacon Sommers and his daughter! As
little as he does know, he has determined to seize upon
this opportunity, to attempt to find out the source of the
slander, and have it contradicted.

The Judge, thus far, was pleased with his reception.
He expressed great satisfaction that his nephew had so
fine a library.

"What paper do you wish me to sign?" inquired the
nephew, without appearing to notice the uncle's flattering
remarks.

The Judge then showed him the paper.

When the nephew had looked over the petition in favor
of David for the very office which that moment he secretly held himself, he must have felt that the position of
his village uncle was slightly ridiculous! It was, indeed,
humiliating enough for the Judge to ask (or beg rather)
a favor from his country nephew, whom he had allowed
his family to slight in every social way, and whom he
himself had only one year before most wickedly contrived to injure, by falsehood to the father of Laura
Sommers!

But the old man had arrived to that point of selfish-

ness, where conscience and honor were only sensitive so
far as he believed himself exposed, or likely to be so.

Had he known what Benjamin knew concerning the
appointment, or even of all the reasons which Benjamin
had for suspicions against his connection with the slander
affair, the present ridiculous tableau of old Bailey in
Ben's library, praying for his political influence in favor
of David, would never have taken place. But since it
did take place, Benjamin thought it a fit occasion to test
his suspicions, which of late had grown much stronger
against his uncle. He, therefore, approached matters with
the artful old man carefully.

"Uncle Bailey," said Benjamin, "what reason have
you to suppose the little influence I may have would do
you any good?"

"I have been told it would. It would certainly do no
harm; and it would be a commencement of reciprocating
favors, and Mr. Baldwin's friends and my friends will be
able to help you in case you should come up for office."

"But, uncle, the names you have here will never secure
that office."

"Do you know that, Benjamin?"

"Yes, sir, I _know_ that!"

"That may be so," replied the Judge; "but from what
I have heard to-day, I believe you can help to secure the
right names. Now, Ben," said the Judge, leaning forward and speaking in a low voice, "will you keep it a
secret if I make you a proposition?"

"It is natural and usual, I believe," said Benjamin,
"to favor those who favor us."

"Exactly so; that's the very sceret! and woe be to the man who betrays political confidence."

"Well, what is your proposition?" inquired Benjamin.

"It is this: take this petition, or get private letters—get the right names, and the day your cousin David gets the appointment, that day I will give you two hundred dollars in gold; (which in these war times you know is as good as five hundred dollars and over, in greenbacks, or any United States paper;) and if you want a hundred in greenbacks to-day to use with any influential friends of yours, you shall have it."

"Uncle Bailey, I have never yet offered money nor received money for political influence. I have never yet solicited an office. If I am a politician, it is only in the sense that I love to defend what I believe to be correct principles."

"Very true, very true," interrupted the Judge; "but then you know we must use the same weapons which others do, or we and our party too, might go to the devil!"

"But wait a moment," said Benjamin; "what I was going to say is this: I don't want your money, but there *is one favor* you can do me, and it will cost you nothing."

"You can command me," said the Judge, "for any influence I can give you. You can, Ben, I give you my word and honor."

"Then," said Benjamin, "write to William Sommers of Niagara Falls, and tell him whether you have any reason to believe I ever treated any young lady in a 'dishonorable and heartless manner!'"

As he said this he looked the Judge steadily in the

eye—in a way that convinced him that Benjamin Bailey had not yet forgotten Laura Sommers!

The Judge was taken by surprise, but assumed great innocence of manner as he replied:

"Why, what on earth do you mean, Benjamin? and where is the need of my writing *that* to Mr. Sommers?"

"Will you do me that favor?" asked Benjamin.

"Why, yes—of course, you may refer Mr. Sommers or anybody else to me on any ——"

Here Benjamin interrupted the Judge, and explained all he knew about the slander; and that he wanted no reference; but wanted the Judge to give him a written statement respecting his habits, honesty, and good moral character—such as would convince Mr. Sommers that the slanderous insinuations were without foundation.

"Why, of course, Benjamin, you refer Mr. Sommers to me, and I should take pleasure in writing to him that I never knew aught against you ——"

"And that you do not believe there is any foundation in fact for the slander which ——"

"Yes, I'll say all I can; just refer Mr. Sommers to me; and I ——"

"No, no, not *refer* Mr. Sommers to anybody," interrupted Benjamin, as he arose and opened his secretary and produced the necessary materials for writing a letter. "What I want, is, for you now to write just what you know or believe about that slander, and let me send your letter *with mine* to Mr. Sommers."

"Why, Ben, of course, I—I can't help what people may say about you or me, or anybody. The least said

about such matters the better.   All I could say about the
matter is, what a certain girl told my wife."

"Then all I ask," said Benjamin, "is that you write a
letter for me to send to Mr. Sommers, and let him—and
me, too—know who that girl is."

"Well, Benjamin, that is what I have no right to do :
that would be dishonorable in me to betray the confidence
the girl placed in my wife, and I should never betray
anybody's confidence!   Take a second thought, and I
think you are too honorable to ask it."

"Now, Judge Bailey, listen to what I tell you.   It is
now about one year since Laura Sommers wrote me a
letter throwing me aside as unworthy her confidence, and
all on account of that base slander.   I tell you, I do not
know even a foundation for the insinuation ; I ask you to
favor me so much as to help me to the facts, so I may trace
it out, and you refuse under a pretense that you are too
honorable to betray the confidence which in this case
means too honorable to correct falsehood !"

"Beware! young man," said the Judge.

"Hear me, then I shall hear you," replied Benjamin.
"What right," he then added, "have you to aid one in
concealing a wicked course because they have trusted you
in the secret?

> "'Who steals my purse steals trash; * * *
>   *   *   *   *   *   *   *
> But he that filches from me my good name
> Robs me of that which not enriches him,
> But makes me poor indeed!'

"To say it is wrong for you to betray a wrong, is but
to say it is right for you to be a confederate to sustain
4*

and conceal that wrong, you knowing it to be such. Judge Bailey, you *know me*, and I know you do not doubt my word. I am seeking, too, to defend my reputation at the very source of this slanderous imputation against me, whatever that source may be."

"Benjamin, you have said already more than I should bear were I not in your own house!" said the enraged uncle, as he rose from his chair.

"Stay," said Benjamin, "one moment, while I tell you why I do not believe that you hesitate to correct that injury to me on the grounds of honor. I now fully believe it is yourself who has set Mr. Sommers against me; for as nearly as I can learn, you are the only one with whom he is acquainted here, except widow Cummings. It is for *that* reason that you cannot help me to contradict the slander. But unless it be contradicted, it is you who have cause to fear the truth, not I."

"Young man, explain yourself!" said the Judge.

"That is what I desire to do, sir," said Benjamin.

"Do you know that I understand something of the secret of your transactions, and especially of that affair on the evening I handed you the letter from Mr. Baldwin one year ago and over? Be cautious, Judge Bailey, and wise enough to do me justice, or the public shall know that secret, too! Will you now correct Mr. Sommers' wrong impressions against me?"

"It is little matter to me," replied the Judge, "what you know; for I have witnesses enough to balance your evidence. And now, rash young man, it is my turn to give *you* warning! Hold your tongue of what you know of that evening," said old Bailey, with a bold look of criminal defiance, "for remember that a case in law depends upon *evidence*, not *facts!* upon who has the most good witnesses, the best lawyers, and the most money! And remember, I tell you to warn you, remember that when you swear against me as to what you alone may know, I may find two or three witnesses to contradict you, and at last convict you of perjury; and by that time you will find you do not abuse gray hairs and Judge Bailey with safety!"

"Now, young man, mark what I, too, have said, and it may save us both trouble, if we are wise enough to come to terms. What do you say? a truce, or shall I bid you good day?"

"I throw myself upon truth," said Benjamin, "and have no truce and no terms to make with wrong. It serves my honest purpose to know what this interview has revealed of you! When gray hairs stoop to threaten wrong, and defend wrong with more wrong, they deserve less consideration than the rashness of youth."

Judge Bailey waited to hear no more, but left the library, and passing through the sitting room and parlor, left the house. As he passed through the sitting room, however, he turned and cautioned Benjamin to remember the warning he had given him.

CHAPTER VIII.

JUDGE BAILEY's interview with Benjamin at the old farm-house, to secure his political influence, had proven not only a failure in respect to the object of his visit, but it had heaped up a combination of troublesome thoughts about other matters, which greatly excited his anger; and, as he emerged from the house and walked down the front yard, he manifested his excited state of mind by making very singular gestures with his walking stick, which seemed entirely uncalled for; also by uttering maledictions against Benjamin, and swearing that Miss Sommers and his own women matters had gotten himself badly mixed up; and that if Benjamin should expose him it would cost at least a thousand dollars to bribe witnesses, besides the danger at his advanced age, of finishing the sale of his soul to the devil; as the time he could yet hope to live might prove too short for redemption! And then he broke out again with an oath:

"But only think of it," said he to himself, "the ill-bred young fellow dared to talk to me of my faults—to me. an old man! as if a man of my standing would'nt find some way to defend himself, right or wrong. The impudent young rascal! If he exposes me in that devilish affair, Adeline must swear it is not so! or I'll cut off her prospects shorter than a bob-tail horse; and I'll have Jerusha swear *her into trouble*, somehow, besides swearing *me out*, if Adeline ever does tell the truth! But I must see Adeline, right away, and give her a hint of my old witnesses, Figsley and Vroman."

"What ails this infernal halter?" he inquired of the knot he had tied to fasten his horse to the hitching-post. "Thank God for one thing," he muttered, "my *wife* is still an active member of the biggest church in the place, and she believes it is a religious duty to hide that infernal foolish affair, or devilish crime, whatever it was! I suppose she thinks it's a pity though, for people of our standing to have to cover up things by falsehood; but of course it is expected people must defend themselves; and so it is, one folly, one sin, one disgrace calls out another."

By this time the halter was untied, the Judge was in his buggy, and away he drove, with his reflections and the unsigned paper.

Benjamin was in no mood to follow the Judge to the front door to take a polite parting; and as he turned and entered the sitting room he found his mother and Matilda very inquisitive and curious to know what was the cause of such an abrupt leave-taking; one of them introduced her inquiries by prefixing "mercy on me!" and the other exclaimed:

"Now, brother Ben, what good does a quarrel do? I thought you could always keep out of a quarrel!"

"What in the world is the matter?" inquired Mrs. Bailey, with intense earnestness.

"Mother and Matilda," said Benjamin, "it was a private matter. Jared Bailey is a greater villain and a bolder rascal than I took him to be; and it would please me if I only knew that there was some mistake about his birth! for he is meaner than any genuine Bailey could be!"

"Mercy on me! what else is going to happen to-day? What is the trouble, Benjamin? Is it politics, or what is it?"

He satisfied his mother and sister with a partial explanation, and left the house, saying he must give some directions to Tom, the colored man, who was at work in the front yard.

Although giving directions to Tom was his ostensible object for leaving the house, it is fair to presume that Benjamin had other thoughts on his mind, which a little walk in the yard might tend to compose. For the turn as well as the termination of the conversation with his uncle in the library, had started unpleasant and perplexing thoughts.

As Benjamin approached the front gate, whence the Judge had driven away only a few moments before, he noticed that Tom was busily talking to himself, and as busily at work by some shrubbery near the alley. He had caught the following sentences before the old colored man observed him, and it was evident that what he said must have reference to Judge Bailey, who had just passed down the alley

"Y-a-s! dat ole fellow wor a heap mad!" muttered Tom. "Fust time I ebber sed 'im *here;* guess it be de las' time, too! Git out ob de way, ses 'e, w'en I warn't in de way a' tall. Y-a-s, I pity de werry hoss dat draws sich a man! Swearin' all de way down de alley—jerkin' de hosse's bridle. I hope 'e git so mad 'e bite his own nose off sometime! I guess Massa Benjamin finest young man *he* ebber seed! I wonder wat 'e means 'bout Miss Somebody; he better not mean Miss Matilda, or I hit 'em five times to wonct 'e come here, 'wen nobody's to home. I wish de Lord de war would give colored folks de right to defend derselves, den his ugly face ebber come here agin, an' he tell me wid 'is big cane, to git out ob de way—wen I wern't *in* de way—I knock 'm wid dis hoe to kingdom come! dat I would."

"Well, 'Uncle Tom,' what's the trouble?" interrupted Benjamin, seeing that the faithful old man was not likely to make a permanent period in what he was telling himself.

"O, nuffen; I wasn't sayin' nuffen to nobody, Massa Benjamin; jes talkin' to myself a little, dat's all."

"What were you talking to yourself for, Tom?" said Benjamin, trying to get the old colored man to explain himself.

"O, nuffen, Massa Benjamin; but you axin me wot for I is talkin' to myself, makes me 'member wot ole Aunt Polly used to say w'en I was a little, small boy, way down in Tennessee, on de ole plantation. 'Monstros sakes!' ses she—."

Here the old man stopped suddenly to make an apology:

"Wal, now, I declar', Massa Benjamin, may be taint speeful for me to tell de story."

"O, yes," said Benjamin, "tell us what you remember about aunt Polly; I always think you mean well, uncle Tom."

"Y-a-s—dat, I allers do, Massa."

Thus encouraged, the old colored man continued, and Ben leaned against the fence and listened, though in a half absent-minded way, as he took up a stick and pro- ceeded to whittle it.

"Wal, Aunt Polly allers used to say, 'monstros sakes alive! wasn't I talkin' to myself 'cause der wasn't nobody else dat I was talkin' to? an' aint it ob course dat w'en I'm alone I's allers in sich good company?' an' den she would jes laugh herself to death, till she sot us laughin' as if we was *all* goin' to die! But bless her ole soul, I shan't never forget w'en dey whipped her little girl—poor Tilly—to death! She died right afore our eyes; and den dey whipped Aunt Polly till de blood run down her back, 'cause she cried so much about de cruel death ob her dear little Tilly—poor, ole Aunt Polly and poor Tilly, too—de whole plantation nebber seed her laugh any more!"

"That was a good many years ago, 'Uncle Tom,'" said Benjamin, as the old man felt for his cotton hand- kerchief.

"Y-a-s, Massa Benjamin," said 'Uncle Tom,' wiping his eyes, which were dim with years and dim with tears that had started at the calling of years agone! "Y-a-s, dat was a good many years ago, but I 'members it plain,

sef 'twas to-morrow or yesterday. "Twas afore I know'd
dere was sich a good man as Gerrit Smith to help de poor
black man, an' dat good ole man, John Brown, what tole
me which way to come, an' foller de north star in de
night time!"

"But, 'Uncle Tom,' you are forgetting to tell me what
troubled you as I just found you talking to yourself
here," said Benjamin, still whittling unconsciously—and
his thoughts were unsteady.

"Y-a-s, now I tell ye, Massa Benjamin, dat man what
come down de alley here—jes drove off wid de big cane
in 'is hand—he wasn't no friend to nobody, was he?"

"I'm very sorry to say, 'Uncle Tom,' that he is a very
bad man," was Ben's reply; and he whittled harder without knowing that he whittled.

"Wal, dat what I spect, w'en he come down de alley
here, swearin' and talkin', an' he look so much like de
hard massa dat tole 'em to whip little Tilly an' Aunt Polly.
O, I wish I could forget dat time, so I nebber 'member it
any more! Dem times wor awful hard."

"Well, 'Uncle Tom,' little Tilly was better off when
she died," said Ben, while the old fugitive slave paused
and again felt for his cotton handkerchief.

"Y-a-s, Massa Benjamin, so she wor," continued Uncle
Tom, after a moment's pause, "may be de ones dat suffer
most here, will hab it all made up in de udder world, if
dey be patient, and lub de Lord in dis world, 'cause we
don't know but cheryting is for de best *sometime!*"

* * * * * * * * *

Here the memoranda furnished by Benjamin Bailey as

to the events of that day, as well as to the interview with 'Uncle Tom,' abruptly closes. And we only know that for a few days afterwards Benjamin spent the time in making preparations to leave for the Niagara District; and that Mr. Baldwin, like a good, kind-hearted, shrewd politician, explained to Judge Bailey by letter how he regretted that influences were such that for this once, he had been obliged to disappoint him about securing an office at present for his son.

CHAPTER IX.

THE autumn leaves, except the constant evergreen, had
begun to change to the tints of red and yellow, and
the setting sun of a beautiful day had painted up the sky
in colors so grandly blended, and had so spread his influence over field and forest, that, only for the knowledge that
it would all so soon change to dreary darkness, one could
have fancied both sky and earth were the scenery of heaven.

In a well-furnished room in the second story of Deacon
Sommers' commodious farm-house, Laura Sommers was
seated alone by the side of a table on which lay the
materials for writing a letter. A half hour had passed
away and she had not written a line. She was undecided
and unhappy; and as she looked out of the window
through the scattering trees to the west of the farm-house,
the beautiful sky and the softened rays of the waning day
only added gloom to her reflections.

She laid her pen aside, arose and approached the
window, and in an audible voice she said: "I *cannot
write*—lest I shall say too much; or they will, to whom I
entrust my secret! I look out upon this bright world
and all would be happiness for me if my own thoughts

would let me forget how I loved him! or even if I could convince my feelings that he is as bad as they told me."

And here overcome by her feelings, the tears started from her eyes; and for a time she thought no more of the bright external world.

For what is brightness without when the soul is dreary within? when the lips are silent for the tremor of grief that has gained control? What though we say, Why submit the will to grief? When the mind is possessed with some certain thoughts, so that there are no other thoughts for the time, to make the will come up to change the course those thoughts drive us to pursue, whether fortunate to us or not, who shall say that the will, *or that which produces will*, can change one instant ere it does! Must not the auspicious moment come? And do not the remote as well as the immediate causes all have their effect to produce the state and quality of mind at the instant? according to the will of Him "who hath ordered every event!"

Laura was not now thinking of the happy friends around her, her father's wealth, nor her own youthful beauty; and who can say the thoughts we are *not* thinking—*they* can come up to rule! And yet, as it is with one, so it is in this respect, with each successive moment! and each successive thought!

At last as the sun-lit scene had faded, Laura again found utterance.

"It is strange," said she, "that Benjamin Bailey is so bad and I could only hear it from *one* family in Fallington. I don't believe it!" and then she held her handker-

chief to her face again and sobbed as she added, "and yet
I do! Father says he knows Judge Bailey would not say
such things if they were not true! and, beside that, his
wife said so, too,—and she is such a pious woman!

And here, as if convinced that her worst fears were
true, she attempted to brush away the bitter tears which
came faster and faster down her cheeks, while she struggled
to resolve again, and perhaps for the fiftieth time, that she
would forget him.

As Laura was giving utterance to her feelings, she was
not aware that a listener stood at the partly open door of
the room.

Poor Dinah,—she was indeed a faithful, simple-hearted
servant; but she had eyes and ears, and she had thoughts;
why should she *not* be inquisitive as well as white girls?
Besides this, Dinah felt an interest in the Sommers family.
She and her mother had once been the slaves of a cruel
master in Virginia; and Mr. Sommers was one of the
Abolitionists who had aided them in making their escape.

Before the Southern rebellion, Mr. Sommers had
donated large sums of money and given personal aid to
provide means for the secret flight of slaves from their
masters into Canada; notwithstanding that he knew the
"Fugitive Slave Law," for giving any such "aid and comfort," rendered him liable to a fine of one thousand dollars, and also to imprisonment.

He had in the course of those transactions, secreted
Dinah and her mother from their pursuers; and as Dinah
was too inexperienced in housework to earn her living or
find ready employment, Mrs. Sommers had, at the request

of Dinah's mother, taken her into her own family to live, and Mr. Sommers had carried the slave mother to Lewiston at night, and placed her in charge of other anti-slavery men, who ferried her across the smooth Niagara River, at that place, to a land of safety.

For the past five years Dinah had received from Mr. Sommers' family the same wages that were given elsewhere to white servants. Her mother had been two or three years married to black Jim, the fisherman, and lived in Canada, just across the river; but Dinah had preferred to live in the family of Mrs. Sommers; she often told her mother she "always was goin' to stay dah, fur she didn't know what do fam'ly could do widout her!"

Dinah was emphatically an eccentric personage. Some said she was simple; others that she was nobody's fool; our own opinion is, that among her multitudinous freaks and sayings she sometimes said very wise things, and, like a great many precocious children, she said and did a great many wiser things than she herself ever comprehended the full meaning of,—precisely as some men by making very foolish blunders have acquired fortunes. One thing was certain: there was none of the Sommers family who claimed for any of Dinah's numerous little annoyances the dignity of impudence.

This was the listener at Laura's door.

Dinah had been sent up stairs to hand a letter to Laura which Deacon Sommers had just brought home from the Niagara Falls post-office. The door, as we have said, was but partly open, but the range was such as to bring Laura in full view of the colored girl. Dinah stopped at the door and listened. She hid herself partly behind the door, at the same time adjusting it so that she could peep through the opening, with so small a section of her countenance exposed that she really believed no chance look of Laura's would discover her inquisitiveness.

As Dinah caught Laura's words, she grew more and more eager to know the cause of her troubles. At first she looked, then she applied her ears to the crevice, and the next instant she directed her eyes toward Laura. She grew excited, and her dark eye-lids peeled themselves back till the white of her eye-balls shone fearfully around their dark centers.

"What in the worl'" said she, in an exclamatory whisper, "am de matter wid my missus Laura! She 'pears awful strange—what dat?—what dat she sayin! De lord ob lub!—why don't I keep still, now—so I hear dat?"

"It must be true," said Laura; and if 'tis, their judgment is right."

"Hark, now, what dat she say 'bout de Judgement!" muttered Dinah, beginning to be superstitiously alarmed—not catching her meaning, and fancying just then she heard a noise in the dark closet at the end of the hall.

"But," continued Laura, just then raising her handkerchief again to her eyes, "I did not, no, I did not like what the Judge said the last day—I was there."

As Laura was speaking the words "*Judge said the last day*," Dinah's superstitious fears were confirmed; she heard the noise in the dark closet plainer than before; while her ideas of Laura and of the white handkerchief to

Laura's face now reached a state of actual confusion and fright; and she ran away from the door and down stairs as fast as she could go.

Deacon Sommers was in the sitting-room reading to Mrs. Sommers the news from the armies in the South. He had just finished reading an account of the surrender of Fort Wagner to General Gilmore, when Dinah rushed into the sitting-room, not venturing to stop till she reached the dining-room door, and exclaiming in a loud whisper, as if afraid the causes of her fright would overhear her:

"O, I's done scart to def! Der is suffin in de dark closet—an Miss Laura—is cryin' 'bout de Judge an' de last day! O, I's so awfully——"

"What do you say about Laura, you foolish thing!" asked Mrs. Sommers with a puzzled expression, as she moderately proceeded to go up stairs.

"I don't believe she has seen Laura," said Deacon Sommers.

"Scart," continued Dinah, "dat I can't hardly say nuffin—an'—an' Miss Laura was stan'in' afore the winder—wid a white cloth over her face. O, I's so fear'd she done gone crazy—cryin' an' talkin' hersef to def—and suffin white on her face—jes sef she wur goin' to be a talkin' ghost! O, I's so sorry for Miss Laura—go up dah, too, Mister Sommers."

"Never mind, Dinah, you are *frightened* about something."

"Dat's what I's sayin', Mister Sommers. I's fear'd Miss Laura is haunted, by suffen, in de dark closet!"

By this time Mr. Sommers started toward the stairway

and Mrs. Sommers had met Laura at the head of the stairs. A few minutes later and all was explained. Laura was not a ghost, with a white cloth over her face; and the dark closet up stairs was all right, as it is in anybody's house. Dinah was sent into the kitchen; Deacon Sommers resumed his reading; and Laura was in possession of the letter which Dinah through all her inquisitiveness and fright, had clung to like a faithful keeper.

As Dinah went out of the sitting-room she was some-what ashamed of her fright, and she muttered in a confused way, as if partly willing to be heard:

"Well, I know'd 'twasn't nuffen', anyhow, but suffen' was de matter; 'twouldn't be nuffen strange if de house *was* ha'nted when dey keep de rooms so dark to scare de flies out. What if de sun-light do fade de carpets, dat aint spooks!"

Our round, revolving world, had not yet hidden all the evening light behind the western arch of lake, land and forest, when Laura returned to the window where she stood when Dinah was her listener.

She saw from the post-mark on the letter just handed her that it was mailed at New York city, from which place Fallington was not many miles distant. The address was in a strange hand; she opened the letter; the letter, too, was in a strange hand, but evidently that of some intelligent lady. The letter was a long one, and she immediately turned to the bottom of the last page to see the name of the writer; it was written Mrs. Hellen Hartley. It was a name she had no recollection of whatever.

5

"Hellen Hartley! I wonder who Hellen Hartley is?" said Laura, as she laid the letter upon the table and proceeded to light a lamp.

"I wish," said Laura, as she touched a match-blaze to the lamp-wick, "that some of these Pennsylvania oil wells would strike something nicer than this *outlandish* kerosene, or they would find some way to get the musk out of it! I prefer geranium myself. What a world this is; it is a good thing that trouble doesn't trouble us any more than it does," added Laura, as she seated herself, and taking up the letter from Mrs. Hartley, she read as follows:

"NEW YORK CITY, *Sept.* 5, 1863.

"MISS LAURA SOMMERS:

"Niagara Falls, N. Y.:

"*Dear Stranger*—I feel it is my duty to reveal to you something about Judge Bailey in Fallington. It may be important to your happiness for life. But as I do not wish to have my name mixed up with any scandal, I want you and your family to consider this letter confidential. I venture it to do by you as I would like another to do by me.

"Last July I made a visit to Mrs. Judge Bailey's in Fallington. It happened I got there the next day after you left. I heard the family speak of you and saw your photograph.

"I had been there about two weeks, when, one evening, as I stood by the window reading a newspaper, Judge Bailey gave me a gross insult. I immediately left the room, and meeting Mrs. Bailey informed her of the insult, and to my astonishment, she at first treated the matter lightly, and then intimated that if I chose to bring scandal upon myself by catching up 'such *little matters,*' I would find it would injure no one but myself; that they *would* tell as much against me as I dare tell against them, and that I would find that they would swear to it, too, to defend their honor, *whether it was true or not,* so if I did not wish to injure myself I had better keep such matters quiet. I then went to my room, but remembering that the adjoining room was over the sitting-room, and that a stove-pipe came through the floor, I went there to listen, thinking the insult gave me a right to hear what they would say of it.

"I will now write you part of what I heard. 'Well, if she makes a fuss about it,' said Mr. Bailey, 'you and Jerusha must swear me clear. You remember what our lawyer said I need only prove. No matter whether it is true or not, evidence is evidence! If I can make out she was to blame, of course it will be nothing to her credit. Tell her then, boldly, that you and Jerusha will swear her into trouble if she is mean enough to get us into trouble.' I suppose she meant Jerusha Vroman. Only think! and she seemed to be such a conscientious girl. Only think! he abuse me, and then defend himself by slandering me!

"But pretty soon they got to talking on what may concern you. I overheard Mrs. Bailey say, 'Jared, I wish David was married to Laura Sommers before you disgrace us all. This is not the only time, Jared, that you've acted like an insane man, and promised it should

be the last! Who knows but Benjamin Bailey knew
Adeline's voice when you abused her in the hall the
time he handed you the letter? Suppose Adeline should
ever get sick, and light-headed, or talk in her sleep about
that, or the way we got our property?' Then the next
thing I heard was Mr. Bailey saying, 'As for Mrs. Hartley, [that's my name,] her father expects all his children
to have some of my property, so there is no danger of
his listening to anything against *me*, even if he knew it
were true. But I'll promise to will Mrs. Hartley the
Hill house and lot if she'll stand by us.' 'No, you can't
do that,' said Mrs. Bailey, 'for you've promised that to
Jerusha.' 'Of course I did,' said he, 'and Jerusha will
get it; that is, if she does exactly as I wish her to do,
and I don't change my mind. But if I need her and
Adeline to contradict anything, they must be on hand.
They talk about conscience! What's the use of talking
about conscience when a thing has *got to be done?* *I've
had* to promise to will the *same* property to a dozen different ones in the course of a few years! *But I had to
do it!*' 'Well, no matter,' said Mrs. Bailey, 'they will
not know who gets it till after we are dead and gone, and
they will not bark much after it is too late to do us any
hurt or themselves any good.'

"They went on in this way sometime. Finally I heard
Jared Bailey say, 'David shall not have that Henriette
Smith, and if she sues him for breach of promise we
must swear him out of it!' 'No,' said his wife, 'I will
not swear to what is not so, *except to save ourselves or the
property;* not for any little thing. And we don't know

as Laura Sommers would have David; and David says all he would have her for is her property!' 'Well, that's enough,' said Jared Bailey, 'and we don't want any such poor trash in the family as Henriette Smith. Of course she'll feel bad—good girl enough—but she is not used to such society as we keep.'

"But, Miss Sommers, I've written enough to warn you what they are. If you doubt what I say, perhaps you can find out something from Adeline Wilderman or others there near them.

" Very truly yours,
" MRS. HELLEN HARTLEY."

CHAPTER X.

"My stars!" exclaimed Laura Sommers, in surprise, as she finished reading the letter from Mrs. Hellen Hartley, which closed the last chapter, "if they are such folks as that, there is not a word of truth in what they told me—about Benjamin; and it is a credit to him and his folks that they do not visit there! Why, how I must have hurt his feelings, and how unreasonable he must have thought us not to let him even have a chance to defend himself! David Bailey! I would not marry him if he were a statue of gold! To say the best, he is only a smart simpleton; his want of good sense has been rendered the more ridiculous by a *little* education! And if that were not so, I don't like the expression of his face. I would rather marry Col. Le Grange, and have him go right off to the army and get shot—so far as *I* would be concerned—though, of course, I don't wish him any *harm.*"

"I'll go and hand this letter to mother, and see what she thinks of it. And then I'll hand it to father and see what he thinks of it. Why! I can hardly believe my eyes."

When Laura reached the sitting-room she found her

father and mother alone; and holding the letter in her hand as she advanced toward them, she said:

"Here, father and mother, is a remarkable letter, which makes things look to me as if we have all been deceived by Judge Bailey—and by Mrs. Bailey, too, instead of mother and I having been deceived in our good opinion of Benjamin Bailey when we were visiting in Fallington."

Deacon Sommers gave a puzzled look over his spectacles, toward Laura and the letter, and the next moment he said, "let me read it, daughter."

"Who is it from?" asked her mother.

"It is from an entire stranger to me—but some acquaintance, it appears, of Judge Bailey's family," replied Laura, handing the letter to her father, "and my stars! you will not believe your own senses when you read it."

Deacon Sommers laid aside his newspaper. The hundreds of soldiers which had been killed in late battles were for a moment forgotten. Two of his own sons who had just enlisted, but who had not yet been ordered to the front, were also out of mind; and Laura's matrimonial affairs now claimed the moment's attention.

Everybody had begun to look upon the sufferings and upon the dangers of the war as something that could not be averted. The horrors of actual warfare made less excitement now than the first gun at Fort Sumter. And a hundred soldiers now killed in battle took less hold on the public feeling than the first soldier killed in the Massachusetts Sixth Regiment, at the Baltimore railroad depot in 1861, while on their way to the defense of Washington.

Such is human nature. The soldier himself, though he shudder in the first moments of battle, he soon looks on and fights on in the midst of blood, carnage and death, without fear or falter! So the public, too, had come to look to matters of civil life, and forget, at times, the horrible state of internecine war. So it was that Deacon Sommers laid aside even the news from the armies in the South, to read a letter that told of Laura's lover.

Deacon Sommers read the letter deliberately and aloud. Mrs. Sommers listened with eager interest. Both were surprised at the contents. Mrs. Sommers expressed her opinion that Judge Bailey was a mean man, and she guessed her first impressions would turn out to be correct, after all.

"Don't be too fast, wife," interrupted Deacon Sommers, "what do we know about this Mrs. Hellen Hartley? And, besides that, she does not contradict a single thing that is said against Benjamin Bailey."

"Father," said Laura, "doesn't that letter show that Judge Bailey is mean enough to tell what is not true?"

"And doesn't it show," added Mrs. Sommers, "that his object was to help David get Laura for a wife?"

"But," replied Deacon Sommers, "it appears David has made no demonstrations to support that suspicion; and even if he had, is it likely that the Judge and his wife would dare state what they could not prove, and what others could show is false? It does seem to me a strange freak that a sensible girl, like Laura, should fall in love with a stranger, like Benjamin Bailey, when she has offers among acquaintances like Col. Le Grange and young Smith, persons of wealth and standing."

"Then you do not think, father, that it is best to notice this Mrs. Hartley's letter, do you?" asked Laura, with some surprise.

"Why, as to that, if I had good reason to believe that Benjamin Bailey is a young man of good morals, good intelligence, good standing, good business abilities, and good habits, and entertaining good orthodox sentiments, and —— "

"Why, goodness sakes! father, there is not anything else good that can be added," interrupted Laura, in a respectful, but thoughtful manner.

"And," resumed the Deacon, "if his means be such as we would think desirable for one like Laura—who has always had everything she wanted—why, then, I should consider it important to inquire into the matter; that is, if you are determined not to be happy any other way."

"As to his means, father, I think a young man of his good habits, with the good sense he has, would be capable of taking care of me, and also help me to take care of what property you, my dear father, are intending shall go with your daughter."

"But, father, I *would* like to ask of you one favor. Will you write to Benjamin and give him the privilege to explain Judge Bailey's charges?"

"I do not think that is necessary; at least, not till we find out from other sources that Judge Bailey's statements are not reliable."

"Well, I can write," said Laura, "to that Adeline Wilderman, which this letter refers to, and perhaps we shall find out that Judge Bailey is a worse man than even

5*

Mrs. Hartley intimates. And, mother, will you write to Mrs. Cummings, and tell her confidentially about this letter, and ask her to write you what she can find against Judge Bailey, towards showing that Mrs. Hartley's letter is true in all it says? I tell you, father, that Judge Bailey does not seem exactly like a saint to me since I've got my suspicions up!"

Mrs. Sommers thought it might be well enough to make some investigation, and finally Deacon Sommers himself said he would make some inquiries by addressing the minister at Fallington, and hoped Laura would then be satisfied.

Deacon Sommers was not a very impulsive man; and even if he had been, it is not likely that he, with man's characteristic habit of looking into the minute points of a tangled case, and pondering out a conclusion after complicating the difficulty by this and that, or some other query—not likely he would have come to so quick or positive an opinion as to what notice he ought to take of Mrs. Hartley's remarkable letter, as his daughter did; for, Laura, with woman's quick decision, dispatched a letter of inquiry early the next morning to Adeline Wilderman.

Five days, or at farthest a week, she considered sufficient time to get a reply, but more than two weeks passed and no reply came. Had she offended Adeline Wilderman by writing as a stranger should not? She had written that Judge Bailey had informed her father of some things which it was important that her father should know positively if they were true. Would she be kind enough to write a reply, and let her know whether the Bailey family in Fallington village could be relied on in all they said against the Baileys who lived about a mile from the village. "We have received," wrote Laura, "some startling information against Judge Bailey. Do you know how he obtained so much property? I have just received a letter from a lady stranger, who tells me you know something of his private character, and as you had been badly abused by him, you might write me some particulars, as it is important to me to know whether his statements can be relied on!"

It may be, reflected Laura, as she thought over these and other things she had written—it may be that this Adeline, though she has been abused, may have some reasons—some interest in saying nothing against Mrs. Judge Bailey's family; or it may be—for it has certainly been long enough for me to have a reply—I was not careful enough in what I wrote, to avoid casting any reflections against her in supposing her to have so much knowledge of such a man's secret history. It does seem, said Laura, to herself, that some things, however innocently intended, and no matter how necessary to inquire about, cannot be spoken of even to innocent parties, without giving them offense; but I cannot help it; it is right I should know, and wrong somewhere if I am deceived. And how shall I know whom to believe, if I must make no inquiries?

Mrs. Sommers now wrote her cousin, Gertrude Cummings, some inquiries; and Deacon Sommers wrote to the Presbyterian minister at Fallington.

It would seem that the marriage of one's daughter—a matter which might effect the happiness or misery of her life-time—ought to have suggested that Mr. Sommers go himself to Fallington, especially when there did appear cause for doubt, and learn, if possible, from personal interviews, the truth of matters. But such a course had not yet suggested itself.

The idea of any deep-laid plot to deceive them, such as novel writers invent, of course was not going to affect *their* family. What they would be told by Mrs. Cummings and the minister would be true, of course! And the idea of Judge Bailey and his wife both attempting to deceive Mrs. Cummings and the minister by some indirect method in order to deceive others, through them, was not likely to be suspected.

Two days after Laura Sommers had written her letter Adeline Wilderman was reading it. Poor Adeline—poor woman! But I cannot in this volume take room to give you the particulars of her life; you shall, however, be able to infer that if ever woman had struggled to cover up the faults, and even the crimes of a man once her guardian, lest his exposure would render another unhappy whom she tried to think had treated her like a mother, and perhaps even drag Adeline herself into the general disgrace which might come about by the blunders of guessing gossipers and erroneous suspicion—that woman was Adeline Wilderman. She had seen trouble enough! It was natural that she should shun the appearance of more. Hence the hasty dispatch of Laura's letter, together with the neglect of Deacon Sommers in writing, were unfortunate circumstances. The former became the cause of giving Judge Bailey notice of impending trouble; the latter afforded him time to plan a concealment of facts; and for a time a successful game of bold, deep and mean deception it was.

For his success, however, he was mainly indebted to his wife and Jerusha Vroman. They suggested the plan, and the three carried it out. One or two of Mrs. Hartley's own relatives were immediately bribed, and otherwise influenced to say with apparently serious regret, that Mrs. Hartley was a *strange woman;* that her story against Judge Bailey really belonged to another family, and that she had applied it to Judge Bailey's family out of spite. This explanation seemed plausible, and partly with this success they succeeded in silencing and perhaps deceiving Mrs. Cummings and the minister's family. In this and other ways they not only covered up the facts, but injured Mrs. Hartley's reputation, for making any complaint about the abuse she had received from Judge Bailey, and for disclosing what she had overheard.

It may be that Judge Bailey's conscience reproved him for slandering one he had provoked to speak the truth; but had he not the heart years before to sacrifice poor Eleanor Grace! and had he not continued to hold a hard hand over Adeline's fears?

Adeline's experience, or rather her broken spirits, had prepared her to silently "endure what she could not cure." She did not, therefore, deem it advisable for her to disclose anything in reply to Laura's letter.

Sometimes she had thought it to be her duty to expose

wrong—to tell what she knew. But she was almost help-
less and friendless; and though she had been cruelly
wronged by Mr. and Mrs. Jared Bailey, it would, she
thought, only make the matter worse to turn even their
selfish friendship into desperate anger against her. Often
had she thought over the time when she lived in their
family; how she had concealed what she knew of his
procuring a fraudulent will from a dying man, and how
she had been induced to sign the will as a witness.

Some twelve years prior to the time of the will-fraud,
and when Adeline was seven years of age, Jared Bailey
and his wife took little Adeline into their family, pledging
her dying mother—and that mother a widowed sister of
Mrs. Bailey—that they would care for her child as for
their own daughter. And yet all the trouble she has
ever known has been caused by being too true to those
who made and broke that promise.

It is now nearly twenty years since she left the rich
Jared Bailey's house and learned the trade of a dress-
maker, that she might be independent of him. It was
her intention then to expose the will-fraud and the defen-
sive falsehoods of Jared Bailey and wife against poor
Eleanor Grace, who had spoken the truth. But her resolution, had it been carried out, came too late to have
benefited Eleanor. She had mysteriously disappeared!
And Adeline, by fear and favor, was finally influenced
to a silence not yet broken.

Jared Bailey's successful attempt to defraud his relatives, (successful unless the bitter end was to come,) and
the heartless means by which he had sacrificed Eleanor,

and silenced Adeline, were not the only private acts of a similar character which he was guilty of. But blundering gossip knew so little of any facts against him that when it made its blundering reports, dependent friends pretended not to believe it, and said in ridicule of gossip, "people will talk, you know!"

It was strange how Jared Bailey had got on so well as he had in the general, seeming favor of society. It was, however, probably owing to two causes; he was rich and cunning. But, then, he was vain and haughty, and tyran- nical when his selfish desires were opposed; and he was illiberal except that his selfish and passionate love of female society led him to many acts of apparent gener- osity and kindness. He was one of those men who would shed tears over the sufferings of a beautiful lady stranger, sooner than give a dime to the starving children of a washer-woman. And so long as any young lady made her diamonds glitter in his house, and also flattered his vanity by even virtuous coquetry, so long he counted her board and trouble nothing, and his carriage or his saddle-horse was at her service and he her humble servant.

CHAPTER XI.

Frightened at last—A Fit—Deeper Injury planned against the Innocent—Adeline's Silence—Rev. Mr. Smoothwell—David Bailey "proposes" by Letter to Laura Sommers.

WITH the knowledge which Adeline possessed of Jared Bailey, and of the course which had been taken to cover up his crimes, she was prepared to put the worst construction possible upon the vague allusions in Laura's letter. "Perhaps," thought she, "that unprincipled Mr. Figsley from Canada, who made out the papers when that poor, sick man signed the wills in Mr. Bailey's house, has said something—has exposed how it was about the two wills! My soul on me! what if there should be trouble, and I brought up as a witness, and then if I swore to the truth John Vroman and that Figsley would swear that I had committed perjury, as Mr. Bailey says they would all have to do in self-defense, and put me in prison!" Adeline's imagination was thus busily at work with unpleasant forebodings when she heard a knock at the door.

She answered the call; and Mrs. Judge Bailey, followed by her husband, entered the room. The usual formalities followed. Mrs. Bailey put on a little more than her usually smooth and friendly manner. After a little preliminary conversation Adeline was about to speak of the letter which she had just received, but the Judge announced his errand first.

"Adeline," he said, "you know what my motto is—when a thing has got to be done, or has been done, there is no use to talk about conscience. What is conscience, any way? Our consciences depend on our judgment, education, etc. We cannot always tell by conscience what it is best to do. Why, the preachers this moment, in the South, are all praying for one side of this war, while the preachers in the North are praying for the other side. One side for slavery, which is a devilish sight worse robbery than the will matters you so often refer to."

"Mr. Bailey," said Adeline, "you call selfishness conscience; and you argue in favor of doing wrong on purpose, because we do wrong sometimes ignorantly. That is your way—not mine."

"Well, Adeline," said Mrs. Bailey," "there is one thing you and I both believe in—friends must hang together."

"Yes," interrupted Adeline, as her eyes flashed toward Judge Bailey, "for if they did not hang together, some one, almost, would hang alone! or get some other punishment!"

But Judge Bailey never appropriated a rebuke which he could possibly think might mean others instead of himself. He knew that Mrs. Bailey and Adeline did not dare to expose him under any circumstances; and to any rebuke from them he usually replied, "the least said the better," and this with a smile that always reminded Adeline of that often quoted line—

"A man may smile and smile and be a villain."

For the opinion or the feelings of those whom he had wronged, but whom he knew would not expose him, he cared nothing; and yet he cared as much as he could care; it was not in his nature to care, and Mrs. Bailey pitied him! She loved him. And she had been known to say respecting him and Miss Vroman, "let them who are without sin cast the first stone," and "let us forgive as we hope to be forgiven!"

"We have come here," said the Judge to Adeline, "to ask a favor of you; for, you know we have been doing you favors almost all your life time."

"Jared Bailey!" said Adeline, with a wild stare, "I am in no mood to listen to your deliberate impudence; and before I die you may fear me as I have feared you!"

"Hush, hush, now, dear Adeline," interrupted Mrs. Bailey, "do be quiet, now! Don't expose anything for my sake, and your own, too. You know, Adeline, that Mr. Bailey can secure all the witnesses, and you none; and now don't, for your sake and mine, too! I don't approve of it, but how can I help myself?"

"Why, then," returned Adeline, angrily, "does he taunt me about *favors*—as if he could make me forget the *injuries* he has done me! Did he not defraud me of the two thousand dollars which was in the real will which that poor, dying man thought he was signing?"

"And haven't we," interrupted Mrs. Jared Bailey, "paid you more than Mortimer Bailey promised you?"

"And haven't you extorted money enough out of me, added Judge Bailey, "for a little affair, lately, which you called a thousand times worse than it was? and haven't

I for more than twenty years paid you the interest on that 'two thousand dollars'?"

"But where is the principal?" said Adeline, "and what reliance can I place in the future on a man like you, who destroyed poor Eleanor Grace by falsehood, which robbed her of a young man who would have made her a kind and worthy husband? you who drove me into sign-ing a false will as a witness, and ever since have fright-ened me into this long silence, by saying the act made me as guilty as the rest of you. If I am a criminal, you have made me such, through fear and ignorance of laws; while it has made you rich and me wretched!" And, then turning to Mrs. Bailey, she added, "and to frighten me into silence about that insane assault, did he not bribe Jerusha Vroman to tell me, after all I did for her, that she would swear to things—true or false—to defend him ; and didn't you intimate the same?"

"Why, Adeline!" said Mrs. Bailey, "you don't—you can't blame us! What else could we do?"

"Adeline," said Judge Bailey, "you act like—purga-tory! What's up worse than usual?"

"This is what's up for you," Adeline replied, produc-ing the letter from Laura Sommers. "You can read it for yourself, Mr. Bailey. *You are already exposed!*"

"Good Lord!" exclaimed Mrs. Bailey; and Judge Bailey reached out his trembling hand for the letter; and when he had read only a part of it his guilty conscience forced him to fear the worst. Mrs. Bailey noticed that he turned pale, and she stepped to his chair. The next instant the letter dropped from his hand; he uttered a groan; Mrs. Bailey supported him in the chair, and cried out:

"O, Adeline! he is dying! he is dying! get the camphor. O, my dear husband, what's the good of all our property, now? O, what shall we do!"

As Adeline was hunting up the camphor bottle, she muttered, "I'm afraid it's only a fit—of his conscience! But if it be the apoplexy—it's awful for such a man to die—such a hypocrite as he has been. The Lord's will be done, though! only I hope he won't die here!"

"Do find the camphor, Adeline!"

"Yes, here it is;" and then she applied the resuscitating remedy to his nose and head, and chimed in with Mrs. Bailey:

"O, what shall we do! what shall we do! if he dies here," said Adeline.

In a few moments, however, he began to revive, and was soon so far restored that by the assistance of Adeline and Mrs. Bailey he walked home.

The next day Mrs. Judge Bailey sent for Adeline, requesting her to bring the letter with her. Adeline went. The letter which Judge Bailey had not finished reading the evening previous was now read, and read again; but after considerable discussion he decided that it was very vague in its meaning; especially about the property. It was decided, however, that Mrs. Hellen Hartley's statements must be put down.

Adeline was again threatened and promised. If she stood by them she would have five thousand dollars willed to her; and when she needed anything it should

be got for her. And if she did not defend them they
would all have to turn against her and give her nothing!

Adeline was once more persuaded—and frightened—
and she promised that she would disclose nothing! "But,"
said she, "I tell you, Mr. Bailey, and mark what I say,
'*your sin will find you out!*'"

"That may be," said Judge Bailey, "but, Adeline, we
cannot help the past, and we must finish up what we have
on hand. You know that John Vroman still lives at
Niagara Falls. Of course I don't fear him. But, that
Figsley, on the Canada side; it costs me a good deal
every year to keep him still. Now, here comes up Benjamin Bailey, attempting to make the acquaintance of
the daughter of William Sommers. Should he succeed
in his object, he would, of course, finally become acquainted with Mrs. Hartley's letter, and that allusion to
the property might revive, in fact it would be sure to
revive the old suspicions—and suspicions might start
inquiry—then if Deacon Sommers should join with Benjamin against us he might supply means; and Figsley
has got to be just dishonorable enough to turn against us!
He makes a great many threats lately, and even keeps up
the old matter about Eleanor Grace—pretends *he* didn't
want things carried so far—that there was enough of us to
cover up the facts and her statements, too, without turning her out doors just for being off her guard and telling
the truth! He says if we hadn't turned her out doors
she would have finally consented to be Mrs. Figsley; and
every time he gets in a rage he threatens that Eleanor
shall have vengeance on me yet, and that her mysterious

disappearance will come to light yet, as well as papers
enough to defend her character; and all this, when at
first, you know Figsley tried to put down her statements
himself!   He's a treacherous *villain*," said the *innocent* Mr.
Jared Bailey, with as much assurance as if it indicated
some virtue in himself to denounce the now dissipated
and disreputable Figsley!   "But," he added, partly with
a view to keep Adeline intimidated to silence, "we are
all in the treacherous villain's power, for I've no doubt
he was just cautious enough to save as many letters and
papers as he needed to injure us with."

"So it won't answer to have Deacon Sommers turn
against us.   And there is only one safe course for us all
to take.   We must at all hazards prevent Benjamin from
having any communication with that family.   If necessary, Jerusha must write Mrs. Sommers that she is the
young lady whom we have said Benjamin treated so
shamefully.   Then I must get some of Mrs. Hartley's
friends to put discredit on what she wrote.   The other
thing to be done is to have Deacon Sommers interested
in our favor by our bringing about David's marriage
instead of Benjamin's with Laura Sommers.   You know,
Adeline, Mrs. Bailey and Jerusha and myself have already
managed to break off all correspondence between Benjamin and the Sommers family; though I confess there
isn't much prospect of David's success in the place of it."

"Mr. Bailey," interrupted Adeline, "I shall have nothing to do with the matter; nor do I know anything against
Benjamin Bailey."

"Have I not told you that Benjamin is no friend of
yours?" said Mrs. Bailey.

"And haven't I told you," said Judge Bailey, with a falsehood on his tongue, "how he talks against you and Jerusha? About that little difficulty I had with you the evening he came to the door to hand me the letter, and you talked so loud—of course I've acknowledged to you that I was to blame ———."

"And at the same time," interrupted Adeline, "you threatened to prove by Jerusha Vroman that *I* was to blame!"

"Well, no matter," said Mrs. Bailey, "he was generous enough by you at last!"

"But what I was going to say," resumed Judge Bailey, "was this: Benjamin Bailey, at the time I talked with him in his library, a little while ago, spoke of the affair in a way to disgrace *you* as well as me. Now my plan is, (if we find it necessary,) to represent to Mr. Sommers that Benjamin on that evening came to see Jerusha, and after treating her in a very dishonorable way, so that I afterwards forbid him the house, he got up that story to injure us all. As for Mrs. Hartley's letter—Jerusha's plan is a good one—we must all declare she told us the same or a similar story about one of her best friends in New York city, and that some of her own family say she is half crazy!"

"Jerusha can tell that story if she pleases," said Adeline, "but I can't, and I won't! The worst you can get *me* to say is, to say nothing, just the best way I know how!"

Not long after the above events Mrs. Cummings called on Adeline, and the minister's wife called on Mrs. Cummings; and Mrs. Bailey called on Mrs. Cummings and also on the minister's wife, and Jerusha called around also. Deacon Sommers had written to the minister. Adeline Wilderman had written to Laura Sommers a reply which amounted to nothing—precisely what she intended it should amount to. Mrs. Cummings' reply to Laura's mother amounted to this: she had known nothing for or against Benjamin Bailey till within the last two weeks; but if what she had heard a certain young lady say was true, he must be a fellow without honor or principle. All she had heard Mrs. Judge Bailey say, was, that she felt very sorry Benjamin was turning out so badly. And from what she could hear from Judge Bailey's family she should think no dependence ought to be placed on Mrs. Hartley's letter."

The minister replied as follows:

"FALLINGTON, N. Y., ———, 1863.
"To WILLIAM SOMMERS, ESQ.,
"Niagara Falls, N. Y.:
"*Dear Sir*—Yours of the 7th instant, inquiring confidentially about Judge Bailey's present standing, etc., etc., was received a few days since. In reply I must say, that I know nothing positively against him. He claims that the stories are all gotten up by his enemies. The rumors in circulation do not, so far as I have learned, gain much credit. His family attend church pretty regularly, and go in the very best society. There is no family here that does more to sustain the church. If any part of what is talked be true, it is probable that the stories are greatly exaggerated. Last Sabbath the Judge and his wife both

partook of the Lord's supper. It is true, however, that the Judge himself is seldom seen in the prayer meeting, but his wife and Miss Vroman are often there, and Mrs. Bailey appears to be one of the finest ladies I ever knew. My wife has just inquired of her about Mrs. Hartley, and Mrs. Bailey says that Mrs. Hartley became greatly enraged because they did not like to associate with her, so they presume that what she wrote your daughter against Mrs. Bailey was made up out of a New York story, which she told Mrs. Bailey and Jerusha Vroman the first day she came there. So we are told.

"We have never heard any stories against Benjamin Bailey, except that we have just heard that Mrs. Bailey and Jerusha Vroman speak unfavorably of him, but do not state anything in particular.

"I am, Sir, very respectfully,

"JONAS SMOOTHWELL, Pastor."

Deacon Sommers was not as well satisfied with the result of all their inquiries, after having received the Hartley letter, as he had hoped to be; but it was thought best to have Laura let the matter rest.

Mrs. Judge Bailey got a hint of what Mrs. Cummings had written in their favor, and Mrs. Smoothwell told Mrs. Bailey that Mr. Smoothwell had written a very complimentary letter for them to a gentleman by the name of William Sommers, living at Niagara Falls. On hearing these things David Bailey took it into his head without consulting his father, to write a letter to Laura. Consequently Miss Sommers was one day favored by receiving the following letter:

6

"FALLINGTON, N. Y., ——, 1863.

"To MISS LAURA SOMMERS:

"*Dear Madam*—Among the varied and numerous incidents of life, there is one subject of daily occurrence, and I may say, as it were, of vast and thrilling importance which is presented, and I may say as it were, daily presented for our consideration, or rather for the consideration as it were, of both sexes. That subject is the subject of matrimony, and after considerable reflection and experience I have come to the determination to offer my hand and heart to some lady whom I can respect, and if you are willing to accept the position, I shall be happy to be informed of your wishes as soon as you can determine on so important a step. It is presumed by me that from your prompt manner of action and your decision of character, as well as from your knowledge as it were of circumstances, that you will be able to decide this proposal within thirty days from date, as I have agreed within that time to give an answer to another lady.

"Very respectfully,

"Your obedient servant,

"DAVID BAILEY.

"P. S. If you will oblige me with an immediate answer, I would make you a visit at Niagara Falls.

"D. B."

This letter Laura never answered. It destroyed what little respect she had ever entertained for David Bailey. She pronounced it the work of an empty-headed dandy, whose education had done him no good. She considered the letter a ludicrous curiosity; but thought when taken in connection with Mrs. Hartley's letter, that it showed at least a motive for what had been said against Benjamin by Judge Bailey's family.

Laura immediately wrote to Mrs. Judge Bailey, asking for the name of the young lady whom they claimed had been so shamefully treated by Benjamin Bailey, and to be referred to any others who knew anything against him. Laura also wrote that a direct and plain answer was important.

It is probable that Judge Bailey concluded that this inquiry had something to do with the consideration of David's letter. He, therefore, directed Mrs. Bailey to refer Laura and her mother to Miss Jerusha Vroman. Jerusha also wrote a short note, stating that she, herself, was the person whom Benjamin had treated as Mrs. Bailey had informed them, but she did not think it necessary to state particulars. This note was inclosed with Mrs. Bailey's letter and sent to Laura.

When Laura received the answer she thought it strange that no reference could be given except to the very person whom Mrs. Hartley's letter had already cast a suspicion against. Deacon Sommers thought the same, and suggested that it tended to show that Mrs. Hartley's letter might all be true.

Notwithstanding David had received no reply to his letter, he made a visit to Deacon Sommers within the "thirty days," where he made even a worse impression on Deacon Sommers than he had previously made on the mind of Laura. His attempts to make matters plain against Benjamin Bailey were so closely inquired into that he lost his courage, and that confused his memory so that he could not keep his equivocations and misstatements consistent with each other, nor with known facts.

It was quite agreeable to all Deacon Sommers' family when he abruptly closed his visit under the impression that he was not destined to be the husband of Laura Sommers.

Judge Bailey and his family began to fear the danger that *in time wrong o'erloads itself!*

CHAPTER XII.

The Detective starts for Niagara—An act of Politeness—Almost a Discovery—A Trick of Travel.

"ALL aboard!" sounded the accustomed voice of the railroad conductor at Fallington station—and then the passengers, who had alighted for refreshments, and who had, probably nearly all, secured their right change for their half-devoured lunch, were hurrying back to retake their places in the cars, and with the usual caution of travelers, to see if coats, shawls, parcels, bandboxes and other hand-luggage, were still in possession of *themselves* and the *seats* whereon they had been left to do the duty of dumb policemen!

There was also the usual supply of additional passengers, among whom, a young man, a little below the average height, slim in proportion, and dressed in a suit of drab, entered the rear car. His personal appearance was tidy and prepossessing; his hair a light brown, and he wore side whiskers, which were of a sandy color; his complexion was remarkably fair for that of a gentleman; his bearing was easy and agreeable, but he had the appearance of being two or three years younger than he really was. He had said his adieus to his friends, who had accompanied him to the depot, and, as the train started he seated himself by an open car-window where the last parting words which he caught, were in the voice of his anxious mother: "Mercy on me, Benjamin," said she, "be careful of yourself; and, don't let any accident happen to you while you are gone; and write to us every day that you can." To which Benjamin replied, "God bless you, mother; and all of you." And as the train bore him away, they saw a handkerchief waved from that car-window bidding them his silent adieu.

Young Bailey's thoughts were too much occupied at first, with other matters, to be diverted by the strangers in a railroad car, or by anticipating the pleasures of travel. He had received a letter of general instructions from his friend, Mr. Baldwin, and was required to report on the first of August to Collector A. of the Niagara District, for special instructions. He had calculated, however, to visit for a short time the points of interest about the great falls, before commencing duty as an officer. Never having visited Niagara Falls, he had preferred not to see the Collector of Customs till he should be at least a little acquainted with some of the localities in a vicinity so noted.

And somehow his thoughts would revert to Laura Sommers and her home in that locality, to which he was approaching, and where he was to become acquainted— and perhaps under circumstances which would add romance to the acquaintance that he had once begun with Laura. He could not help thinking how pleasant it would be to visit Laura and her friends had not cruel fate allowed him to be misrepresented, and separated

them from him. One moment he thought he would go
and see Mr. Sommers and insist on offering some proof
of his innocence of any dishonorable course, and offer
references to persons of standing in Fallington; and the
next moment pride, delicacy, and the thought of the
reception he might receive, discouraged him.

If Benjamin tried to think whether he had any friends
and acquaintances residing at Niagara Falls who could
post him up and show him about, it was not an unnatural
thought; and there is many a weary house-keeper residing at the Falls whose patience has concluded that such
ideas are not *unusual*, even among the most distant—
acquaintances! "It is wonderful how popular it makes
one with all their old acquaintances—with all their *new*
acquaintances—with father's old neighbors and with the
acquaintances of your wife's second and third cousins,
whenever they come from distant parts to visit the Falls!
come to see you a couple of months in such a delightful
place—come to make you a good, long visit—I declare!
said they, before leaving home, it is too warm weather to
keep house! Too warm for them to keep house? Did
they think of others?"

Of course this little satire doesn't mean everybody, for
there are, no doubt, many sensible people who don't even
visit their friends enough at Niagara Falls, because, either
nervously or humorously such reflections have been suggested.

I am certain, however, that Benjamin Bailey would not
have thought of hunting up a fifteenth cousin whom he
had never seen before with the sole intention of spending

the summer months under their hospitable roof—"to see the falls."

But as the train speeds along towards Laura Sommers' home, nobody that has ever been in love will blame Ben Bailey for wishing it were so that he could make a visit at Deacon Sommers'. But he does not feel permitted to do so. He thinks, however, that possibly he may gain a favorable acquaintance with some friend of theirs who may sometime favor him so far as to induce Mr. Sommers to furnish him with the secret facts about the slander, that he may be able to vindicate his honor; though he presumes that Laura has long ago ceased to think of him!

When the train reached the city of Rochester our new detective felt a strange interest in the words of the conductor as he called out to the passengers: "Rochester! Passengers for the Niagara Falls road change cars!"

The train stopped; and then followed the usual rush and the usual variety of passengers—home-folks and foreign visitors, bound for the Falls—citizens of the frontier villages, of Niagara Falls, Niagara City and Lewiston, and way-passengers on their private business, and travelers for the great West via Suspension Bridge, and at this time an additional variety of characters occasioned by the war of the great rebellion; some of whose missions were as secret as that of Benjamin Bailey's.

Our new detective entered the Niagara Falls car in time to secure a seat by himself; but as the crowd came into the car they began to claim their right to a seat by the side of those who occupied the room intended for two persons. Some, who had previously taken possession of

a whole seat designed for two persons, placed their traveling bags with themselves in the seat to give the appearance that the whole room in their seats was claimed.
And various were the tricks of old travelers for securing
the most room exclusively to themselves.

Two elderly gentlemen entered the front door of the
car in which toward the rear, Benjamin was seated. They
appeared to be well acquainted with each other, and
looking for a seat together. Just before reaching Benjamin Bailey they politely asked a gentleman, occupying a
seat alone, where two could be seated, if he would oblige
them so much as to take a seat with that gentleman—
pointing to the vacant seat by the side of Bailey—so they
two could sit together, as they wanted to chat a little.

The man thus accosted, replied that he presumed the
two gentlemen could find seats enough in the forward
cars! The *manner*, however, in which this individual
"presumed" what he evidently knew nothing about, was
in keeping with the probability, from the number of passengers, that he believed no such "presumption!"

The two gentlemen made no reply to this indirect
refusal; nor had they hardly time to have done so ere
Benjamin Bailey politely offered and vacated his seat for
their accommodation. They thanked him and accepted
his offer; while he took a seat with another gentleman
near them.

The older one of the two gentlemen remarked to
Bailey, that "he hoped it might happen in his way sometime to do him a favor in return."

"Gentlemen," said Bailey, "it seems to me that so
6*

small a favor is only a common civility; and your polite acknowledgment already leaves no balance in my favor."

"Well, at any rate," pleasantly replied the same elderly gentleman, "I think you are deserving of our good will, and I don't very often make mistakes in my first impressions of people."

"Thank you for the compliment," returned Bailey, with a very perceptible blush, and a manner altogether such as pleased the two unknown gentlemen, and called out a remark from the one who had not spoken, "What a difference," said he in an undertone to the other, "there *is* in people!"

"Yes, indeed," responded the other, "and it only takes a trifle besides a man's countenance to make us read his whole character!"

Benjamin Bailey had now turned to his newspaper. And now let us inquire, who is that elderly gentleman, who, as well as his friend, has formed so good an opinion of Mr. Benjamin Bailey as a stranger? Ah! that is a secret which Benjamin little dreamed of at that time, or he would not so soon have forgotten the compliment just paid him—not even to read of the prospect of a fight between General Sherman and the rebel General Hood at Atlanta. No, no; for that elderly gentleman is Deacon Sommers of Niagara Falls! The other is the Collector of Customs of the Niagara District.

But as Mr. Sommers and the Collector entered into conversation together, and other matters attracted Bailey's attention, the link of conversation was broken off, and was not renewed; which, otherwise might have led to a

very embarrassing recognition of names between Mr.
William Sommers and Mr. Benjamin Bailey; in which
case, it would probably have been a perplexing puzzle
for Deacon Sommers to have reconciled his "first impressions" of the stranger on this occasion, with the opinions
he had formed through another source; and, had supposed
himself still to have of one Benjamin Bailey residing
near the village of Fallington !

With the thoughts which must have been brought up,
under all the circumstances, and in the presence too, of
the Collector, to whom Benjamin was soon to report for
duty as an officer of customs, the occasion was not a
desirable one for recognition! and much less for an
explanation! It was better, therefore, to happen as it
did; though it was a long time afterwards before Deacon
Sommers knew that he had ever seen Benjamin Bailey;
and, that, without knowing it, he had formed as favorable
an opinion of him as had Mrs. Sommers when she and
her daughter first saw him during their visit at Fallington a little less than one year previous to this time!

As we have intimated elsewhere,. Benjamin Bailey had
traveled but very little; hence, the strategic movements
by a gentleman and lady to secure plenty of room in the
car for themselves, had attracted Benjamin's attention,
when he first took his seat, before the train had started.
And he soon had opportunity to notice the success of
their stratagem, as he now sat in the next seat behind
them.

They had entered the car in time to find two car-seats
together, unoccupied; they laid a satchel and some arti-

cles of over-clothing in the empty seat in front of the
one which they personally took possession of. This gave
the seat before them, which they had turned to face from
them, the *appearance of having been claimed by some party
who had stepped away for a moment!* and, as the gentleman behind it seemed to manifest no interest in the
matter, no one of course ventured any inquiries; passengers in search of a seat, and even the conductor, of course
supposing that *that* seat was "occupied!"

But now the train was under good headway, and all,
in that car at least, had become seated, by crowding in,
two and two. The plan has succeeded. The jolly
couple in front of our new detective, now turn over the
mysterious seat in question, to their own advantage; the
gentleman at the same time remarking to the lady that
"every trade has its tricks and this is one of the tricks
of travel!"

"Possibly," responded the lady, "by the time we arrive
at the next station the conductor may compel us to make
another 'move,' and we shall lose this fine advantage!"

"Very true, they may come and put a verbal 'attach-
ment' on our extra 'room' and drive us into closer
'quarters,' unless I claim to be a Major General, and thus
make it out a 'military necessity!' that we keep the
advantage."

"I'm afraid that wouldn't work," replied the little
woman. "You don't look Major Generalish enough!"

"Then I would try another point of argument—I would
claim it by 'right of possession,' and put on the assump-
tion of a lawyer. Wouldn't I look like a lawyer?"

"Yes, *appear* like one—in a bad cause!"

"Then I would tell him to commence his suits, and I would beat him on 'time;' and try *that* argument to make him let us alone!"

"But," retorted the little lady, with a roguish smile, "suppose the conductor and his brakemen should use a more forcible argument than your quibbles?"

"Then I'd tell him—as the South tells Abraham Lincoln—that 'it is unconstitutional to use force,' and that all I ask of him or his brakemen, is, 'to let us alone!'"

"What if they should take *both* seats away from us, then, and put us off the cars into the bargain?"

"If they tried that, I would scare the brakemen off by reminding them that these are war times, and that the President has suspended the writ of habeas corpus! They would'nt know what it means, but that is the way politicians frighten voters now, you know."

"Don't mention politics—I hate both parties."

"How so?"

"Why, because they tell such miserable falsehoods, and talk such intricate nonsense, and then have to fight about it!"

"Would you rather talk about the *fashions?*" retorted the gentleman, in a joking manner.

"O, yes! certainly; a magnificent change of subject—presto, of course; for they do say there are such delightful styles out this month!"

"I presume so," was the reply; "silk dresses that trail a half-yard on the dusty sidewalk, without the slightest regard to good sense or neatness."

"Yes, a full half-yard!" interrupted the lady, without noticing the last part of his remark. "Such long dresses give immense grace to one's figure! and, by the way," said the sociable Mrs. Smith, (if that was her name,) "that reminds me that we are going where silk is very cheap—unless the Canadians want too many 'greenbacks' for a dollar—too much of our money for too little of theirs!"

"Hush! remember the customs officers are more strict than they used to be when you crossed the Suspension Bridge before!"

That means smuggling! thought Benjamin Bailey. And as he took notice that he might identify them, his eye fell on a name on their traveling bags, lying on the seat in front of them. Of the name and such other matters as he thought best, he made a note in his diary.

It was one of the peculiar qualifications of Ben Bailey that he had acquired the art of writing short-hand, and he was in the habit of keeping a very full journal in that way. By this practice he had become able to write with much rapidity, and to this we are indebted for many particulars of incidents which are related in this volume.

CHAPTER XIII.

The two Detectives—A Laughable and Mutual Deception—Benjamin learns something of Niagara Falls and Smugglers.

WHEN the train reached Brockport Bailey took his traveling bag and went into the next car, where he seated himself by the side of a man whom he found very talkative, and who said he had lately moved from Niagara Falls. Bailey asked him a great many questions in relation to that locality, and about business there, and he wondered if it was not easy to smuggle across the Niagara River in some places.

At this moment the conductor was making change with a man seated just before them, and as he turned to look at Bailey's ticket he remarked to Bailey that "a man is not very smart if he cannot smuggle without being caught at it."

Not long after the conductor had made this remark, a shrewd-looking man came in from another car and took a seat just behind Bailey. And though at first he only seemed interested in his newspaper, he gradually managed to get into conversation with Bailey, and the opportunity became a good one as the stranger in the seat with Bailey got off the train at the next station. The man with the newspaper grew more and more sociable, and no two smugglers could have sooner or more easily worked their way to the question of smuggling than did these two strangers, Bedan and Bailey.

Now, the fact was, this man who was courting Ben Bailey's attention, was an old officer of customs, and well known as such to all the railroad conductors whose trains ran to Niagara Falls. For three years back he had been constantly traveling as a detective, and frequently on this road. The conductor at this time having heard Bailey speak of smuggling, fancied it would be well to put this detective on his track, as he happened to be on board the train.

Knowing the circumstances it does not now seem very remarkable that the new detective, Ben Bailey, and the stranger with the newspaper, found themselves so easily drawn into conversation in which each one was trying to learn what he could of the other. Without a knowledge of these circumstances it certainly would have seemed singular to have noticed what a propensity these two passengers so soon had for asking questions of each other, and how willingly each was to learn any facts on the subject of smuggling.

When the old detective—for a blind—turned the subject upon the weather, or the crops, or the railroads, he noticed that the young man shortly returned to the questions about the Niagara River; the custom house; the cost of articles in Canada; the duties and the inducements for smuggling; from which he concluded that the young man had either the most extraordinary curiosity in the direction of custom houses and smuggling, or else he was one of the most verdant, yellow-haired Yankees that ever contemplated his first speculations in that line of business. Bailey, on his part, had formed the decided opinion that this fellow-traveler hated the government, the taxes, and custom house officials in particular; and that he was, probably, an old smuggler.

Their conversation, up to this stage of con lusions, had been designed on both sides "to call each other out." At first it was common-place talk, then a little skirmishing, to find out each other's business and each other's views on free trade and smuggling.

The following is a portion of what was said, neither party for one moment suspecting that the other was a detective:

"I have lately heard considerable about smuggling," said Bailey. "They say they watch smugglers pretty closely. How many officers have they right about the Falls?"

"Not so many that one need be afraid of them," was the reply of Bedan.

"I suppose when strangers wish to speculate that way, they generally hire some persons living on the frontier, who are acquainted with the business, to get the goods across the river, don't they?" inquired Bailey.

"Frequently, but it is easy done by anybody, one way or another."

"Is it true that a great many get rich just by getting goods from Canada into the States without paying duty on them? or is it," said Bailey, "more dangerous than profitable?"

"Profitable! I'll be hanged if it isn't," said Bedan. "There is one man, in particular, who lives in Tonawanda, half-way between the Falls and Buffalo, who has made a fortune at it! principally by smuggling whisky; and made it all in about a year back!"

"How do they manage to avoid detection?" inquired Bailey.

"O! that's a secret which belongs to the business. Perhaps I could tell you more about that than it would be for my interest to tell!" was Bedan's reply.

"What can you have to fear from me?" replied Bailey, feeling quite elated with the idea of getting acquainted with a real smuggler. "I am," said Bailey, "an entire stranger on the frontier, and don't know one of the officers there; and besides that, if you are in the secret, and can convince me you have been smart enough to make money out of it yourself, I am willing to pay you for posting me up."

"Well, what do you want?" asked the old detective, for he began now to suspect Bailey knew more of the frontier than he pretended, and also flattered himself he had well-nigh won Bailey's confidence as a smuggler himself.

"Well, for instance," replied Bailey, "how could you assist me, suppose I should buy a few barrels of whisky on the Canada side? Have you any means of getting it across the river?"

"Perhaps I have," was Bedan's reply.

"I suppose the *perhaps*," said Bailey, "means, provided I paid you enough for running the risk."

"Perhaps it does!" returned the old detective, pretending a little caution, "and perhaps it means we don't help any stranger into the business till he begins the business first, himself. This is the rule, and I know they wouldn't post me up till after they knew I had smuggled something myself, as a sort of confidence initiation. But for all I know to the contrary, you may be better posted on smuggling than I am," said the old detective, with a kind of suspicious laugh.

"O! no, upon my word," said Bailey, "I was never at Niagara Falls in my life."

"Since we have talked so much, then," replied the old detective, taking out his tobacco-box and filling his mouth with a huge quid of tobacco, as if he were thinking of something else, instead of the voracious quantity—"since I've told you my views on free trade"—he resumed, as soon as his tongue had rolled the "fine cut" a little out of the way of his organs of *speech*, "I should like to have you regard what I have said as a private matter; and if ——"

Here, happening to remember the etiquette of tobacco-users, he extended the remnant of a paper of tobacco, with the polite invitation:

"Here, stranger, beg your pardon, take a chew?"

"No, thank you, you will have to excuse me."

"Ah! don't use the weed, eh? but as I was going to say, if you will tell me candidly whether you thought of dealing in whisky, or anything in which you would need a boat, I can tell you who are the best and most cautious men for you on the frontier between Buffalo and Youngstown."

"I thought, sir, of getting acquainted with the business first."

"Hang it!" thought Bedan, "this is a queer fellow. He is bold as a fool before he begins the business; or else he's playing a game of curiosity for his own amusement. I can't make his intention nor his business correspond with my impressions of the fellow, I can't; I'll be hanged if I can!" thought Bedan, instead of making an immediate reply to Bailey's last remark.

After a moment Bailey inquired: "Are you interested in any boats doing that kind of work? if you are, I shall be pleased to see you and your friends after I have visited the Falls a few days."

"Hang it!" thought Bedan, "he *means* to smuggle, whether he ever *has* or not!" so the old detective replied: "Well, as your talk seems to mean our kind of business, I would say, I have a few very fine, fast boats, and I shall be happy to do you all the favors I can *consistently!* But until you shall be admitted into the organization of 'free traders,' you and I must keep each other's secrets from other smugglers! For instance, in connection with smuggling you are not to mention my name, nor I yours."

"Precisely so; a thing we shall not be very apt to do till those convenient titles of our individualities become known between ourselves!" said Bailey, with a suppressed laugh.

"Ha, ha! very true; my name is Bedan, George Bedan."

"And mine is Bailey. But I was going to ask, how you manage to evade the officers?"

"That's the very secret—that's the trade. It's like medicine for the asthma; one medicine don't suit every case; you have to change it according to symptoms."

Bedan could account for his own boldness of conversation about smuggling, because he was no smuggler, except he did so for a blind to detect others, but when he saw Bailey's want of caution about his probable intention to smuggle, he concluded he must be one of those unaccountable Yankees, we sometimes meet with, in search of adventure and speculation. And he anticipated easily catching him in his attempts at smuggling.

To Bailey's inquiry as to the best hotels about the Falls to stop at, Bedan replied:

"If you wish to pass as a gentleman of travel, above the suspicion of smuggling, you must take up your head-quarters at the very best houses. And if it is your intention to bring rich dress goods across from Canada, such as silk and silk velvet, etc., or jewelry, and such like, it is a pity you have not provided yourself with a lady assistant. But perhaps you have done so?" inquiringly added the old detective.

"No, I have no lady with me."

"Well, we can arrange that; what you can't find along Niagara, you can't anywhere. With the present style of ladies' dress, you can easily understand how they can conceal and bring over three or four hundred dollars' worth of goods at once, right before the eyes of the officers, and all the while appear as innocent as little lambs. Of course, the gentleman accompanies the lady, and crosses the Suspension Bridge, either on the cars or in a carriage procured of one of the most innocent drivers in the world! who will report for you 'nothing aboard,' with the intention, if the carriage is seized, of swearing that he could not of course have known that the lady had concealed goods aboard. You see I'm posted, and if you want any help I'm on hand."

"By George!" said Bailey, "you do seem to understand it. Do you keep any carriages for that purpose?"

"No, but I can tell you whose carriages have never been caught yet! If you have got the capital to carry on the business I can give you plans enough. But we fellows who understand the frontier, and all the 'tricks of trade' there, expect a liberal percentage for our aid in such matters whenever you succeed."

"O, certainly," said Bailey, "if I find you are the right man, and if I conclude to risk your plans after seeing how you manage the matter a little, I can raise some funds, but I might not meet your expectations, for I am only a country-bred chap, any how; and like the poorer class of editors, we don't deal much in luxuries; probably in other respects we don't resemble editors. Farmers generally have to work hard, you know, and don't grow rich fast, and besides that, they don't handle large amounts continually, like merchants, and bankers, and speculators; and I've no doubt it is this difference which cultivates different ideas of liberality, and greater or less caution as to using or investing money. So you must bear with me a little till I become accustomed to your views of liberality and right, and to your customs generally!"

"Our customs! you know we don't believe in *customs*," said Bedan.

"No, not in *custom-house* customs, of course, but in, at least, the custom of avoiding customs!" was Bailey's laughing reply.

"Ah! precisely so! I am acquainted with some customary ways, as well as some very *un*-customary ways in that line; else, of course, I should be a very poor pilot for 'free traders' to employ to aid in getting their goods across the Niagara into a port of safety!"

"A port of safety!" thought Bedan; "perhaps it is mean for me to deceive the fellow; but if men will break the laws they must *expect* a detective will trap them if he can, and bring them to punishment." Such were Bedan's secret reflections; while Bailey at the same time rested for a moment on the last remark of the "smuggler's pilot!" and privately thought,—"All right! I've been lucky enough already to stumble on the right man to let me into the smugglers' secrets, and into their very camp, I suppose, if I choose to go there. But it's thundering queer," thought Ben Bailey, "that smugglers are so bold in their talk; especially to a stranger like me—though perhaps that's the secret! he takes me for a country fellow, with a little money on a speculating trip, ready for a little smuggling, and being in the business himself he can make a little something on what he helps me to smuggle. I don't know what kind of officers they have in the custom-house service, but this old smuggler, or chief aid in some branch of their business, evidently don't honor *me* with the suspicion that I could possibly be such an officer! Well, if I lack anything in appearance, and it turns to my advantage, so mote it be," thought Ben.

The old detective and the new occupied the time in conversation on smuggling and other subjects, if we deduct an occasional pause, till they reached the Falls; before which time, however, it had been arranged that Bailey should drop a letter in the Niagara Falls post-office to let Bedan know where and when he could meet him, and to do this so soon as Bailey should be ready for

CHAPTER XIV.

In due time the train stopped at the village of Niagara Falls, and our two detectives, Bailey and Bedan, who had deceived themselves, as badly as each had deceived the other, separated in the crowd of passengers.

Bailey concluded to leave his trunk in the railroad baggage-room, and sometime during the day to return for it. Of course an experienced traveler would have had himself and his baggage taken directly to a first class hotel; but Benjamin Bailey took a notion to spend a little time looking about the place, and to decide from his own observation as to where he would select a boarding place. He first went forward to the baggage-car, and had his trunk placed safely in care of the baggage-man, to whom he paid a liberal fee. He then passed by the first group of porters and hotel runners in the most perfect safety; notwithstanding the greatly exaggerated and fearful accounts given of this whole class at the Falls by an occasional newspaper correspondent, who in some instances may have left the hotels angry at not being able to offset his board-bill against what his pen would or would not say in the newspapers, he claiming to be a highly-

7

salaried correspondent, though writing under an assumed name in consequence, (as he has previously intimated to the landlord,) of his great modesty!

Had the porters and runners been as bad as sometimes represented, the regulations at the depot, at this place, are so excellent, and so strictly enforced by police officers and railroad employees, that passengers as they get off the cars, have ample room and opportunity to look after their own baggage, or walk into large and commodious sitting-rooms of the depot without being confronted, or troubled with questions or solicitations.

Those who drive an omnibus for any hotel, occupy a small space at a proper distance, and passengers may converse with these porters by approaching them, or pass directly to and through the sitting-rooms of the depot. As they leave the depot they will usually, during the summer season, find from ten to twenty elegant carriages waiting along the platform at the west side of the depot, which is about eighty rods from the great cataract. Carriages are also found waiting at various points close in view of the falls and rapids.

Bailey emerged from the passengers' sitting-room, and was immediately upon the side-walk at the corner of the streets. The sharp eye of a hackman in an instant detected him as a stranger, from the manner in which he looked about to view whatever the streets at this point, in four directions, allowed him to see of the celebrated little village of Niagara Falls.

Writing these pages as I am upon the banks of Niagara, and having a familiar acquaintance with doings in this locality, I can assure the reader that very many of those engaged in the hack business at Niagara Falls, are reliable, intelligent, and respectable, business men; many of them driving their own carriages for their passengers.

As in every other business, there is occasionally a peculiar character among the hack-drivers at Niagara, and such was Mr. Gulliver's driver.

"Do you wish to hire a carriage, sir?" said Mr. Gulliver's driver, in his most beseeching manner to our new detective.

"No, sir, not at present. But may I inquire how far it is to the Niagara Falls?"

"O, only a *short* distance, sir; I am going right there; get aboard, sir; take you there for twenty-five cents."

By this time the driver had stopped the carriage close by Bailey, and he accepted the very reasonable offer of the driver and got into the carriage, without the least idea whether a "short distance" means a quarter of a mile or two miles and a quarter. But how can he refuse his patronage when only such a trifling sum as twenty-five cents is asked by a driver who has so evidently intended the offer as a favor, seeing he was "going right that way" with his carriage!

"How far did you say it is to the falls?"

"Only a '*short distance*,' sir," repeated the driver, as he cracked his whip and turned his horses down Falls street, intending to take his passenger in view of Goat Island, and drive along Mechanic street in view of the rapids and towards the Ferry House, on which route a large portion of the falls can be seen from carriages.

"There's a good many places about here that strangers go to see, and to get different views of the falls. People might think before they come here that all there is to do, to see Niagara Falls, is just to come here an' stand an' look at 'em—from almost anywhere in sight of 'em; but everybody finds when they get here that these 'ere falls is a mighty big thing afore you get all 'round 'em. Anybody needs a whole day, with a carriage, to see all the points of interest."

"I should not suppose it would take a long time to see the falls after you get to them," said Bailey.

"Yes, but it's a dum sight worse than just walkin' around a big hay-stack!"

"I presume so," said Bailey, smiling at the driver's odd comparison.

"That's the International Hotel on the corner here," said the driver; "and the other big, rough-cast structure right by the rapids here, is the Cataract House—both good houses, tip-top fare and everything."

"Good many visitors stopping there?" inquired Bailey.

"Not a great many just now. Probably about five hundred at each house."

"Say, driver, did you say you were going right to the falls?"

"Yes, sir, there's the rapids, right there. Don't you see how the river dances about on a regular rough-and-tumble?"

Bailey acknowledged that he did; and here the driver turned down the short street between the two large hotels, and in a moment more stopped his carriage near Goat

Island bridge, which crosses the rapids just above the American fall.

"There," said the driver, "just below us you see where the water pitches over; but the big part of the fall—the Horse-shoe fall—is over beyond Goat Island, on the Canada side. There's seventy-five acres in that island right at the brink of the falls there. But you see, stranger, that the falls are a dum sight the biggest!"

"But we can't get a good view of the falls here, driver," said Bailey, starting to get out of the carriage.

"Of course you can't get a *good* view of the falls if you get out here. But I can drive to a place where you can get a better view. *You'd like a better view, wouldn't you?*"

Bailey thought the driver a very *clever* fellow—very *sociable*—so he resumed his seat, and the driver resumed his business, which was to keep his passenger interested in hopes he would extend his patronage to a longer ride. The driver started up his team and in a few moments he called the attention of his passenger to a partial view of the falls upon the Canadian side of the river.

"Magnificent! sublime!" exclaimed Bailey.

"Do you see," asked the driver, "that fine, large, yellow building on the opposite side of the river, with double piazzas extend——"

"Never mind your large buildings and piazzas," said Bailey, continuing his intense gaze towards the Horse-shoe fall. "Hadn't I better get out here, so I can walk round somewhere and get a better view?"

"Would you like to go where you can get a *front* view

of the falls?" asked the driver, while his horses kept on a slow trot.

"Why, yes, I would."

"Well, that is what I was going to tell you; you see that yellow establishment, large building, double piazzas extending around two sides?"

"Yes."

"Well, that's the Clifton House—that's where Jenny Lind stopped several weeks when she nightingaled it so in this country. In fact it's where the Prince of Wales stopped, and where every noted person makes a stop before leaving the Falls. You see it was built there because there is the best view—a 'front view' of the whole Falls, on both sides of the river; and it's kept in the very best, tip-topest style. They take greenback money, and only charge the same as the best houses this side. It's across there you must go to get the best view— a front view!"

"How far, driver, do you have to go to get there?'

"O, not a 'great' ways—just around by the railroad Suspension Bridge."

"How far off is that bridge? I always thought it was close by Niagara Falls."

"No, but it's just 'below' here—only a 'little ways.' There's the Whirlpool, too, a mile below the bridge, which everybody goes to see. You can go to it upon either side of the river. And there's Buttery's Rapids, which strangers go down to see, just below the bridge, by a saw-mill which runs by a curious contrivance of long, wire ropes, two hundred and fifty feet off—down the bank—

in the rapids! And then a mile further down the river, there's the Devil's Hole, a queer place in the river bank, with a spring in a cave; and there was an Indian massacre there once. Then just beyond the Canada falls is the battle-ground of Lundy's Lane, and near that a curious burning spring. And so I could tell of points of interest all around this vicinity for a whole day's drive. If you would like to go and see some of the best places, as far as you have time to-day, I'd be glad to take you as cheap as anybody will!"

"Say, driver, where are you taking me to?" inquired Benjamin. "It seems to me you have got almost a mile away from the falls!"

"Why, of course," replied the sociable driver, "you are not bound to ride any further than you wish to; but wouldn't you like to cross the bridge and go up on the Canada side, where you can get the best view of the falls? Take you up there and give you all the time you want, and only charge the regular price—a dollar and a half an hour."

It was true that this was only the legal rate. But Benjamin Bailey's knowledge of team-work in the country, at three or four dollars per day, and of Smith's livery charges for a horse and buggy in the dull village of Fallington, led him to ask the driver with a look of surprise, if people generally paid such prices here.

"Why, of course, stranger; only think, this hack and horses cost fifteen hundred dollars; and it's only four months in the year that strangers come here, and they are so rich and so many of them, that they keep every hack busy."

"O, if it is the market price—all right, of course," said Bailey."

"Say, stranger," said the driver, getting off the subject of prices, "speakin' of rich visitors, I wonder if some gentlemen don't come here to get acquainted with rich young ladies? There's an awful sight of weddings here, and diamond rings, and dances, all summer."

CHAPTER XV.

The Hack-driver continues to interest Benjamin—Other Strangers—Another Custom House Officer—Gulliver's Driver—Smuggling talked of—Hints of how it is done.

THEN they came to the spot where Blondin, the French rope-walker, stretched his rope across the Niagara river in the summer of 1858. Here the driver stopped his horses a moment, and recounted the daring and wonderful performances of that great gymnast on his rope over the deep abyss, in which runs the rapid river below the falls.

Although this driver was suspected by some strangers of telling fictitious stories to interest passengers, and of exaggerating trifling incidents which had occurred about the falls, in order to be considered an interesting guide, still we must do him the compliment to affirm that such was not the case.

On one occasion a waggish stranger, who had employed Mr. Gulliver's driver, and had humorously encouraged his narration of items of interest, jokingly asked him, why he lied so about everything but Blondin?

"Why," said the driver, in reply, "I'm almost afraid to tell the *whole truth* about that Frenchman, because it sounds like a bigger story than anything I could get up. So you see I always feel as if I *was lying* about him *when I'm telling the truth!*"

7*

As the driver pointed out to Bailey the spot where the rope, the first season of these performances was stretched across the river, from " White's Pleasure Grounds," Bailey inquired how far across the river it is at this point.

" About eleven hundred feet, sir."

" Is it possible," inquired Bailey, "that Blondin actu-ally walked across there, on a rope, as the newspapers told it, with a man on his back ? "

" I beg leave to be eaten up by cannibals, sir, if he didn't! I saw him do it, myself; and there was at least five thousand others lookin' on the same time."

" How much did the man weigh ? "

" One hundred and thirty pounds, sir; and besides that, the tough, little Frenchman carried a balancing pole in his hands which weighed forty pounds, sir."

" I declare, said Bailey, "that made one hundred and seventy pounds—nearly equal to three bushels of wheat; and of course the man could not get off the rope-walker's back, and get on again for fear of falling; so there was no way of resting until he carried him clear across."

" Get off his back and get on again while on the rope? So help me Jehosophat! that is just what he did do a half a dozen times ! "

" Don't you find it hard work to make folks believe that story, driver? "

" Yes, sir, but Blondin always did all he advertised to do; till at last everybody would have believed he could walk across on nothing if he'd said so ' "

" What else *did* he do? "

" What else? he took a good-sized sheet-iron stove,

with a length of pipe on it, out on the middle of the
rope, and cooked buck-wheat cakes there for refreshments.
And at another time he took a strong-made chair out
there, balanced it on the rope, and stood up in the chair!
And one night he walked across with a torch-light at
each end of his balancing stick, and when he got half
way across, all of a sudden the lights dropped off into
the river, and everybody was scart to death; they could
not see whether he fell into the river or what had become
of him, but no, sir —— "

"What in the world," said Bailey, half doubting the
driver's word, "could he do if it was dark as that, and
his light went out?"

"Well, everybody waited awfully, for as much as five
or ten minutes, and although they was scared all to shiv-
ers, they kinder had faith in him; so they held their
breath, and in a few minutes they heard the crowd on
the other side of the river makin' the awfulest cheerin'
you ever *did* see! We knew then he'd got safe over
Jordan, an' 'twas just his own trick—he didn't need any
light!* Then the next season he put his rope across
just below the Suspension Bridge, and at the time the
Prince of Wales was here lookin' at him—and the bridge
and river-banks were lined with spectators—I'll be eaten
up by cannibals if he didn't walk across on his rope, on
stilts three feet high! he did, sir!"

"There, driver, that's enough! At any rate it is all I
can possibly believe!"

"Well, it's as true as Jehosophat! and I 'spose if any-

* These incidents are literally true.

body rides with me they always want to know all the points of interest; and it's no good to hire a guide about the Falls if he jest takes you around and don't tell you nothin' what there is to see! I've had gentlemen what's use to travelin' give me five dollars more'n they agreed to many a time for understandin' my business!"

"That is the great railroad suspension bridge, is it, just before us?" inquired Bailey.

"Yes, sir, that's the animal."

Bailey gazed in mute astonishment till the driver halted his team behind another carriage, waiting his turn at the toll office, at the entrance upon the bridge.

Here the driver (as was his custom with all his passengers) told Bailey that people in general liked to ride across the bridge in their carriage going over, and coming back they could walk on top, by the side of the railroad track, so as to see the whole bridge.

At this moment in a little office opposite the toll office, Bailey observed a man examining the contents of a valise which a gentleman had just brought in his hand from off the bridge and from the Canada side. He also noticed that the man so examining it, was attempting to soften the surprise of the owner by saying: "Why, my dear sir, I don't inspect your baggage on the grounds of any suspicion that you are actually smuggling; but this is the rule of the custom-house, with every one."

"I don't believe any such nonsense!" replied the man with the valise, "and I don't care about being humbugged in this way by officers that want to show a little of their brief authority, looking at my old clothes."

This was the first customs business which Bailey had ever seen done; and he suddenly concluded that he would like to stop and have a little talk with the officer, and look about the bridge. So he informed the driver that he would not, probably, go to the falls on the Canada side that day, and proceeded to get out of the carriage. He then asked the driver how much he should pay him.

"About a dollar and a half, sir," said the driver.

"All right," said Bailey, but as he handed out the money he again silently thought of Smith's livery in Fallington, and although the driver had made only the usual charge allowed by the authorities, and Bailey saw that he could only blame himself for not having made a definite agreement for the distance he had allowed the driver to serve him, yet judging from Smith's livery in Fallington, he believed that this driver had overcharged him, and yet he rather admired his shrewdness. Then Bailey thought suddenly of a stroke of policy. It was a common saying of his, that "no matter how good a man's cause is, it needs good management, and even good principles on this planet can not afford to lose sight of shrewd policy!"

It occurred to Ben that he needed, or at least might need, the friendship of just such a fellow on the frontier as this odd character, and so he told him in a smiling way, that he would like a little private conversation with him.

At this the driver turned his team a little one side, and Bailey beckoned to him in a confidential way, which caused the driver to descend from his carriage, when

Bailey proceeded to astonish him, by saying in a low tone :

"Well, driver, your infernal shrewdness convinces me that you are just the fellow to help me, for good pay, in a little *private business* that I propose to do. Perhaps I can turn a little *money* into your pocket if you can help me. I don't want a man that has got any conscience, and I am satisfied you would suit me," said Bailey, with a peculiar smile which rather pleased the driver.

"What in the name of Jehosophat do you mean?" whispered the driver.

By this time Bailey had again opened his pocket-book, and the driver observing him to take out a two dollar greenback, changed his smile from a doubtful expression to one of evident satisfaction, which Bailey was careful to observe—to read his man.

"There," said Bailey, putting the money into the driver's hand, "that is your first instalment; call it for what you please."

"All right," said the driver, "every man has got his price! and I am of course no exception to that rule."

"I expect to stay around here some months, so there will be time enough, driver, to arrange particulars. Where can I see you?"

"I drive for Mr. Gulliver; here is his card; he can tell you where I live. But, say! if I can get a passenger here in a little while, I'm going across to the falls on the Canada side, and you can go along and I won't charge you a cent more. Honest, I won't!"

"I'll see; perhaps I will go. But, driver, do carriages cross this bridge at all hours during the night?"

'Of course they do, same as they do on any other road," said the driver.

"And you are an old guide?—perfectly posted on both sides of the river, are you?" said Ben, in a confidential tone.

"Of course I am," whispered back the driver, "and I know exactly where to drive to. But you must pay for the wine and take care of yourself, too, if that's what you mean!"

"I don't exactly understand you," said Bailey.

"And perhaps I don't you," replied the driver, who took Bailey to be a fast young man, with plenty of money to waste in dissipation on a spree at the Falls!

"Well, it's no matter whether I understand you," said Bailey. "I want you to understand me; will you keep a secret?"

"I will, sir, if I am paid for it!"

"Well, you have found me liberal to begin with. Now tell me how is the best way for me to get some silk dress goods across from Canada without paying this infernal duty of sixty per cent., in gold."

"Well, I 'spose I know a few of the tricks—been about here long enough—been a guide and a hackman ten or eleven years about here—and smuggling isn't a thing that's very scarce in these parts. And it's nothing very wrong, as I can see. If 'tis, I happen to know that the richest of them will smuggle silks a dum sight quicker than any hack-driver! But I don't calkerlate to risk this carriage in the business, no how; for Mr. Gulliver is a straight-forward man — the man that owns this carriage is."

"Well, perhaps you know some better way," said Bailey.

"No, not that; I mean——well—management! Ye see, suppose now, yourself and lady —— "

"But I haven't got any lady!" interrupted Bailey.

"Well, couldn't ye get one, if 'twas necessary? I'm *supposin'* a case! Suppose yourself and lady—all the better if there was two of 'em—were stoppin' here at a first class house, say like the Monteagle, right there in sight, and suppose you hire me with a splendid carriage to take you across on the Canada side to see the falls and Table Rock, or what there is left of it since it tumbled down; well, suppose the women (ladies, of course,) go into any hotel where youv'e got the silk all ready— couldn't a lady tie a whole piece of silk around her just as easy as she could a big hoop skirt, or an old fashion bustle? Jehosophat! I should like to know if she *couldn't!* "

"Yes, I see," said Bailey.

"Well, 'spose you paid me ten dollars for takin' you over there and back, you don't think I'd be fool enough to know anything about it, do you? Not if the court know herself, and she think she do, as Esquire Dickens always says when he declines a small marriage fee— because it's too small!"

"Exactly so," said Bailey, smiling, "and yet I prefer to wait till I see you get some others safe across in that way; of course I must be cautious, Mr. driver."

CHAPTER XVI.

THE driver with whom Ben Bailey was engaged in a low conversation, though eagerly listening to the proposition about smuggling, at the same time was on the watch for passengers for his carriage. In a little time the driver noticed a gentleman and lady whom he knew to be strangers from the interest they manifested in looking at the bridge, so he asked in his professional way:

"Have a carriage to go around and see the Falls, sir? and the Whirlpool on the Canada side, sir?"

"I hardly think we shall have time," replied the stranger, in a good-natured way. "We've only an hour or two to look around before we are to take the cars for the West."

"That will be plenty of time, sir, if you take a carriage, sir. Take you to the falls on the Canada side or on this side, either, for a couple of dollars," continued the driver.

"Well, if you can get us back in time to take the next train for the West, I guess we will go across the bridge and up to the falls on the Canada side, and then to the Whirlpool," said the old gentleman.

"All right, get right aboard," said the driver, opening the door of the carriage—"plenty of time!"

The two new passengers took seats in the carriage; the driver closed the door, and got a chance to whisper to Bailey: "It's all right between you and me; get aboard—on the seat with me. I see you intend to go in for your line of business, and you see I understand mine in every department of it."

"Exactly so," said Bailey, with a significant smile, while he gave the driver a familiar hunch with his elbow, as if they had been smugglers of old acquaintance!

In a moment longer the carriage was before the toll office, and Bailey on the seat with the driver. The driver whispered to Bailey to pay the toll-man twenty-five cents, which Bailey did, and asked no questions. The toll-man then informed the clever old gentleman in the carriage that the toll was "one dollar."

"How is that?" said the passenger.

Bailey himself having just paid twenty-five cents for his own toll, was a little curious too, to know the meaning of the one dollar charge.

The driver fearing that the high rate of toll might break up the prospect of his bargain, informed his passengers of the fact that that paid for coming back also.

"Do you charge a half dollar each for passengers to cross this bridge and return?" asked the old gentleman.

The gate-keeper explained that the toll was "twenty-five cents for each passenger, and fifty cents for the carriage."

"See here! driver," said the clever old man, "you

have made a contract to take us to the falls and back on the Canada side for 'two dollars.' Now I suppose it belongs for you to do as you agreed, which you was aware you could not do without paying this toll. So what have I to do about the toll?"

"Why, passengers always do pay their own toll," said the driver. "So you see I couldn't have thought nothin' about takin' any advantage of you!"

"How innocent!" thought Bailey.

"Yes, that *is* the custom," said the toll-man.

"Yes! and some mighty queer customs, too, travelers find that ever traveled much. But sometimes I think, as I did about this war, that it's best to endure all manner of evils, as they come, than it is to fight ourselves out of one trouble into a dozen others! So here is your dollar for toll!"

"Driver, how long is this bridge?" inquired the clever old man.

"Eight hundred feet, sir."

"Pretty big toll, but a magnificent structure!" said the stranger, as they entered upon the floor of the bridge which was tightly covered overhead, but open like net-work at the sides.

"Driver, what was the cost of this bridge?" inquired Bailey.

"About four hundred thousand dollars in 1855, when money was like gold," said the driver.

"Hark!" said the lady, "what is that overhead? Why, that's the cars, isn't it? I'm afraid to go while the cars are over our heads!"

"O, that's nothin'," said the driver, "there's freight or passenger cars or engines goin' over almost all the while."

"Why, it sounds so *frightful!*" said the lady.

"Yes," said the driver, "till ye get a little used to it. There was a feller riding here with me the other day that said it sounded to him very much like *distant thunder close by!*"

"Don't the bridge sag any, when there's a heavy train on?" inquired the stranger.

"They used to tell that story to make passengers go some other route; but it don't sag more'n it allers did. It kinder has a little mite of sag where the train is, and a little mite of rise where the train isn't! But it's stouter'n Jehosophat! this bridge is. May be you would like to hear me tell you something 'bout this bridge that's mighty queer. Well, in the winter it arches itself right up in the center twenty inches higher than 'tis in the summer time. Looking out there to the left, would you think them Niagara Falls was two miles off? Well, they be, and right under this bridge it's two hundred and fifty feet down to the water. And there's a water-wheel down there with a long shaft that turns the flour-mill, just by the toll-office there. Now look through the other side of the bridge, down stream. Do you see how awful rough them rapids is? Well, do you 'spose any boat ever went through there with any live man on it?"

The passengers presumed not.

"Well, as true as Jehosophat! there was once three live men went down through them rapids on a little steamboat. You see there was a small steamboat built,

and used for a pleasure and ferry-boat, where the river is
pretty smooth, just above here, and close below the falls;
but when this bridge was built it didn't pay to run the
boat, so one day it absconded down through them rapids
to get away from a mortgage, where it could run in Canadian waters on Lake Ontario. Mr. J. R. Robinson, the
man the guide-books tell of doing such daring things
about the falls and rapids, was the captain on that trip,
but nobody but the current was boss; Robinson himself
was thrown hilter-skilter, and the smoke-pipe went to the
deuce, and everything tumbled through like Jimminet-
tee!"

"Driver, is all this true, you are telling?"

"Of course 'tis, it's no use for drivers to tell big stories
about what happened here, lately; but when it's something further off, we have to tell it just as we get it!"

"Right about the middle of the bridge once, about
sundown, there was a man murdered."

"Bless my soul!" exclaimed the lady, "what! somebody murdered right here, on this very bridge!"

"Yes, and the folks had a talk around that the feller
was goin' to get clear 'cause they couldn't tell which
country had the right to hang him! for, don't you see,
one-half of the bridge is in Canada and tother half is in
the United States. But at last he settled the whole matter himself."

"Why, how could he settle a murder?"

"By jest dying in jail."

"What was the murder for?" asked the old gentleman.

"O, they were partners, and both too mean to live; and one of them got so mad he thought so, and killed his partner for the privilege of being hung himself! The way 'twas, when one stole anything he wouldn't divide!"

"And another awful thing happened here. An old resident—I knew him well—picked out the very center of this bridge, on the north side of it, and sat down on that railing, and waited until two of his neighbors came along, and then after talking with them a few moments, he suddenly sprang from them and leaped off into the rapids! You can't imagine what awful feelings them two friends of his had as they watched him falling two hundred and fifty feet! They say it took four seconds, and they heard him strike the water."

A few questions from the passengers, and at last to the great relief of the lady, the carriage had passed the bridge; the driver had handed the tickets to the toll-man at the Canadian end of the bridge, and had reported "nothing aboard dutiable," to the officer of Canadian customs. He then drove up the carriage road close by the high bank of the river, which was the usually traveled road to the Clifton House, the Museum, Table Rock, and the falls on the Canadian side, and the Burning Spring and the battle ground.

"Yes, and there was a love story happened on the bridge three or four years ago," continued the driver. "You know those three things, love, murder and suicide, do get mixed sometimes."

"A love story on the bridge?" said Bailey.

"What kind of a happen was that?" said the lady;

"and why didn't you tell us that story while we were on the bridge, instead of such horrid things?"

"Well, there was a couple (a feller and a girl) who came here from way off in Toronto, or Hamilton, or somewhere else in Canada, and got a United States minister, one of the preachers here, to come out on the bridge and marry him and his girl."

"Quite romantic!" said the clever old man.

"May be that was it, and may be he wanted to puzzle the lawyers," said the driver, "on jurisdiction, in case he hadn't no right to marry the girl!"

"Bless my soul! what won't folks think of?" remarked the lady.

"Talk about getting married," said the driver, "you ought to see what a host of Canadian couples come across this bridge to the American side to get married, 'cause the justices nor the American ministers don't make no bother marrying folks, but in Canada they have to get licenses and advertise, and you know some folks get off the notion before that time!"

"Driver, how did they manage to get the bridge across this place?"

"They sent the first of it over with a kite—I mean they got the first string across with a kite—and then drew the first wire over by that string. When they was windin' wire around them big wire cables that reach across the river over the four stone towers that the bridge hangs on to, by the wire rope suspenders, there was two of the men fell off the scaffold."

"Bless me! and they was drowned, weren't they?" said the lady.

"Drowned! I rather think they was! In the first place, they were killed a falling so far; and then they were killed by striking the rocks on the slope of the bank afore they got into the river; and then the rapids finished 'em by 'drowning' 'em, or tearing every rag of their clothes off; as it always *does*, if anybody is ever found after falling into any of these rapids—which sometimes they ain't."

"It's a wonder," said Bailey, "if there were no more accidents, building a bridge over such a place!"

"I believe there wasn't, though," replied the driver. "But there was something here, afore they finished the bridge, a great deal worse than accidents! In these two little villages, (each side of the river,) there was over a hundred died with the cholera; and half the folks that wasn't dead left the place. There was a whole family of three died in one Irish shanty on the Canada side, and the folks around it was so scart they actually burnt the shanty with the bodies in it! as they were afraid to carry the bodies to bury them!"

"Was that really so?" interrupted the old gentleman.

"Why, that was awful!" exclaimed the lady.

"It's as true as Jehosophat!" said the driver, "for what I've told you, so far, is what I have known myself, since I've been a guide about these falls. I know it individually! And what's more, I had the cholera myself, and was dead more'n two hours, or ——'

"Hold on driver!" said the old gentleman.

"Whoa!" said the driver to his horses, pulling up on the reins.

"No, no, not stop your horses," said the old gentleman with a hearty laugh, "but do you really think you were dead two hours?"

The driver loosened his reins, snapped his whip, and replied, joining the passengers in the laugh:

"Two hours, if at all; at any rate, I was *collapsed;* and all of 'em said I was *good* as dead; and I know I wasn't *'live* enough to *know* it, if I wasn't dead! I guess I would have died any how, if it hadn't been for something that cured me just at the last minute!"

But we have other things to notice, and we must omit what further took place on this ride; simply saying that the rest of Benjamin Bailey's experience this day was similar to that of thousands who visit Niagara Falls.

8

CHAPTER XVII.

IT was near dusk when Benjamin Bailey returned to the Niagara Falls depot and transferred his baggage to the Cataract House. The day's events, its interest and its excitement, had left him neither opportunity nor appetite for a meal at tea-time; but he immediately went to his room, where he occupied the evening in writing letters home to his friends; not forgetting to inclose a sprig of cedar as a relic plucked from the bank of Niagara.

His journey by railroad, and his first impressions of the Falls and its surroundings, drew him into lengthy epistles; and, even Gulliver's driver, not only as a character himself, but on account of the incidents he had related, was given a special paragraph among the matters of interest in Benjamin's first day's experience at the Falls.

And for the benefit of the reader, we will here state that all the incidents which Gulliver's driver related on that occasion, so far as we have recorded them, were substantially correct, if we except his account of having once "had the cholera himself, and been dead with it more than two hours," which latter incident, if it ever did occur in the experience of Mr. Gulliver's driver—or of any other person—we have no knowledge of the facts, though we were at the Falls during the cholera season of 1854, and well recollect the incident of the three bodies burned in the Irish shanty, on the Canada side of the river.

After two or three days spent as a visitor about the Falls, though keeping his eyes open to his prospective business as a detective, Benjamin Bailey reported for duty, and special instructions, to the collector of customs; on which occasion, as he approached the door of the collector's office, he observed a man just leaving the office in an opposite direction. He only caught a glimpse of the man's face, but was almost certain he had seen him somewhere, before; but did not quite identify him as George Bedan, his smuggling friend, whose acquaintance he had made on the cars! When Bailey entered the office the collector was busy signing some papers as they were handed him by his deputy. Benjamin, before speaking, waited a few moments till he caught the collector's attention.

Their eyes no sooner met than they recognized each other. It was not the recognition, however, of persons acquainted, and yet they knew more of each other than at this moment they were conscious of; for Mr. Baldwin and the collector were personal as well as political friends; and it was by a mutual understanding between them that Benjamin Bailey had been appointed as the friend of Mr. Baldwin. But the collector this moment recognizes

Bailey only as the stranger who extended to himself and Deacon Sommers the courtesy referred to on the cars. But this was an introduction for which they who are careless of the smallest acts of kindness and courtesy, may be more than repaid the cost of this volume, if Benjamin Bailey's act in this one instance shall remind them to perform similar acts of kindness, which surely will in the end, result in their own happiness as well as that of others. And Bailey recognizes the gentleman whom he now suspects may be the collector, as being one of two strangers to whom he gave up his seat in the cars.

"May I inquire, sir," said Bailey, addressing the man he thus recognized, "if the collector of customs is present?"

"I am the person you refer to; take a seat, sir," said he, with a good-natured smile of recognition, "I shall be at liberty in just a moment."

"Any time, at your convenience, Mr. Collector," Benjamin replied, taking a chair.

After signing his name to a few more papers the collector approached Bailey, saying: "Isn't this the gentleman who gave us the seat in the cars the other day?"

"Yes, sir, I remember seeing you on the cars, but had no idea then," said Bailey, with a smile of surprise, "that you were the collector of customs to whom I had a letter of introduction from the Hon. Mr. Lyman Baldwin, through whose kindness, together with your own, sir, I have the honor to report to you for duty." And Benjamin had scarcely finished his reply before he had presented the letter to the collector.

"Ah, indeed! Is this Mr. Bailey?"

"That is my name, sir."

The collector expressed his pleasure at seeing him, and introduced him to his deputy as a new officer for the secret service. The deputy and Bailey entered into conversation and the collector read the letter from Mr. Baldwin.

"Kingsley," said the collector, addressing the deputy, "have we any news of the smugglers at Youngstown?"

"Nothing, besides the kegs of whisky seized last night in Mr. Chewbrick's sail-boat."

"Mr. Bailey," said the collector, "are you acquainted with any of the places along the Niagara River?"

"Only what I have seen since arriving here on Tuesday; have never been in this section before; but in some respects I hope that may be an advantage; it may help me to appear all the more natural, if I am inquisitive among the smugglers."

"Yes, we can sometimes take advantage of a misfortune," replied the collector, smiling.

"If," said Benjamin, "it prove a misfortune, I must at least see that it does not get unnecessary advantage of me."

The collector, after a little general conversation—very little, for he was a man of executive ability, not words—gave him some special instructions, and requested him to call again the next day at two o'clock, when he would introduce him to an officer who had been in the secret service two or three years. "Mr. Bedan knows all the smugglers that own boats, and he can post you up about them, as well as the tricks which others play to defraud the revenue."

As the collector mentioned Bedan's name, Bailey was on the point of asking the detective's Christian name. Then it flashed across his mind that the man whom he had just seen leaving the office was dressed like the Bedan he had talked with on the cars, and had taken to be a smuggler. He was of the same size, his clothes of the same color, same style, and his side whiskers were the same. It was he, without the least doubt. But Bailey did not deem it best to introduce a subject to the collector, which he and Bedan both, might think involved a joke to be kept between themselves—for both had been equally deceived!

When Bailey left the collector's office he rambled along the river bank on his way back to the Cataract House. On entering a small piece of woods, about three-quarters of a mile from the Falls, he fell in company with a stranger, with whom in a little time, he became quite sociable. They admired the scenery together. When the stranger found Bailey was from the country, he thought there was no business like farming; he had always followed it; he owned a nice farm out West; he believed, too, that the farming community were more independent and more honest than any other class of people.

Had Benjamin possessed the experience of some old police officers, he would have been at least more likely to have thought of a class of traveling pick-pockets and swindlers, who make their occasional visits to Niagara Falls, as well as other places of fashionable resort—and would have looked more critically at his new companion; in which case the Western farmer's hands would have looked to Bailey more like following some "light-fingered" business than "holding the plow!"

As it was, there was nothing in the appearance of the stranger that inclined Bailey to suspect that he might be other than what he pretended; nor, did he even think of swindlers, pick-pockets or robbers! What if the stranger was loitering about that little strip of woods that one could almost see through? Wasn't there just as good an apparent honest object for one stranger to be there as another? Wasn't Bailey there himself to admire the scenery and enjoy the grove?

They had just passed through the strip of woods towards the falls and the village, when they met a man with a small valise, who, in fact, was a confederate of the first stranger, and both were black-legs. The second stranger made some inquiries, such as any stranger might be likely to make. "Could either of the two gentlemen tell him what the short canal, which seemed to have no other present use than to make an island of the village of Niagara Falls, was intended for?"

Respecting the canal, Bailey had himself made inquiries concerning it, and was able to tell him, that it was intended to furnish water-power for manufacturing pur-poses, but after expending three or four hundred thousand dollars upon it, it had ever since lain idle.

"Ah, indeed! Well, gentlemen," said the man with the little valise, as he opened it, "let me show you an improvement which I think one of the greatest discov-cries of the age. Of course you need not buy it if you don't choose to."

"On those conditions," said Bailey, "of course I can have no objections to looking at what you wish to show, sir."

"I have but little time to spare," said the Western farmer, "as I wish to meet a friend at the Cataract House."

The man then took a vial from his valise, which he said was a composition for silver plating. He proceeded to show what lasting wonders it had wrought, and could be made to do, as he said, on any smooth metal. He silvered over a brass spoon or a spoon of some badly tarnished metal, which, when done, he declared would last ten years without wearing off!

To this, however, Bailey ventured to suggest a proviso, "that it be kept carefully wrapped in a soft piece of *chamois* skin, laid away in a dry place, and carefully left there."

"O, no, I guess that's a good thing," said the "Western farm" man. "How much a bottle do you ask for it, sir?"

"One dollar for the four ounce vials, and fifty cents for the two ounce," was the reply.

"And how much is the lowest you take?" asked Bailey, with a joking smile.

"The same as I ask for it, sir," returned the disguised black-leg.

"See here," said the first stranger to Bailey, "that *is* a good thing, no mistake! See! you can't rub it off one mite!"

Bailey looked at it; tried to rub it off; and remarked

that "it *appeared* pretty good, but it would take some time to try it *a year!* though perhaps hot dish-water, or strong vinegar might try it in *less* time, pretty well!"

"See here," said the "silver-polish" man to Bailey, "you talk as if hot water, or vinegar, could penetrate silver!"

"O, he's only joking," said the "Western farm" man. It's no doubt a good thing; in fact, it looks like some I've tried myself; I silvered over a set of the worst looking spoons you ever saw and an old teapot, two or three years ago, and they look as good as genuine silver yet! and have been in constant use ever since. It's called a big discovery in our section; but it's hard to find a bottle of it now; and I'll buy a bottle of you."

"The recipe for that article cost me a hundred dollars, and I *know* it is good; and when a man tries to show *just what a thing is,* and you can *see* it, what is the use of thinking everything and everybody is a cheat and a humbug?" said the "polish" man, showing the tarnished spoons and the polished ones by contrast.

The "Western farm" man took the silver plating compound and handed the "polish" man a five dollar bill, which he looked at sharply, and then asked Bailey if it was good.

Bailey looked at it, but said he was no judge of money; which was precisely what these two black-legs desired to know.

"What will you take for the recipe?" asked the pretended farmer.

8*

"I've sold a good many recipes for twenty dollars," said the "polish" man.

Finally a bargain was made at fifteen dollars. But on looking in his pocket-book the "Western farmer" found he would have to give him a fifty dollar bill to change.

The "silver plate" man took the fifty dollar bill, saying, "it's a good bill, but I haven't got money enough with me to change it. Perhaps your friend here can change it," and they both made a very innocent and inquiring look toward Bailey.

Bailey hesitated a moment, but finally said "he did not like to change such large bills, for the reason as he had already told them, that he was not a good judge of money!"

This of course did not suit the plan of the two "confidence men;" for, the bill was a counterfeit; and, it was their business to pass it. But they had gained a point; they found he had money with him. How are they to get it of a man so cautious? It was not a safe hour for robbery; though one or two instances of daylight robberies had occurred some years back in that vicinity.

"If this gentleman don't like to risk changing the bill I will get it changed," said the "farmer," "at the Cataract House, where I am stopping, if you will go back to the village with me."

"Yes, but that will make me later to the Suspension Bridge than I like to be," objected the "polish" man.

"Perhaps you would cash a draft of fifty-one dollars for me?" said the "farmer" to Bailey, "and I can exchange back with you, as soon as we get to the Cataract House."

This game of getting off a fraudulent draft as security for money, for "just a little while," is a game which has been successfully tried on strangers at the Falls and elsewhere, who have seen and read too little for reasonable caution.

But Bailey declined to cash the draft, giving as a reason that he was not acquainted with the parties!

Bailey's new companion and the "polish" man, now, both joined in cursing out an opinion, that "no man could be so devilish disobliging, unless he was some outrageous scoundrel, that didn't want to show what kind of money he carried!"

Suddenly at some kind of signal, understood by themselves, they both sprang to their feet, and each presenting pistols to Bailey, the "Western farm" man declared "if he stirred hand or foot they would blow his brains out;" for, said he, "since I've been walking with you back here, you've picked my pockets, and that is why you dare not show the money you've got!"

"And I *saw you do it!*" said the other.

"Raise your hands while this man searches you for my money, or you are a dead man—and we fling you over the precipice!" said the innocent farmer.

"Men, I am unarmed, and of course in your power," said Bailey, who had carelessly left his revolver in his trunk.

The "polish" man searched Bailey first for weapons; finding none, he took his money; but returned his pocketbook and papers.

"Now complain of us and we complain of you. Your

life is safe till you make complaint—and we are safe if you do complain, for *I can prove you took my money!*"

At this moment Bailey saw a man approaching near them; and, for a moment felt a sense of relief; but the next moment the "Western" man astonished Bailey by calling out to the new comer:

"Say! stranger, perhaps you *saw* this young man pick my pocket back there?"

"Yes, sir, I did, and am ready to swear to it!"

"Well, I've got my money back!" said the "farmer."

"If such witnesses were common," ventured Bailey, "law might as well be abolished! for it would soon become a 'remedy' worse than any disease!"

"I bid you good day, sir," said the "Western farm" man to Bailey, as he walked away in an opposite direction from the Cataract House.

"And if you don't want to buy a bottle of my silver plating compound, I may as well be going, too," said the other, as he walked off with the "farm" man. "But, say! you better have a bottle, it would polish up your manners!"

"I say! stranger," said the "farm" man, "if you make us any more trouble, THERE *is an honest witness! and* HERE——*a revolver!*"

"It don't look, now, as if I were in a position to trouble you!" muttered Bailey, as he started toward the "Falls" village; and noticed that the new comer was slowly walking in the same direction.

"Then you are going to swear you saw me rob that man, are you?" asked Bailey of the new stranger, eyeing his dark visage and long, black beard.

"Why, of course I should have to swear to the *truth!* the truth is the only thing I *could* swear to!"

"And you would advise *me* not to complain, if *they* don't!" added Bailey, with a slight appreciation of the tragic ridiculous!

"I certainly should," replied the stranger, with an air of disinterested indifference, and apparently turning to take a look at the river scenery.

"Do you know those two men?" asked Bailey.

"No, sir, I don't make myself intimate with strangers, when traveling!" he replied, as he ceased walking, braced against his cane, held his lighted cigar in his delicate fingers, and gazed at the high, rising mist of the falls, as if he were some sublime meditator, too devoted to let such a small matter as a highway robbery divert his thoughts from the soul-inspiring scenes of Niagara!

Bailey felt, now, more inclined to increase his pace toward the village than to waste time with this mysterious witness; who, whatever he might appear in court, was to Bailey clearly an accomplice of the other two villains, and whose part in the plot was, to be a "witness," to swear the guilty free, or assist to intimidate the injured and the innocent from making complaint!

CHAPTER XVIII.

"THIS will never do," said Benjamin to himself, as he quickened his pace—"never do for me to be outgeneraled by black-legs and robbers the very first day I have reported myself for duty as a detective of smugglers! This is no small matter; it may get into the newspapers, and it must not go there as it stands now. The only merit the public seems to recognize is *success*. Even an honest failure gets more disgrace than a successful humbug, or than a profitable bargain gotten up by deception and fraud. Why, if these very scoundrels had got their counterfeit money or forged drafts on me, strangers as they were, they would have been called 'sharp,' and the Lord only knows what the public would have called me! As it is, I hereby give Benjamin Bailey notice that he must capture those thundering scamps, dead or alive. Deacon Sommers and Laura must not have the chance to hear that Benjamin Bailey was a coward! But, of course, I must have weapons. It would have been only brave foolishness for me to have resisted two armed highwaymen, unarmed as I was."

The first house to be reached was the Frontier Hotel. Benjamin soon entered it, exhibiting no small degree of excitement, in spite of his efforts to appear otherwise.

"Give me a gun!" said he to the landlord, "I must capture two highwaymen in twenty minutes, or they will escape! There is no time for delay or explanation! Give me a gun—a rifle, shot-gun, carbine, pistol, anything, the best thing you have!"

As might be expected, Bailey's sudden as well as his excited appearance, created no little excitement in the bar-room. One Dutchman held his half-emptied lager beer glass by the handle, while he inquired of another German, better versed in English:

"Was meint der mann? Was ist gethan? Ist der teüfel hier?"

At the same time a soldier handed Bailey a large revolver, and the landlord produced a double-barrel gun.

"Mein Gott!" exclaimed another Dutchman, who had just emptied his glass of "lager," and stood bewildered by the movements, and the hasty English of those who best understood Bailey.

"Mein Gott! ist die gun schus some dings? Der mann ist viel mad, don't he? Vot for vill he make some dead mans?"

"Are these loaded?" asked Bailey.

"The revolver isn't; but here are some cartridges," said the soldier.

"The gun is well loaded," said the landlord.

"Is there any policemen at hand?"

"I've sent for one up town," replied the landlord.

"And he will probably be here, be jabers, by the time you don't want him!" added an Irish porter.

"Cannot wait an instant," said Bailey. "Whose buggy is this, before the door?"

"Mine," said the landlord.

"Send a man to drive me a mile or more, and I'll overtake the scoundrels!"

"Und I go mit sie," said one of the landlord's porters.

"Hier!" said another Dutchman, coming from behind the bar with a large cavalry pistol, "hier ist einander shootsen ding waan sie will maken some powder in!"

Benjamin seized it, and with loaded gun and two empty pistols—the latter he thought might answer for a show in arresting the robbers—he and the porter, for a driver, jumped into the buggy, and the next moment were riding rapidly down the river road. A sharp eye was kept along the bank, but they saw no person, not even the mysterious witness, till after riding about a mile and a half, Benjamin saw two men disappear from view, near the end of a high board fence, close by the railroad. He pointed them out to the driver, who informed him that there were some desperate bad characters living in the house close by there.

"Faster, then, and I'll get out at the end of that fence and head them off. My gun is all right, but this thundering revolver isn't! But no matter, if we can get near the rascals; you take this big pistol, and take aim when I do!"

"Der teivel! und sie tinks I shoots waan sie shootsen auch! und dis ding go nit, mit no powder in!"

"But will you make believe, all but the shoot?"

"O, yes, I scare dem. I go mit sie, all but die shoots!"

A few moments later and the well-broke livery horse was left standing in the road; while Bailey stood at the end of the fence. His double-barrel gun was in a position for instant use, and a part of a revolver could be seen projecting from his side pocket. The two robbers were facing him at a doubtful distance for the aim of their revolvers, but not for Bailey's gun.

"Halt, scoundrels, or you are dead men! You are our prisoners!" exclaimed Bailey, in a voice that left no room to doubt his intentions.

The two robbers halted, and as they whispered to each other, Benjamin continued:

"Disobey one order and I shall take pleasure in demonstrating the fact that this gun will shoot twice—at a very short interval!"

The Dutchman, too, assumed the appearance of having a commendable amount of courage, making a very significant demonstration with the big pistol, as he moved within supporting distance of Bailey, and exclaimed:

"Dis be der bolice!"

The robbers saw that their late acquaintance was in no mood to be trifled with. Bailey had assumed command.

"Before you make another move," said he, "take out your revolvers and lay them on the ground!"

This order was silently obeyed.

It is probable that the robbers decided to show no signs of guilt, and to rely on the evidence of the "mysterious" witness to clear them; though their first intentions may have been to secrete themselves till dark, at some point down the bank of the river, which Benjamin's quick movements had frustrated.

"Raise your hands!" ordered Bailey. "Higher, as I did mine, when you rifled my pockets; or this gun shall rifle your bodies!"

"Now keep together, and march to the right! There, halt!"

The robbers again whispered to each other, but obeyed orders.

The Dutchman, by Bailey's direction, secured the weapons of the robbers, and in due time all were in marching order for Niagara Falls village. The two robbers advanced in the road, in front of Bailey; the porter driving behind them.

"Hands away from your pockets, there!" said Bailey. "You can keep my money with you, you honest 'Western farmer,' and you 'silver polish' man, till we reach the Justice's office!"

In due time the captives were marched into the village, where a police officer now made his appearance, and took them into custody.

Bailey's money was found on the person of the "Western farmer." In due time the two highwaymen had their trial. By marks upon two of the bank notes Benjamin proved the money to be his, and where he had obtained it. The "mysterious witness" appeared, but refusing to answer certain important questions which would have probably led to an exposure of his own true character, no confidence was placed in his testimony. The robbers were convicted and sent to prison.

The evening of the robbery and the next day, the bold and energetic manœuver of the stranger who captured the two robbers without waiting for policemen or other assistance, except to procure weapons and a conveyance, was the subject of talk among the strangers at the hotel, as well as among the citizens of Niagara Falls village. Who is the man that marched those robbers into the village? was one of the questions which almost everybody asked, but which nobody seemed able to answer to anybody's satisfaction. The next day after the affair, Deacon Sommers was in the post-office, and he asked the same question of the post-master.

"I have heard two stories," was the reply. "Some say it was Bailey. I supposed at first that they meant one of the Baileys living in the village here. But Dawson, the livery man, says Gulliver heard that it was a stranger stopping at the Cataract House—says he is a young man, rather slim, and not very tall."

"Did Mr. Gulliver hear what his name is?" inquired Deacon Sommers.

"I declare, now!" said the post-master, "I cannot remember whether Gulliver said his name is Bailey or not. But he said they called him an intelligent-looking fellow—had sandy whiskers and was well dressed."

When Deacon Sommers got home he told the news; gave the description of the young man who captured the robbers, as one account gave it, and the name, Bailey, as another rumor had it.

Laura Sommers declared it to be her decided opinion that that description and the name, Bailey, meant Benjamin Bailey, and nobody else! and she wished she could see him, if he had come to Niagara Falls; she could not see the need of being so delicate, or so something, that they would not let Benjamin know the facts, and defend himself, if he could. She was satisfied from what they had already heard, that Judge Bailey was a "miserable sinner!" and that he ought to blush every time he read those words in the prayer books!

"Why, daughter," suggested Deacon Sommers, "even if Benjamin Bailey is a good, common sort of a young man, it could not have been pleasant after things got as they were!"

"Father, now don't you think that it was an act of injustice for us not to give him an opportunity (when he so politely requested the privilege) to show, if he could, that he had been misrepresented?"

"Well, daughter, you know it cannot be helped now. And there was the young minister, here, a much better husband for you, if you could only think so; and there is Col. Le Grange. The Colonel is a good fellow—always has been an anti-slavery man; and there is no doubt but he is wealthy. The minister, too, he gets a good salary."

"Father, in reference to the minister, what more could I say than that I *dislike him?* or, of the Colonel, I do not *love* him? In deference to my father's good judgment, and in obedience to his expressed wishes, I have been able to refuse the one I loved! but marry one I do not love? No, dear father, never!"

And with these words the tears came to her eyes, and she left the presence of her parents, and went sad and sorrowful to her room.

"Why, de Lord sakes!" said Dinah to Mrs. Sommers, the next moment after passing Laura in the hall, "de massa sakes alive! ef Miss Laura don't hab Benjamin she won't hab nobody! Hih, he! I wouldn't say dat ef I had——two beaux! I heer'd Massa Higley say, once, down South, dat it was agin' de Bible to be so mighty pertic'lar! Ses he, 'where would de world been by dis time ef de fust man and de fust woman, an' all der childers had a been so mighty pertic'lar?'"

"There, Dinah," interrupted Mrs. Sommers, "you may sweep the dining-room out, now."

"De Lord sakes! Missus, hih, he! does ye know what Miss Laura axes me, yesterday? hih, he!"

"Why, what was it, Dinah?"

"Wal, when I tole her dat I had sweept her room out, she axes me, '*out where?*'"

"Did you tell her, Dinah?"

"I tole her not to be skeered, 'cause I could sweep it all in agin ef she said so; but she didn't say nuffin after dat, hih, he."

"There, Dinah, you need not talk any more, now."

"No, ma'am," said Dinah, as she left the room.

"Husband," said Mrs. Sommers, "suppose you and I make a visit to Fallington in a few weeks. You have not visited cousin Gertrude's family in several years. These letters are so contradictory we can tell nothing about them. Suppose their minister did say, that so far as he could find out the facts, things had been exaggerated against Judge Bailey by his enemies. After all, you cannot say but things look bad against him. I don't

believe Mrs. Hartley's letter can be *all* false.   Then everything Judge Bailey or his family say against Benjamin —
see how afraid they are of having it inquired into!   They
would not for a long time even tell the girl's name who,
they said, could tell such hard things against Benjamin
Bailey.   And then when they *did* tell us, it turned out to
be one in their own house—Jerusha Vroman—the very
one whom we have heard of before with no credit to herself or to Judge Bailey, either!   Why, nobody has
started anything against Benjamin Bailey that we have
heard of, but what came first from them!"

"It is an unpleasant affair, anyhow," said Deacon
Sommers.

"Unpleasant, of course, but when they call him a half-
witted fellow, why, I saw enough of him to know they
could not say such things without some base motive for
it!   I begin to think that Mrs. Hartley's letter is true,
and that Judge Bailey had some idea of helping his son
to get Laura for a wife, long, long before David's letter
to her!"

"Tut, tut, wife, it does not look very likely that Benjamin Bailey, and David Bailey, and Judge Bailey, all
fell into such extravagant admiration of Laura, and that
the old Judge contrived a game against Benjamin, and
hired Jerusha to tell such down-right falsehoods as you
must think she has told, and all to help David to get a
girl he had not at the time asked for!   And did not
Laura, herself, know that David was paying attention to
another girl?   Even if Judge Bailey be a bad man, I can
not see that he could have had at first any bad motive to

deceive us; it would be a queer man that would get up falsehood and trouble without motive to prompt him."

"And yet," said Deacon Sommers, putting in a cautious proviso, "it may be that I was wrong, and your first impressions and Laura's were right—time may tell! I do blame myself for not taking more pains to find out the facts and to know more about Benjamin Bailey. And in two or three weeks, perhaps, we *had* better make a visit to Fallington, so that I can satisfy Laura how things are, if we can find out."

CHAPTER XIX.

A Singular Comparison of Letters — How a Minister proposed to Laura — How a
Colonel proposed—Laura's Opinion of them.

A FEW moments after Deacon Sommers' last remark, recorded in the preceding chapter, Laura reëntered the room with a package of letters, and asked her father if he would please read and compare Benjamin Bailey's first letter to her with the minister's and the Colonel's, and then say if he did not think Benjamin's the best in every respect.

The Colonel's letter was received by Laura almost immediately on her return from Fallington; and the minister's four or five months before Benjamin Bailey's arrival at Niagara Falls. Laura had given to each a respectful and decided answer, that she could not reciprocate the sentiments expressed in their letters.

Deacon Sommers would have been pleased either with the minister or the colonel for his son-in-law. The Deacon was a high Calvinist, as well as an anti-slavery man, and when the minister, the next Sabbath after the Fort Pillow massacre of Union negro soldiers, prayed that the Almighty would "destroy the rebel armies and send them quickly down to hell,"* the Deacon approved every word

* This is an exact quotation from the prayer of a Presbyterian clergyman, made in a village near Niagara Falls.

of it, and liked him better than ever. He also admired the colonel as a man entertaining the same "radical principles," and as a man who possessed the kind of courage necessary to aid in carrying out the mundane portion of the preacher's prayer.

The idea of comparing the first letters written by these two suitors and Benjamin Bailey, the Deacon remarked, was a matter of no importance, and he believed he had learned the substance of them when first received.

"But you have never seen them together," said Laura, "and perhaps a comparison with the minister's letter might convince you that Judge Bailey was at least mistaken as to Benjamin's being a young man of very 'inferior abilities,' having a 'poor education,' etc. I cannot help forming some opinion of people by their letters! It takes a good deal of good sense, in my opinion, to write a good letter; and it means as much sometimes as dollars and cents! I don't like egotism in a letter nor in a minister. I don't like to hear a minister talk as if he expected the congregation to believe him an inspired interpreter of scripture. And I don't like a man any better because he happens to be a colonel, and thinks his lips were made to hold tobacco—or to be too commanding!"

"Daughter, you are getting severe in your criticisms," said the Deacon, with a smile.

"Not much more severe, father, than our minister was with the rebel slave-holders, not long ago," responded Laura, with a blush. "But I wish you would read and compare these letters, father, just to please me, this once."

9

Finally, Deacon Sommers was prevailed on to read the letters. First, he read Benjamin Bailey's, which ran as follows:

"FALLINGTON, N. Y., ———, 1863.

"MISS LAURA SOMMERS:

"*Dear Stranger*—If there be those who might in strict etiquette criticise me for writing this letter to a lady to whom I am probably unknown, I can but hope that my reasons for doing so, with the honorable intentions which I bear toward the lady I am addressing, will be kindly regarded.

"I have seen you on three occasions, but have merely learned your name, and that yourself and your mother are visiting at Mrs. Cummings'. Seeing no prospect of a favorable opportunity for an introduction to you through acquaintances, I have thought it not improper to address you this letter.

"As an assurance to you of my sincerity, and of my consciousness that no one can say aught against my moral character, allow me to say, that I have always lived near Fallington village, and consequently your friends, if you desire, can easily make inquiries concerning me. To make this letter a better introduction of myself, I will state that I am the person whom you probably saw in conversation with Mr. Baldwin yesterday, as yourself and Miss Cummings came into his store. You may have also seen me at church. I occupied the pew in front of Miss Cummings and yourself last Sabbath.

"I should be happy to make your acquaintance; and with that purpose, may I ask the favor of an interview, at the house of your friend, at such time as will be most convenient to yourself?

"Anxiously awaiting your reply, I am with sentiments of high esteem,

"BENJAMIN BAILEY."

"Yes, daughter," said Deacon Sommers, as he finished reading the letter, "there is a sort of candid, honest and sensible look about that letter, I admit. But seeing the writer of it face to face, I might get a far different impression of him."

And yet it is not four days since Deacon Sommers did see him! If he could now know that the writer of that letter to his daughter, was the same young man he had so lately met upon the cars, with whose manners he had been so pleased, how it might disarm his prejudice! And then, could the veil of falsehood be turned aside which has been thrown between the Sommers family and Benjamin Bailey, what changes might it make! How it might effect the happiness of the innocent, and disclose the motives of the guilty! When and how will this take place? Or, will secrecy forever hide and shield the guilty to let the innocent suffer?

To the remarks of her father, at the close of Benjamin Bailey's letter, Laura made no reply, but anxiously watched his countenance as he took up the minister's letter and read as follows:

"N——— ———, 1863.

"DEAR MISS SOMMERS:

"Your dear father has granted me permission to write you this letter. You may be surprised at receiving the first intimation of these sentiments in a letter instead of my calling to talk with you about the matter. But I feel too deep an interest in your welfare, both earthly and spiritual, to say what I would in words that pass away with speaking; and which in this form, of a letter, we both might wish to keep as a memento of an *era* in our lives.

"I have long thought that if I were a married minister I might be more useful among my dear flock. Indeed it was an objection among some of the dear people which they raised against my taking charge of this church and instructing them in spiritual things, that I was not yet married; and they would perhaps do better to pay a larger salary to another clergyman who had a wife. I therefore ask the pleasure of seeing you at your home to-morrow evening to express my views on some essential points, and leave it with you to consider whether you would be willing to be my wife, in which case if you are not already orthodox in religious belief, I should take great happiness in instructing you as well as my dear congregation, in the truth respecting spiritual things and the true meaning of scripture.

"I am, your affectionate pastor,

"REV. JONAS CREEDLY.

"To Miss Laura Sommers."

"What do you think of that letter?" asked Laura, noticing that her father was about to take up the colonel's letter without expressing any opinion of the minister's proposal.

Deacon Sommers replied that "he thought the minister's letter might have been better adapted to his object as well as to his subject."

"Yes, I think so, too," said Laura, "and I don't see how any young lady could like a man who would write her such a letter. It seemed to me when I first read it that he had a confused idea that he was writing to a small child, to a young lady, and to his 'dear flock!' It was difficult for me to determine whether he was intending to marry for love or to advance his business as a preacher; or whether he would be my husband or my spiritual school-master! Before I would marry such ridiculous egotism, and such spiritual impudence, I would rather marry Col. Le Grange, as I have said before, and have him go immediately 'in the front of battle,' as he said, 'and lay down his life on the altar of his country!'"

Laura smiled, as she added: "Please read the *Colonel's* letter now. No matter if you did read it when I first received it. You see it is my fortune to get letters that bear reading *twice.*"

Deacon Sommers smiled, and proceeded to read the following:

"N—— ——, 1863.

"DEAR LAURA:

"It is with no little anxiety that I write this letter. In the little acquaintance we have had you cannot have failed to notice that I have been more than pleased to be in your society.

"I now write you this letter to offer you my fortune, and my sincere affections, and to declare that I love you as I love life itself. For, without your society, or at least without the hope that I may sometime in the future, have you to cheer my home, I shall be wretched, and life to me be of no further value.

"If I have any fault in your eyes which it is in my power to correct, I pledge you my word and honor it shall be my greatest happiness, influenced by your charms, and for your sake, to correct them. You can ask no sacrifice I would not willingly make for your sake. I admit that from some remarks which you have made to me, I have little expectation that you will accept my proposal; but I await your answer, and if your reply be unfavorable, I can only add, in proof of my devotion to you, that I shall then seek the front of battle to lay down my miserable life on the altar of my country; for I shall have, myself, no further use for life.

"I am yours only and forever,

"LAFAYETTE LE GRANGE."

In the course of reading this letter Deacon Sommers' countenance several times manifested a slight struggle between a smile and an effort to be serious. For while he thought the colonel's letter too extravagantly in advance of Laura's feelings to gain his object, it certainly was a serious question who was to be the future husband of his daughter. And when finally he handed back the letters to Laura she very naturally expected her father would express an opinion as to the comparison of the letters. For a few moments Deacon Sommers was silent. But Laura, with exceedingly good tact, desiring to find out the impression which alone the comparison had produced in her father's mind, remained silent also, till her father spoke. At last he said:

"Daughter, such letters addressed by a gentleman to a lady upon a subject so generally embarrassing, are the most difficult of any in the world for a man to write. I know how it was when I was young!"

"I perceive, father, that you mean what you say as an apology; and as you are so much of a friend to the minister and to the colonel, too, I conclude you are apologizing for *their* letters—not Benjamin Bailey's!"

"But is not the apology a good one?" asked Deacon Sommers, smiling.

"Perhaps it is; but it is better still, where none is needed," was Laura's quick response.

At this reply Laura's mother gave a smile of satisfaction. And Laura added, "that she admired Benjamin Bailey's letter, and did not like either of the others; and that she did not believe one word coming from Judge Bailey, or from any one under his influence."

Deacon Sommers admitted that the hearsays had become badly mixed; and he regretted that he had not visited Fallington before things got into such an unpleasant state. In fact, Deacon Sommers himself, had begun to suspect that all was not right with Judge Bailey. He had never known much of him, and for a number of

years past almost nothing.   It had occurred to him that
Judge Bailey and his family might have more than one
motive for deceiving the minister in Fallington, as well
as the Cummings family; that through them they might
deceive others, and thus be enabled to sustain themselves
in society.

But the barrier between Laura and Benjamin was not
yet to be removed; and there was little prospect that it
ever would be removed.   Deacon Sommers thought it an
unpleasant matter to meddle with.   No action was decided
upon; and Laura saw with regret, that results were still
to await the uncertain events of time; and that she could
do little to hasten them.   Years might pass away—her
life might pass away—ere the truth would come to light.

What strange barriers—what thin veils sometimes
exist between the opinion we *do* form and those we
would form, if the veil which hides some secret truths
were drawn aside.   Sometimes the barrier between is
innocent ignorance of some fact, and sometimes falsehood
has placed it there.

There was, indeed, a faint, lingering hope, returning
now and then to Benjamin and Laura, that the obstacles
thrown between them would sometime and somehow be
explained away,

> For true love needs but little hope
> To keep that little long,
> And when that little once is broke
> 'Tis often mended strong.

CHAPTER XX.

TIME passed on—time is a noted traveler in that direction—and Deacon Sommers made a visit to Fallington; but circumstances so turned that Mrs. Sommers could not accompany him. He thus lost the benefit of what a woman's visit could have learned of fact and rumor.

It was common talk, however, that is to say, every confidential friend told her confidential friend, under strict injunctions of secrecy, as she preferred not to get the ill-will of the Bailey family—told of numerous scandalous things that had lately come out against Judge Bailey and Jerusha Vroman; and also of the heartless course which Mrs. Bailey, driven to defend him, had taken to frighten Adeline into silence, and to destroy her credibility, should she speak the truth. It was told, too, how Adeline, in a late severe sickness, in some delirious moments, had said some strange things; at one time charging Judge Bailey with a crime almost incredible; then how she blamed herself for having helped Mrs. Bailey to conceal Jerusha's trouble.

And yet the very persons who whispered these things
9*

the most, but the most privately, said among themselves,
"well, *we* don't wish to have their ill-will; they are wealthy;
they can do us favors, and should we openly appear to
believe the truth against them, they might pay us badly
by starting falsehood against *us* to *our* injury! We can
not respect them, of course, but we can treat them as if
we were not supposed to know how things are! We must
look to our interest! We can stand it as long as the
minister and the deacons do." And the minister and the
deacons thought it wouldn't help matters to say anything.
So Jared Bailey and his two or three interested defenders
seemed to keep possession of public respect more than
was a reality.

By continued favors, and also a bold cunning, in which
Mrs. Bailey and Jerusha were perfect masters, they
secured either the good will or good opinion of Mrs.
Cummings, as well as of the minister's family; so that
what Deacon Sommers vaguely learned of facts, from
other sources, they half-innocently smoothed over. Indeed, it was a worldly failing of the Rev. Mr. Smoothwell, which he, himself, however, mistook for one of his
Christian virtues—that he was always ready to counsel
great forbearance and forgiveness in all special or individual wrongs where even necessary notice was likely to
interrupt the harmony of subscribers to his salary; while
he taught in a more distant sense, that on account of
Adam's transgression wrong-doers *deserved* no mercy.

Mrs. Cummings, too, though she never submitted to
wrongs against herself, without fanning a spark into a
blaze, felt a remarkable indifference to wrongs against

others. Hence in the latter cases, when it was for her interest to cover up wrong, she, like the Rev. Mr. Smoothwell, believed it to be her Christian virtues which led her to forbearance! In such cases it never occurred to her that such a course could be carried far enough to encourage evil-doing.

Deacon Sommers, however, had heard things against Judge Bailey in the nature of several criminal assaults, which were of a character to corroborate the statements in Mrs. Hartley's letter to Laura; and which alone rendered Jerusha's statements in defense of Judge Bailey entirely inconsistent and improbable; and hence tended to confirm the stories against herself. Also, to the further astonishment of Deacon Sommers, all he could learn against Benjamin, was traced to Jerusha and Judge Bailey's family. Mrs. Cummings informed him that Adeline Wilderman declined to talk about other people's quarrels. Deacon Sommers, therefore, learned nothing from the source to which Mrs. Hartley's letter referred.

When Deacon Sommers returned home, he said that "he was obliged to admit that he could hear nothing against Benjamin Bailey, except what had lately started from Jared Bailey's family. He was also satisfied that Jared Bailey was *as dangerous a man as he dared to be!*"

He regretted that he had no opportunity to see Benjamin Bailey, who, he learned, had "gone West on private business," and would be gone several months at least.

One evening after Laura had asked her father innumerable questions about his late visit to Fallington, she sat carelessly picking the hem of her handkerchief, when

her father suggested that perhaps by spring Colonel
Le Grange would be home, and she might think better
of him.   "As for the scandal in Fallington against Jared
Bailey, and the unaccountable course his wife takes,"
added Deacon Sommers, "I fear it will yet disgrace the
whole Bailey name; for half the folks would never take
pains to inquire *what* Bailey, and never find out what
motive the Jared Bailey family had for turning over their
own scandal against Benjamin Bailey."

"Father," said Laura, after an unusual space of silence,
"I want your permission for me to write to Benjamin
and tell what that Jerusha Vroman says about him!"

"You may do that if you choose, after seeing Colonel
Le Grange once more."

A smile of satisfaction lighted up Laura's countenance,
as she replied:

"Then I shall be delighted to see the colonel just as
soon as he can come!"

*   *   *   *   *   *   *   *   *

The day after Benjamin's experience with the two
black-legs, the account of which was closed in Chapter
XVIII., he called according to appointment at the custom
house, where the collector was to give him instructions
and introduce him to the old detective Bedan, who in a
short time entered the room.   Bailey and he stared a
moment at each other in mutual surprise; and though
they instantly recognized each other, they manifested no
recognition until the collector, introducing them, had said:

"Mr. Bedan, this is Mr. Bailey, a gentleman who will
assist you in looking after smugglers."

"Well! well!" said Bedan, shaking hands with Bailey, "this either explains things or else it doesn't! By Jove! I guess we've been practicing on each other a little!"

"O, you've seen each other before this!" said the collector.

"Yes, Mr. Collector, on the cars, last Tuesday, I took Mr. Bailey for a smuggler!"

"And I paid Mr. Bedan the same compliment!" retorted Bailey.

"Ah, ha! I see," smiled the collector.

"I believe Mr. Bedan is to find the *boats*," added Bailey, "if I conclude to smuggle a little whisky!"

"Yes, ha, ha! I *was* to find them, but *now* it will belong to Mr. Bailey *to find them*, himself!"

The conversation now turned upon the duty which had best be assigned to Bailey. It was finally decided that Bailey, being an entire stranger, should manage to make the acquaintance of smugglers, and learn where and when they purchased their goods, or smuggled them. He was also to send any information by telegraph, in the secret cypher, understood by the collector, his deputy and detectives. He was to avoid being seen much with other custom officers or about the custom house.

Several weeks from the date of the above conversation Bailey arrived one evening in the railroad depot with important news for the collector.

"Any news?" inquired the old detective, in a whisper, as he happened to meet Bailey in the depot.

"Before forty-eight hours," replied the new detective, at low breath, "I can tell the collector where and when to have a seizure made worth ten thousand dollars!"

"By Jove!" whispered Bedan, "twenty-five hundred dollars for your share; the same for the collector, and five thousand for the government, wouldn't be bad for you to begin on, Mr. Bailey!"

A few minutes later and the two detectives were having a private conversation in the Exchange Hotel.

"What is the case you've just worked up?" asked Bedan.

"It is this: they are shipping flour and mill-feed to Buffalo from one of the St. Catharines mills in Canada. They have entered at least a dozen boat loads, free of duty, at the United States custom house, under a fraudulent entry, by reporting the flour and mill-feed to have been manufactured from wheat raised in Canada; when in fact the whole is dutiable, because made from American wheat—a kind of violation you see of the present Reciprocity Treaty."

"Well, by Jove! Bailey, as many times as I've read up custom-house matters, ɪ never thought of the Canada mills making that dodge! But, Bailey, those mills have Canada wheat and American, both, and how can we ever know which kind of flour or shorts they ship into this country? It seems mixed up with one of those queer laws which great statesmen sometimes make, as if on purpose to be avoided or misunderstood!"

"But if I have read our custom-house laws rightly," said Bailey, "we are justifiable under reasonable suspicion, to make a seizure, and then it rests with the owner to prove the goods were properly reported for duties; and if free of duty, why, then of course the oath that must be made to make a 'free entry,' ought—whether it does or not—to cover the facts under which the free entry is made; and if required, the importer ought to be able to prove the facts otherwise than by his own oath, simply. In this case, however, I found there had been no Canada wheat, or flour, or mill-feed, in the mill for six weeks past. While I was there a vessel from Chicago was unloading wheat grown in the Western States; and I tell you it was provoking enough to hear those Canadians talk sympathy with a slaveholder's rebellion to ruin our country, without our letting them get any more advantage than the Reciprocity Treaty already allows them! I declare, it seems to me our country will serve them right to annul that treaty."

"Yes," added Bedan, "and turn Fenian, too, till they stop giving aid and comfort to Jeff. Davis."

Bedan now suggested to Bailey that he attempt to get the confidence of some of the parties smuggling whisky across the river from Chippewa in Canada, at which place there was a large distillery. It was his opinion there was a newly-organized band of smugglers. "The inducement at this time," said Bedan, "is about two dollars per gallon! enough to tempt some who pass for very respectable people; though it is not considered quite so aristocratic to smuggle whisky as it is silk or broadcloth; a thing which on any frontier, *custom*, in spite of custom houses, seems to have 'sanctioned and sanctified,' as Henry Clay once said of slavery! So you see, Bailey, we must look out for respectable people as well as midnight desperadoes. If there is a new company of smugglers, they,

like the old ones, are sharp enough to have their secret
spies watching customs officers. They, of course, have
men each side of the river, and a regular system of talking signals for day and night. They can signal danger,
and where to land and when to land. We must have a
new spy in their camp; you being a stranger might
safely act for awhile, and then on special occasions we
can also engage others."

Bailey's success in the detection of the smuggled flour
and mill-feed made him willing to risk a few adventures.
He, therefore, favored the suggestion. And Bedan went
on to give a little of his own experience in that line of
detection.

"I got into one of the smuggler's secret organizations
some two years ago," said Bedan, "where they operated
down at the mouth of the river. But after I had managed to get two or three smugglers arrested and their
boats and goods confiscated, they somehow got up a suspicion against me. An old fellow started it by name of
Chewbrick. He claimed that I was very much such a
man as Jonah was—the real cause of all the late troubles
that befel their boating! which fact, so to speak," said
Bedan, with a smile, "was true! You see, in a moral
point of view"—here Bedan stopped to press a fresh supply of tobacco into his mouth, as well as to consider how
he was to finish his "moral point of view"—"you see,
Bailey, like a certain passage of Scripture, so in a moral
point of view it was with me, 'no man can serve two
masters.' So I served the government instead of the
smuggling organization! Of course I was under the

necessity of being slightly *hypocritical.* We, of course, consider our business right and honorable, but *they didn't!*"

"Why, yes, Bedan, I justify a detective in this way. He acts as an officer of the law—not as an individual. It is as right to detect and catch criminals as it is to shut them up to punish them! It must be as right to catch a murderer by deception as it is to hang him with a rope, and the same principle applies to detecting lesser crimes!"

"Precisely so; but it would have amused you, Bailey, to have seen the manifestation they gave me of their opinion of officers of our profession, when one of their spies came with information that I was a custom-house detective, betraying them! I was alone with them, on the bank of the river, about midnight; alone with a half dozen smugglers, and the very worst men I ever knew. They gave me a very brief, mock trial, and convicted me of being a 'deceptive and treacherous scoundrel!' 'It was their opinion,' said one of the mildest of them, 'that I didn't deserve an honorable discharge from any decent band of robbers! and much less from the fraternity of *free traders!*' Another declared that 'it wasn't safe to give such a villain a safe acquittal!'

"At the moment I started to escape from them, I had occasion to believe myself in danger! And, by Jove! the discovery the next morning of two bullet holes in the flying portion of my coat, confirmed me in the opinion that I hadn't taken my departure any *too* quick; and that in all probability, I had lost their confidence! And, furthermore, Bailey, on that occasion I don't think they were shooting to frighten me! There was too much

meaning in those bullet holes! For several days afterwards I also felt a sore sensation, putting me in recollection of heavy cow-hide boots which had come before the
shooting, into forcible contact with indiscriminate portions, so to speak, of my mortal body!"

After some further conversation our two detectives
separated.

Four days later the canal-boat, loaded with shorts and
flour in Canada, was towed out of the Welland Canal;
and on reaching Buffalo the expected fraudulent entry
was made, when the boat and cargo were seized by the
officers of customs.

Benjamin afterwards received a letter from his friend,
Mr. Baldwin, in Washington, congratulating him on
being the first to detect that class of unlawful entries.
The government thereafter took extra precautions to
collect duties in similar cases, and many thousand dollars
was saved to the country before the Reciprocity Treaty
was, in 1866, finally abrogated by the United States.

Benjamin next attempted to gain the confidence of
some of the whisky smugglers. For this purpose he
took lodgings at a tavern in Chippewa. The boisterous
nonsense, the profane and obscene levity of assembled
drinkers, smokers and topers, in the bar-room, on the
first evening, sickened him of his undertaking. His
mind reverted to his country home, and to his sister's
cautious warnings, and his own resolution on that afternoon when the telegram announced his appointment.

From these reflections, however, he was soon startled
by hearing the landlord address a man with a gray beard

by a name which he had heard his mother speak of in connection with his grandfather Bailey's will!

"I say, Figsley," said the landlord, "take my advice to-night, and go home sober!"

"Whose business—Mr. Tibbles, is *my* business?—so long—as I've no wife—and—no *children* as I know of—I think, Tibbles—I could stand—about one—glass more!" bewildered out the man addressed as Figsley.

"I'll be d——d if you get another glass *here* to-night," replied landlord Tibbles. For landlord Tibbles feared that too much drinking (his idea of too much) might make his bar-room unmanageable.

"Say, Tibbles, say," hiccoughed Figsley, with a wicked grin, "do you — you think — you would — ever be— damned, wholly—on my account—eh?"

"If not, I *ought* to be, for selling liquor to such men as you!"

"I'm glad to hear you—say so!" retorted Figsley. "It's a good confession—worthy to be—said before any— priest of your parsuasion!"

"At any rate, Mr. Figsley, you can't have any more *here*, to-night."

"Well, I'm—dev'lish glad—to hear you say so—to a man of my education — Mr. Tibbles — glad you've re-formed. I think all—the more of you for it—*I* do, Mr. Tibbles!"

So saying, he took a huge quid of tobacco from his mouth, crammed another in, and staggered out of the bar-room into the street.

Here a man, apparently a day laborer, with old age

hurrying upon him, approached the bar. His poor but well-patched clothes and clean shirt collar, bespoke the efforts of a patient and enduring wife. He called for a glass of whisky. Landlord Tibbles placed the decanter and tumbler before him. The poor old man filled the glass to the brim; then placing one hand on the handle of the water-pitcher, he raised the whisky with the other to his lips; then he hesitated, and leaning over the bar whispered something to the landlord.

"I've told you times enough," replied the landlord, with the most blasphemous oaths and curses, "that I don't *trust* my liquor till no Saturday night!"

The old man still hesitated, when landlord Tibbles, with a new set of oaths, ordered him to let the liquor alone, and set down the glass. But the poor slave to drink making no reply, turned the coveted fluid down his throat and slowly went from the bar, bearing both shame and abuse.

One of the company remarked to another, sitting near Benjamin:

"If Pat was as big a rascal as old Figsley, he could get money to pay for his whisky without coming down to that!"

"Did you ever hear how old Figsley gets his money?" asked another.

"I know what I think about it," replied the first. "It's my opinion he and that Vroman on the other side of the river, are doing a mighty good business smuggling!"

"Figsley! Figsley!" thought Benjamin, at the first

mention of that name. "Possibly this is the Figsley who was a witness to my grandfather's will. But his surprise was still greater when Vroman, another name to the will, was spoken of with Figsley. If such men, he pondered, were witnesses, no wonder that Judge Bailey was suspected of something wrong in a will so contrary to my grandfather's known wishes. Who knows what time may not develop? And what a fool I have been that I have so often and so easily yielded to opposing circumstances. Is this the way to fight the battle of life? No!" said Benjamin Bailey, to himself, almost audibly, "and if I let Judge Bailey deprive me of Laura Sommers, and do not devise ways to aid time in bringing out the truth, I shall *deserve* to lose her!" And he resolved to know more of these two men. If Judge Bailey's secret history were in part known to them, perhaps here was an opportunity to detect something more than smuggling—something tangible for himself, and convincing for the ear of Mr. Sommers.

But Benjamin could not penetrate yet that hidden future, so dark to mortal eyes; and so he little dreamed how much was soon to be lighted up as that future rolled into the present—lighted from what seemed to be accidental sparks on the tinder of time's events.

O, how searchingly then will their "sins find them out" and "bring sudden destruction" upon them!

CHAPTER XXI.

WHILE Benjamin Bailey is endeavoring to perform the duties of his office at the various points on the frontier, and is especially gaining the confidence of one smuggler from whom he hopes to learn important secrets for himself, as well as the government, let us notice an adventure of Miss Laura Sommers among the reminiscences of the custom house.

A new officer of customs, Mr. Seth Dobbins, had just been appointed. His duties were with passengers and their baggage arriving in the cars from Canada upon the Great Western Railway, which runs across the celebrated suspension bridge into the United States, terminating at the depots of the Erie and the New York Central Railroads, where the passengers at this time changed cars for the East or South. In the hurry of changing cars a better opportunity for smuggling goods, concealed under the clothing worn by ladies, had been afforded here, than by walking or riding across the lower floor of this peculiar transit from one nation to another. But now new orders had been given by the government. All women suspected of hav-

ing any dutiable goods concealed among their wearing
apparel, were to be required by the officials to report to an
inspectress. To create a suspicion of smuggling, it was
considered enough if an official was informed that the
American ladies had been seen to enter Canadian stores.
Sometimes the very clerks who had sold the goods were
secretly engaged and paid by detectives as informers!

One day several highly respectable ladies, among whom
was Miss Laura Sommers, were seen to cross the suspension bridge on foot and to take the cars in Canada. Our
old detective, Bedan, took that same train, got off at the
same station. Less than two hours afterwards the collector of customs received a telegram in secret cypher,
which meant a description of these ladies. Then immediately Dobbins, the new officer, received special orders.
When the next train arrived, these ladies and a large
number of others, were surprised when officer Dobbins
requested them to report to the lady officer, whose room
he pointed out.

Now it happened fortunately for Laura's friends, who
were with her, that through caution, they had arranged
to have their goods taken charge of by friends living
upon the Canada side of the river till some subsequent
day, when they would call upon these friends, be seen to
enter no store, secrete their goods upon their persons, and
return, like nine-tenths of all who cross the bridge, without justifiable suspicion of smuggling.

But Miss Sommers had been less cautious. She did
not leave her new purchases upon the Canada side in the
care of friends for a future visit. Like hundreds of

others she more than half believed that she had a clear title to what she bought "for her own use and with her own money, and not to sell again." She had purchased a merino dress pattern and some velvet for trimmings, which, for reasons that she afterwards expressed to officer Dobbins she had concealed under the mantilla she that day wore. There had been little prospect of any lady escaping; for Dobbins believed that with silk at half price, no lady would hesitate to buy at least ribbon enough for bonnet strings. After having taken his oath of office to be faithful in collecting the duties, he acted upon principle, and, being a new officer, counted nothing too small to collect; till, at last, he was blamed by the collector for annoying the public by obeying orders too strictly.

Of course, then, Miss Sommers and her lady friends were required to report to the inspectress. Laura's friends (thanks to their caution) passed innocent! but her own purchases were found. And a few minutes later the merino dress pattern and the velvet trimmings were delivered into the hands of officer Dobbins.

Miss Sommers then inquired if she could have the goods by paying the duty upon them.

Mr. Dobbins hesitated; Miss Sommers was beautiful; Mr. Dobbins had already thought so, and was embarrassed. He remembered his oath, and yet he wanted to please the fair girl before him, and he said:

"Madam, I regret very much—in this case—that I am obliged to deprive you of these goods. Indeed, I would be glad to pass them unnoticed, if it were not for my oath of office."

"I beg your pardon, sir, but I think it is generally believed by the best of our citizens that a custom-house officer has no right to take articles purchased for one's own use. They think it ought not to be considered smuggling, sir."

"I suppose, Madam, that the concealment of the goods would be evidence of intention—to—smuggle." Then Dobbins was angry at himself for the way he had said this! He might have used some milder word than smuggle! So he added: "I'm sorry, but I suppose that that is why the government does not allow me to give back the goods and take the duty in such cases."

"No, sir, I beg your pardon again; the concealment does not, in my case, prove that I intended to smuggle—only I was afraid you officers would be so unreasonable as to charge me duty when I knew that a great many smart people say we have a right to buy such little things for our own use on the frontier here."

"Your reply," said Mr. Dobbins, smiling, "is a very good one. Concealment because *officers might be unreasonable* is another motive, I admit. I presume, however, that you do not reside here, or, are not acquainted with the rules of the custom house."

"Yes, sir," said Miss Sommers, smiling at the confession she was about to make, "I do reside very near here; and I am acquainted with the custom of people getting a great many little articles in Canada without paying duty!"

"You turn my reasoning very well, Madam; and yet,"

10

said the new officer, "it seems strange to me that so many people think it right to——to do so."

"Some of you officers call everything smuggling; but we don't! When we buy a yard of ribbon or a dress, we think it is ours; and I'm sure it is no *moral* wrong!"

Mr. Dobbins had never before seen Miss Sommers, to his knowledge, but he began to be certain that he admired her. And his conviction seemed to grow stronger that she was beautiful! What she had said, and how she had said it, pleased him. So he said with as much suavity as he could:

"Then you do not think it wrong for ladies to—avoid the laws about duties, do you?"

"Wrong?" repeated Miss Sommers, in a low voice, and as if to gain a moment's thought before replying, "No, not wrong—in one sense." And then addressing her friend, Mrs. Fairfield, who had been making some inquiries of the inspectress, she added as a further answer to Mr. Dobbins' moral question in reference to smuggling: "Do *you* think, Mrs. Fairfield, that ladies, who are not allowed to vote on any law whatever, are bound to believe in high tariff, and in *prohibiting* trade, because politicians do?"

"No, Miss Sommers, I do not," said Mrs. Fairfield; "neither do I believe that because a custom-house official is legally right, that we are therefore morally wrong!" Mrs. Fairfield, however, was very agreeable in her manner of expression.

And officer Dobbins smiled while he remarked, "that he supposed everybody ought to obey the laws."

"I think," rejoined Miss Sommers, "that it is worse to make some laws than it is to break them. I know that my father was proud of the fact that he used to violate the Fugitive Slave Law. He would keep slaves over night, and give them something to eat, and help them to get into Canada, away from the slave-catchers, in spite of the law!"

"But this young lady was not bringing goods here for sale," said Mrs. Fairfield.

"Are you going to be so strict, sir, as to keep my dress pattern?" asked Laura.

"I am obliged to do so, Madam, by orders in such cases, from head-quarters."

"Will you be kind enough, sir, to tell me where is head-quarters? I'll go and see if I have done such a great wrong."

Mr. Dobbins very politely referred her to the office of the collector, but said that "even he had no right to restore the goods, because the law required them to be sold at auction by the government."

"I have been told," replied Miss Sommers, "that the officers get one-quarter of all the goods they seize."

Although she endeavored to soften the remark with a good-natured smile, yet Mr. Dobbins thought he knew that her intelligent blue eyes looked as if she intended to hint that officials for that reason were over-strict. That she did so intend her remarks I have no doubt. Mr. Dobbins was embarrassed; and before he could reply Mrs. Fairfield had told Laura that the collector also gets one-quarter of the proceeds from seizures; and that one-half goes to the government; she thought everybody on the frontier knew that. Then the ladies walked away from the presence of Mr. Dobbins and the inspectress. But as they turned to go Mr. Dobbins was certain that Miss Sommers had replied to Mrs. Fairfield, that "if the officers were all interested then her dress pattern had gone to the dogs!"

The first moment that Mr. Dobbins found himself alone, he had a little talk to himself. "Just my kind of luck, exactly," said he, "falling in love at first sight, with a stranger. Confusion! a slight aberration of mind, already! Of course a '*stranger*' *if at* '*first*' *sight!* They say that love is blind; and I should say that I should say so—under existing circumstances. Mr. Seth Dobbins, allow me to say that you—that is, I—haven't any chance at all. I don't think, Seth, that she would care even to make my acquaintance. Her dress pattern, with all its little fixings, which she bought with her own money, etc., is in my custody—your custody, Mr. Dobbins—and the collector's—and it is her expressed opinion that it has gone to the dogs!"

"Let me see! I treated her politely, and she smiled and acted good-natured, and so did I; and 'a faint heart never won a fair lady!' Her name is Miss Sommers— so the lady called her—and she lives near here; and Seth Dobbins must make some opportunity to make her acquaintance!"

"What *could* she have meant," said Dobbins to himself, the next day, "by saying that goods in the hands of officials had 'gone to the dogs?' Did she mean it as a hopeless or a sarcastic expression?" Then, too, the expression was not a very refined one; but he told himself that very well bred ladies—and very amiable ladies, too, under perplexing circumstances, did sometimes unfortunately, use unchoice expressions, so that, as Mr. Dobbins was charitable enough to suppose, they could not be charged with the vanity of thinking themselves perfection. So it troubled him most to decide what was her meaning. Finding that Mr. Riggs, one of his brother officials, was well acquainted with Deacon Sommers' family, Mr. Dobbins ventured to ask him his opinion on the ambiguous expression.

But Mr. Riggs preferred to let the attractive Miss Sommers manage her own case; consequently he assured his bachelor friend that it was impossible to say which meaning she had intended; as it was impossible for him to understand what impressions they may have made upon each other under the peculiar circumstances of the introduction.

If his friend Dobbins were "in love *de facto*"—Mr. Riggs had heard the village lawyer say *de facto*—then in his opinion, all that Dobbins could do, was "to manage his case judiciously!" Perhaps it would be best "to wait future developments and treat the symptoms homœopathically, that is specifically as they come up." "By all means," said Mr. Riggs, with emphasis, "until you understand this case act homœopathically. Don't make things worse before you try to make them better. Don't add more difficulties, and thus amputate what little prospects you may now have."

As Riggs used the word *amputate*, Dobbins smiled; and then Riggs did the same, and turned his high-sounding nonsense into something more like practicable advice. "Dobbins," said he, "get some middle-aged lady friend to find out and tell you what Miss Sommers thinks of that new officer, Mr. Seth Dobbins. Then you can tell what to do next."

"Mr. Seth Dobbins," said Dobbins, addressing himself, after leaving the presence of Mr. Riggs, "in the first place, you—I—had better let this affair rest till this seizure matter is a little out of her thoughts." And then the ambiguous expression recurred to him again—whether Miss Sommers had meant to intimate that customs officers were like a set of watch-dogs. But then he knew that she had made a fruitless application to the collector; and the thought now came to him that this would prevent her from further blaming himself. Dobbins thought over the matter a great many times during the weeks that followed preceding the time when the dress goods would be sold at the auction sales. He dreamed that everything would finally turn in his favor; that he would see Miss Sommers at the auction sales, and that he would look so well in the eyes of Miss Sommers that a very romantic courtship would follow—and then a wedding.

When Laura Sommers left the collector's office, without recovering her dress goods, she began to believe that the new officer, who had seized them, had, after all, tried to be very agreeable. And I have no doubt that she thought of two circumstances: how easy the conversation had been prolonged with the new officer; how short and

unexplained was everything with the collector. The collector was a man of years, and thought only of the law
and the facts; while Mr. Dobbins had before himself
prospective matrimony.

Not long after the seizure of the dress pattern, Laura
Sommers noticed among the items of seized goods advertised in the village newspaper, to be sold at auction, in
the custom house, "*Ten yards of purple, merino dress
goods*," and "*Twenty-four yards velvet trimming;*" and
she resolved to be the purchaser of her lost dress goods.

The day for custom-house sales at last came round.
It was a beautiful morning, and before 10 A. M., the hour
for the sales to begin, there were a good number of ladies
and gentlemen waiting in the sales-room of the United
States custom house; a large, square, stone building on
the north side of the railroad, and within fifteen feet of
the passing trains just before they enter upon the great
suspension bridge. If you ever passed this bridge during
a visit at Niagara Falls, you have noticed the building.

Among the items to be sold were three dress patterns
of Irish poplin and *six bottles of brandy;* all of which had
been found evenly divided on the persons of three gen-
teel and respectable ladies, who had come across from
Canada in one of the fine carriages attainable by the
pleasure travel of that locality. These ladies, accompanied by an elderly gentleman, all having a wealthy and
aristocratic appearance, had passed officer Riggs, and
becoming the unfortuate objects of his suspicion, he had
directed the ladies to report to the inspectress; when the
said articles were found and seized.

Mr. Riggs was, therefore, early at the place of sale, feeling a patriotic interest in seeing the poplins and the brandy sold at a good price, in order that the *government share* of the proceeds would aid in reducing taxation. Of course it was pure patriotism, for the government share was just double that of officer Riggs! At least this is as plain as the patriotism of some who at this time were enlisting in the army as privates, with the understanding that they were to be promoted to captains and brigadiers! O, how we overpraise men in high positions, sometimes, who are kept patriotic and faithful because it is their stock in trade! while oftentimes the poor, ill-paid and self-sacrificing private soldier has been censured and perhaps dishonorably discharged, because he could not submissively bear all the exactions and manners of (in many cases) *inferior* superiors!

The small auction-room was crowded; some of the gentlemen, therefore, were standing in an adjoining apartment, among whom were Benjamin Bailey, Bedan, Dobbins, Riggs, and other officials. Mr. Dobbins, however, was occasionally going about the room where he hoped Miss Sommers would be present to observe him. Benjamin Bailey, at a proper time and place, would have been overjoyed to meet Laura Sommers. But now he desired not to be recognized by any of the Sommers family— not till he should be permitted to vindicate himself to Mr. William Sommers against his still unknown slanderers, did he desire to meet her from whom he would have to part so sadly.

Most of the goods had been sold, when the auctioneer

at last put up the poplins, one dress pattern at a time.
Riggs, who had made the seizure, started the bidding at
fifty cents per yard. At first the bidding against him
was very light, and to all appearance the poplins were
likely to go at less than half their value. But the auctioneer was a true officer of the government; and after
having raised his hammer as if for the "last warning,"
he seemed suddenly to relinquish the idea of striking it
off at so low a bid, and after a moment's pause he said,
with a forced seriousness of tone and manner :

"Ladies and gentlemen, I am astonished that you will
look calmly on such a scene as this! This is not merely
sacrificing *Irish* poplin, if these goods are to be sold at
half their value. They are the property of the United
States—of your own government! Will you see its
property wasted or thrown away for half price at an
auction? At this rate, how shall we ever pay our
national debt of twenty-five hundred millions of dollars?
And yet you who pretended to be patriotic citizens, and
are even willing to send all your poor relations into the
army to bleed and die for your country—you seem con-
triving not to bid against each other! *Seventy-five cents*
only is bid! and is there no lady here who will help run
up this dress pattern, which is going at *only* seventy-five—
seventy-five cents ?"

"Eighty cents," said a new bidder.

"Eighty cents," repeated the auctioneer, "eighty—
going at eighty; who'll give the dollar? worth three
times the money, and going at eighty cents."

10*

"Eighty-five, is bid—ninety—going at one dollar, one dollar, one dollar."

And the auctioneer went on crying off the bids; at which monotonous business we will leave him a moment to notice a sample of the talk among the by-standers.

Said one lady in an undertone: "Don't bid so fast—not so quick—make the auctioneer think your bid is the last one!"

"Why, yes," replied the lady, "if you seem willing to pay a high price, the others will stop bidding against you."

Another young lady whispered:

"Mother, don't bid till they've sold a few dress patterns; then there will not be so many buyers!"

"You heard," said another, "how that new officer, Mr. Dobbins, seized two merino dresses, three poplins, and ever so many things from Laura Sommers, did you not?"

"Yes, I know all about it; she told me herself. Only it wasn't ever so many things, at all; she only had one dress pattern and a little trimming; nothing more."

"O, my! I heard she had more than she could carry."

"And you believed it?"

"Why, I didn't stop to think!"

"I guess if everybody did stop, once in a while, to think, we shouldn't hear so many big stories."

"Well, she did have the Irish poplins, of course, for they are selling one of them now!"

"Does that prove that Laura Sommers ever had them?" was the argumentative reply.

"Why! here is Laura, now," said the other.

"Of course, I am," said Laura, smiling, "and I'm here to have my merino dress pattern; and father says, if I wish to, I may buy a dress here for Sophia. You know that new officer, Mr. Dobbins, took one of her's, that she was bringing from Canada, awhile ago; and she is a poor girl, too, and she plays the organ so nicely for our church, you know."

CHAPTER XXII.

Dobbins gets Deeper in Love with the Deacon's Daughter—Troubled with Nervous Mental Inquiries—Excitement at the Auction—The Mysterious Bidder.

THE auctioneer was now offering the last of the poplin dress patterns.

"Eighty cents," bid Mr. Dobbins.

"Eighty cents! eighty, going at eighty cents—and *is* it possible, ladies, that you will allow these custom-house officers after taking so many things away from your friends—allow such fellows to bid off these fine, Irish poplin dresses at half the real value?" Here the auctioneer, who was himself an official, smiled at his own allusions; and everybody else smiled, while he continued: "Will you—can you allow all this, after taking the trouble that so many of you have to bring such things from a foreign country, across this romantic river? Possible that these goods are going at only eighty cents per yard? at eighty, eighty, eighty—*at* eighty cents!"

"Eighty-five," said a stranger.

"Ninety," spoke the low voice of a lady, which Mr. Dobbins did not recognize.

"Ninety-five," offered Mr. Dobbins, looking through the open doorway from the adjoining room.

"One dollar," spoke the voice which Mr. Dobbins had just overbidden.

"One dollar, one dollar; the gentleman's bid of ninety-five is lost, by a fairer bidder, and shall I hear any more than one dollar?" said the auctioneer, turning his eyes from the last bidder towards officer Dobbins.

Thus involuntarily directed, the two bidders also met each other's gaze. Then Mr. Dobbins knew that he had been bidding against Miss Sommers. He bowed with all the grace that embarrassment permitted. And Miss Sommers, whatever she might have done had the opportunity for recognition been less sudden—did sufficiently recognize officer Dobbins to excuse him for the bow that he gave her. He was certain, too, that she bowed in return; but it was so slight that it worried him. It was in vain that the auctioneer cried on for another bid. Mr. Seth Dobbins had ceased bidding. Miss Sommers had again turned his brain into nervous mental inquiries! Did she yet blame him for the seizure? Had she now recognized him because he had performed that unpleasant duty so politely and kindly? Or, might it not be, after all, that she had glanced at him just an instant, to see if his bids had been made against her, knowingly, instead of her having a desire to give him a polite recognition? And then it flashed over Mr. Dobbins—what if she were to get the impression that he had bowed only to recognize her in connection with the unpleasant seizure of her dress pattern. If she did not think so at the moment, she would on reflection. And why not? Had he not had the ungallantry to bid against her? True, he had not known that it was she, but to her it may have seemed, or would seem, that he did know. And this worried him.

Then as to the matter of a lady buying a few dollars' worth in Canada, as Miss Sommers had done, he had learned since, that no one in the best society of the village thought any harm of it; and he was sure that he wanted Miss Sommers to think now that he, too, thought no less of her for it.

It was no mistake of Laura's that she thought that she distinguished a deep blush of embarrassment on all of the unwhiskered portion of Mr. Dobbins' face; and afterwards the more she thought of it the plainer she knew that she had noticed a quiver of his mustache. This impression, however, may have come through her imagination.

The auctioneer got no other bid, and the poplin dress pattern was struck off at what was, in those war times, not more than half its value.

"There," whispered Laura to Miss Percival, "I've got a nicer bargain for Sophia than either of us made in Canada."

"And a much *safer* bargain," added Miss Percival, with a smile.

"Yes," responded Laura, "it was too bad for *us* to lose our Canadian goods when *the rest of you* always have such good luck!" And then before Miss Percival could put in a rejoinder, Laura proceeded to declare that she did not like custom-house officials; especially the one who had just bid against her; but she would just like "to know if that Mr. Dobbins did that on purpose!"

"O, you don't like him," whispered Miss Percival, very perceptibly enlarging the orbs of her lovely blue

eyes, "but you *would* just like to know what he is thinking of you!"

"No, not that; but I was just thinking——"

"O, no, you don't like him," interrupted Miss Percival,
"but you *would* just like to know if he stopped bidding
the moment he saw it was you, and made that interesting
bow—on purpose!"

"Are you afraid that he is going to like me?" retorted
Laura, good-naturedly.

"I? I never spoke with him. But I hear that he is
the best one among the whole dozen officials in this place."

"Best one? how? best fellow, or best officer?"

"The best *beau*, I mean. What else *should* I mean?"

"But, Clara Percival, you can't think he wants to be
my beau—seizing my dress pattern—bidding against me.
Doesn't it look as though some unlucky star had fated us
to an unfavorable acquaintance?"

"'Truth is stranger than fiction,'" said Miss Percival.

And Miss Percival might have added that gossip is
stranger than either. Mr. Dobbins was a new officer, and
whatever is new gets into the mouth of gossip. Gossip
had said that Mr. Dobbins wouldn't be thought much of
here, if he persisted in being so strict about small purchases; and then gossip contradicted itself, and declared
that Dobbins allowed the policemen to smuggle all the
whisky they wanted—and the Justice, too! and that
Dobbins permitted some ladies to pass him that were
"completely loaded down" with smuggled goods. Mrs.
Limberlingual, whose tongue sometimes runs faster than
her thoughts, declared that "she had heard, with her own

lips, that Sophia What's-er-name, had told somebody, that Mr. Dobbins, or Doublebins, or some of the officers, *didn't pretend to suspect some folks!*" Mrs. Listenviel, on the contrary, had asserted "that there was no truth in this report—else she would have heard of it—and consequently that Sophia had said nothing of the kind; and that it wasn't true if she had!"

There is no place in the world like a small village for gossip to develop itself into *perfect* imperfection. It is only necessary that something either does happen or does not happen, when straightway somebody feels inspired to see that said something has a relation to other possible or impossible events. Consequently gossip said everything about everything, but on account of gossip's known weakness in such matters, neither his truths nor his falsehoods seemed to injure any one; probably because the one was known seldom to be separate from the other!

It had been reported very confidentially among a very few that Mr. Dobbins was holding a correspondence with Miss Sommers, and that they were engaged to be married, and that Mrs. Fairfield had said so. Mrs. Fairfield, however, had been inquired of, and she affirmed that she had never said so, and never had heard such an intimation. All she remembered saying was, that at the time of the seizure of Laura's dress, she had noticed their "*holding quite a conversation!*" or in reference to that conversation she may have said that "they were quite engaged." She remembered saying that Laura Sommers was a sensible and high-minded girl; and no doubt respected officer Dobbins for the honesty which made him do his duty; and perhaps admired his pleasant way of doing an *unpleasant* duty.

But we must now return to the auctioneer, for he is announcing that he "will sell 'a purple merino dress pattern,' which was imported into this country from across the river, he presumed, by a lady of taste; and consequently everybody present could rely upon the goods being of the very best style and quality. He presumed that the lady must have forgotten to report it to the custom house!"

By this time the auctioneer had displayed the goods, and it had been whispered among the by-standers that it was the dress pattern which Miss Sommers had purchased in Canada. The auctioneer called for a bid, but for some reason there was a reluctance to bidding. It was usual for the seizing officer to start the bidding, and see that the goods were sold as high as possible. But in this case officer Dobbins had told himself that he should do nothing of the kind. Miss Sommers he now knew was present, and he was certain that he would not interfere with her dress pattern any further.

Mr. Dobbins was in love, and he knew that he was in love; and under the unfavorable circumstances he feared that he was hopelessly in love. And again he was troubled with mental questions: hadn't he better write a short note to Miss Sommers to apologize? And what could he lose by asking at the same time the pleasure of making her acquaintance?

But Mr. Dobbins realized the fact that it was easier to ask himself questions than to give himself satisfactory answers.

"How much is offered?" cried the auctioneer.

"Fifty cents a yard," said Miss Sommers.

"It is Miss Sommers, the lady who lost the goods, that just made the bid," said Mr. Dobbins, as he passed officer Riggs and detective Bailey, "and out of compliment I hope the villagers will not bid against her."

It was well for the present comfort of both, that Mr. Seth Dobbins and Mr. Benjamin Bailey did not know that they were rival lovers!

"Is it possible," cried the auctioneer, observing the reluctance to bid, "that you will see this fine merino sold at one-quarter its value? Where is your patriotism thus to stand by and see your country's property sacrificed?"

Nobody seemed inclined to bid against Miss Sommers. This was, indeed, a compliment to Laura Sommers among her neighbors. The man of mental inquiries knew it, and asked himself if she would ever forgive him, and then if she would love him. He must wait and see! Haste would surely dash away his little hopes.

But how about the other? the one who once knew that Laura loved him! He, too, was waiting. He was waiting for truth to reveal the assassins of his hopes. He knew that the innocent were often destroyed by the guilty. For himself he was sad and almost hopeless. Perhaps it were well if Laura, so long as she were forbidden to see him, believed him unworthy. He knew that she was then in the auction room and his heart beat in gladness for her over the pleasure she must feel to know that her village neighbors so evidently intended the compliment in refusing to bid against her on this occasion.

The auctioneer had raised his hammer for the "last call," when a man of mysterious character—mysterious because that which *was* known indicated to the villagers that there was much more that *should be known*—approached and examined the merino. While he was turning the cloth over and over and tearing the edge to try its strength, a voice inquired:

"What does John Vroman want of such a dress—a man that abuses his wife as he does?"

"May be he's going to hire his daughter Jerusha to come home again," said another.

"Can't dwell. Going at fifty cents a yard," said the auctioneer.

"Fifty-two cents," said John Vroman, with as much attempt at dignity as if the villagers had always respected him—and there *was* one class who had deceived "old Vroman" (as they called him behind his back) into an idea that, do what he would, his money would keep a few true friends around him.

"Sixty cents," was bid by Miss Sommers.

"Sixty-two," said John Vroman.

"Old Vroman," said a rough voice, "is bidding to spite a dacent family, be jabers! because they are afther knowin' that he's an ould hypocrite, an' it's meself that's knowin' it, too, be jabers! for twinty years or more."

John Vroman was grinning as if all that could be said against him were mere jokes! But if Benjamin Bailey had heard the name John Vroman, he might have thought of suspicious circumstances related of the will of Benjamin's grandfather.

"Eighty cents," said Miss Sommers.

"Eighty-five," said old Vroman.

"One dollar," was then offered by Miss Sommers.

And still John Vroman advanced the bid. The by-standers seemed to be looking on with interest; and Miss Sommers, determined to release herself from their attention, by bidding so high that John Vroman could make nothing by another bid, so she offered:

"One dollar seventy-five cents!"

The auctioneer cried off the bid. Nobody wanted old Vroman to win the battle. Nobody now believed that he would. But just as the hammer was raised to strike off the goods John Vroman raised the bid ten cents!

"Do bid once more, Laura," urged Miss Percival.

But Miss Sommers declined to do so. Then it became evident that old Vroman had won the battle, and much regret was manifested by the by-standers.

"I fear it might give offense, or I would buy it for her!" said Mr. Dobbins to Mr. Riggs.

Just at that moment, and as the hammer was descending the last time a voice in the adjoining room was heard to say:

"Two dollars!"

The voice was low, but the auctioneer from his elevated position saw and knew the bidder, and in a few moments his hammer went down:

"Going at *two dollars* a yard—and sold—to a gentleman!"

"Good!" exclaimed a half dozen voices, when they saw that old Vroman at last had lost the battle.

At the sound of the voice in the adjoining room Laura Sommers was startled; she thought it so much like that of Benjamin Bailey!

The velvet trimmings were then put up and were struck off with only one bid, to Miss Sommers. It was noticed that the one who had bidden off the dress did not bid against her! When the auction sales were closed and Laura walked away, she said to more than one of her friends, that she wondered if anybody knew who it was that got her dress away from that John Vroman. But no one knew. Days and weeks passed and she often wondered if it was a freak of her imagination, or some strange coincidence of voice, that had made her think of Benjamin Bailey.

CHAPTER XXIII.

In Chapter XX., we left Benjamin endeavoring to
make the acquaintance of smugglers. Omitting some of
his successes and some of his failures, we now notice him
again in connection with Figsley and Figsley's associates
at Chippewa.

There was an old, dilapidated dwelling, at this time,
standing on the Canada side of the Niagara River, near
the shore, and a short distance above the falls and rapids.
This building belonged to Figsley, a part of which he
always rented to some fellow smuggler. One of the
rooms, on the ground floor, he occupied himself, cooking
his own meals. For Figsley had one virtue, (it might
have been one of necessity,) he had never married to
degrade a wife and innocent children by his own life.

By various strategems Benjamin had at last won the
entire confidence of Figsley, so far as concerned smuggling. He had bought a row-boat of him, and hired him
to assist in smuggling several articles across the river,
and to pilot him to the different landing points. And
finding that he and one Bergman, who lived in a lone

snanty a half mile distant from Figsley's, were in the confidence of a new party of whisky smugglers, Benjamin laid a plan to win their confidence more positively, before asking them too many questions about themselves or others.

Bedan, with two other officers, was to be on the watch. Bailey was to be with the two smugglers, and when he found what landing they desired to make he was to advise them to make a different landing, but finally to yield to their choice. Then, while on the river, Benjamin was to indicate to Bedan, cautiously, by signals with his dark lantern, at which of the landings the smugglers might be met. For it had been arranged that Bedan's party were to make a mock attempt to arrest Bailey with the smugglers. And Bailey was to keep the officers back by firing blank charges at them from his pistol.

All this had been planned to induce the smugglers to put implicit confidence in their new comrade, Bailey, and thus be led to confide their secrets to him. It was also to insure Bailey's safety among them by preventing any suspicions that he might be a secret detective.

The plan was most gallantly carried out. Benjamin was the last one to get into the smuggler's boat on their retreat from the landing where Bedan and his party had made a pretense of attempting to take them—and of course had been most ingloriously defeated!

Figsley had arranged to have a team in waiting at a distance from their intended landing, but their plans being frustrated, they now took young Bailey's advice and made their way to Navy Island on the Canada side

of the river, where they secreted their cargo of whisky
to await a more favorable opportunity. The party then
repaired to Figsley's room, where the two smugglers
unanimously gave Bailey the credit of being the hero of
the night; believing that they had been saved from arrest,
and their whisky from seizure, by his bravery and "presence of mind!"

But their "hero" insisted with a modest smile, that he
"did not deserve so much *credit* after all. For," said he,
"the officers *appeared* to be scared to death at the very
first discharge of my revolver! when the truth is, *I did'nt
expect to hit the scamps*, for I'm not a very good marksman
even in the daytime!"

"Say," said Figsley to Bailey, "did I ever tell you
now old Chewbrick got the officers out of the way one
night, so that he engineered a little boat load of liquor
across the river at Youngstown?"

"No, Figsley; and you know I'm always fond of listening to a good trick against these impudent officers!"
said Bailey.

Figsley moved his chair and was about to begin.

"Here! this will never do," said Bergman.

"What's the trouble, now?" asked Figsley.

"Trouble! Isn't whisky the first thing? And then,
do you expect me to listen to a yarn till you lend me
your old meerschaum?"

"Very true! and a very great oversight!" rejoined
Figsley.

After whisky, Figsley proceeded:

"Well, it was down near the old fort where the Niagara

goes into Lake Ontario at a very moderate pace; for the river gives up its ravin' jumps and its exasperated jigs a half a dozen miles, you know, before it gets to the fort, and down there behaves itself splendid! Of course, Bailey, you don't understand that locality as well as Bergman and I do.

"Well, Chewbrick and his son had agreed to get ten kegs of whisky across there from Canada, and land it at a short ravine just above the fort for a man by name of Robertson, who was to be there with his team; or within reasonable notice, from eleven till one o'clock on a certain dark night.

"But, Bailey, you ought to hear Chewbrick tell that story himself, at some of our club meetings! And the beauty of it is, it's a *true yarn*, all but the *coloring*, which Chewbrick always tells a *shade* different.

"Well, 'Blowhard' was on hand, (or Robertson, which is the same thing,) wagon and team, and oil-cloth coat, for it was a rainy night. I tell you they are the nights to pick out for our business, after all. Do you suppose any of them corrupt, black republican officials, are going to be on watch quite so closely such nights?"

"I should be afraid they would," said Bailey, "for you know they get a quarter of what is seized!"

"Yes, but there is an offset to that. They stand just as good a chance of getting a dev'lish good thrashing from us; or," said Figsley, turning towards Bergman, with an exulting laugh, and extending a complimentary allusion to Bailey's late firing at the officers, "they might chance to get one of Bailey's bullets!"

11

"But let me see, where did I drop Chewbrick? O, yes! Chewbrick," Figsley resumed, "had sent his son and a hired man over to a point on the Canada side where the whisky was to be loaded into the boat. And Chewbrick himself was to stay on the American side and watch, to know if the officer on watch left his duty before midnight, the time for another officer to take the patrol. As soon as old Chewbrick found the coast clear, he was to raise and lower the light of his lantern, so that his son would know when to start with the whisky. When they saw this signal his son was to show a light moving up and down a few moments, to notify Robertson, who was then to get his team in readiness as soon as possible. You see in case the custom-house officer did not leave, then, old Chewbrick was to get him out of the way—out of the way (I mean) of Robertson and the boys.

"Well, about eleven o'clock old 'Brick' saw Mr. Officer go home—followed him, and saw him enter the house. You see it was a leetle too rainy for Mr. Officer! But Chewbrick was an old fox. How could he tell certain whether the officer would *stay* in the house, or whether the other officer was not to come on duty at that hour for that night. So old 'Brick' waited awhile, thinking which of a half dozen plans he would adopt. But all the while he kept near enough to the officer's house to know if he came out. In this way, however, old Chew. soon saw he was going to lose an indefinite amount of time. So he changed tactics; he went to the officer's door and rapped.

"'Good evening, Mr. McQuade,' said old 'Brick,' putting on a patriotic face to the officer, who opened the door, but had hardly time to reply before old Chewbrick, says he:

"'Say! McQuade, there is one of the darndest, meanest 'rebel sympathizers' in the whole North, going to smuggle over ten kegs of whisky to-night! I just heard of it in the bar-room at Schneiderberger's.'

"'Are you sure of it?' asked McQuade, 'and who told you?' says he.

"'Well, that's my business,' said old Chew., 'but if you want to catch the meanest man you ever saw, and will give me five dollars in case your part of the seizure comes to twenty-five dollars, I'll show the very spot where the boat will land!'

"The officer, of course, accepted the proposition at once. So McQuade and the old smuggler (or free traders as we call ourselves *politically*) went down the river bank to the very spot where nobody was to land; and just where old 'Chew' wanted to show his son the signal-light; and about a half mile from where the whisky was to be landed for Robertson!

"But stop," said Figsley, "I'm a little ahead of my story. The officer had a dark lantern with him which he was inclined to keep open too much to suit old 'Brick,' for it might have confused things, you see, if his son had seen the movement of that extra light. Then to put a climax on top of that, Chewbrick says that McQuade made some awful suspicious inquiries—wanted to know what Chewbrick needed a dark lantern for—how long he had had it, etc. But 'Chew' told him it was one he had had ever since Pierce was President; that he used to be employed nights to help one of the secret detectives on the same business he was on that night!"

"*Same business?* O, I see! of course 'twas," said Berg-man.

And here they all gave a hearty laugh; and Figsley improved the opportunity to take an old tobacco-box from his pocket and supply his mouth with a little "fine cut."

"Now the first thing was," said he, resuming the story, "to get rid of McQuade's light. So Mr. Chewbrick con-cluded to have his own light go out by *accident;* so he opened his lantern, wondering what *ailed his light!* and somehow, says 'Chew,' the light went out! Then says he to the officer, 'McQuade let me take your light so I can lead the way!' Of course the officer was willing to do anything to help matters along, and so he handed over his lantern.

"Now Chewbrick began to fear another difficulty. What if the other officer should come on duty and go down to the landing where Robertson himself was ex-pected to go, on seeing the signal from the boat. So Chewbrick stopped suddenly, and says he, 'I wonder if we better not go and wake up the other officer to come with us?'

"'No,' said McQuade, 'he was out all last night and he wouldn't come; for he is half sick, besides!'

"'All right,' said Chewbrick, pleased with the infor-mation; 'they are only a man and a boy anyhow, and you've got your revolver, haven't you?'

"'Yes; but let the scamps get away with their bodies,'

said the officer. 'If we get the boat and the whisky, it will be all *I* care to bother with this dark, rainy night!"

"Finally they reached the spot where Chewbrick was to give the signal to his son to bring over the whisky. Now you see it would not answer to have officer McQuade see him do that little exploit. So old 'Chew' pointed up stream with his hand close before McQuade's eyes, and wondered if that wasn't a light away off there!

"But after looking and watching a few minutes in every direction *up stream*, McQuade declared that *he* 'couldn't see it!'

"Of course while old Chewbrick was pointing up stream with his left hand, he was, with the other cautiously moving the officer's lantern up and down for a signal to his son down stream! And this he did till he saw the signal light in the boat answering him.

"And the same signal in the boat for himself, you see, Bailey, also notified Robertson to be ready with his team at the landing below.

"The next thing was to take up the officer's time, which old 'Chew' did by finding themselves a place of conceal-ment, and occasionally swearing, that it was strange that the smugglers hadn't come across, and that he knew the scamps intended to smuggle across ten kegs of whisky before one o'clock that very night. And he knew that they *intended* to land it at that very landing.

"At last Robertson had got his load of whisky a good bit away from the lower landing, and on the way to a place where it was to be secreted. And Chewbrick and the officer went home, old 'Chew' pretending to be swearing mad at his disappointment, while the officer endeavored to console him, presuming the storm had made them give up crossing that night!

"Pretty well done," said Bergman, "but before I had the misfortune to lose my character I did some shrewd tricks myself, watching and misleading customs officers. Why, at one time I was paid by the custom house for detecting smugglers, when, in fact, I was giving information the other way! But, like every other kind of deviltry, it didn't last long before something turned up, and I got suspected; and here I am now, all the worse for what little success I ever had in that line.

"The fact is, there is too little honor with most devils among themselves! Why, Figsley, you know I got up that hose and pipe plan by which more than twenty thousand dollars worth of whisky has been smuggled into Buffalo and Tonawanda; and all I got was fifty dollars for the secret; except the positive assurance that if ever I revealed anything about it except in the *regular* way, to the members of the *regular* club, by their *regular* sanction, at their *regular* meetings, and all such dev'lish conditions, why, then I was to be waylaid by a blow upon my head with a professional sand-bag, or gagged and taken to the rapids, and there thoroughly drowned, after first having my skull broken in by a bludgeon!"

And here Bergman went off into terrible oaths, calling everybody dishonest, and declaring that the unequal division of property in this world, made it right to demand and enforce a better distribution of it, in any way it could be done safely, whether it was called highway robbery, Wall street robbery, or contract swindling, or any other business, for each man to get his share!

"Say, brother Bergman," spoke Figsley, in a low tone, "your confounded talk reminds me of a brother villain I knew more than twenty years ago, whose financial mean- ness I could always *excuse* easier than the *selfish advan- tage and heartless meanness with which he treated his female victims.* He had a habit of swindling them into friend- ship, abusing their confidence, and then cheating them out of his promises; because, at last he would exact more than even human weakness could consent to. But what you particularly reminded me of was a sharp trick of his rascality to produce a very unequal division of property; which, though the trick pays *me* well enough, I always despised him for getting *two girls* into trouble about it—which I afterwards found he did, the unmanly devil—partly to punish them for their *virtue*, and partly *to frighten them into concealing what they knew against him!* Poor *Eleanor!* she left his house though, and *Adeline*, too, soon after.

"Adeline was always in fear of his malicious slanders, as well as losing a portion of the property, which old Mr. Mortimer Bailey had intended for her; but which this Jared (blast the illegitimate bastard) promised to restore a part of to Adeline in case she kept still!

"But this is more than I ever told before. This is bad whisky, Bergman. And, see here! how do I know but this young dare-devil is a son of his? it's the same name! What is your first name, Mr. Bailey, and where are your relatives? But, really, you don't resemble the man I spoke of!"

For an instant a chill went over Benjamin Bailey, and he was at a loss how to answer. The next moment he decided it would not do for him to be discovered as a relative, nor even as an acquaintance of Judge Bailey; and much less as one of the heirs referred to. He also feared the possibility that Judge Bailey might learn his whereabouts, and write exposing him, as a detective, to Figsley; an idea of itself which produced no comfortable sensations. So he answered that men in their business were not fools enough generally *to be known by their real names, when it could be avoided.*

"Bravo!" said Bergman. "A man after my own heart! Let us drink to the health of our *hero of the night!* 'Brave as a lion—cunning as a fox!'"

The dodge was effectual: and Benjamin felt a sense of relief. And when that night he left Figsley's house, for his lodgings, he felt that the suspicions about the will, years before, had been well-founded, and he had now double reasons for frequent visits to Figsley's!

CHAPTER XXIV.

WE now pass over a short time, to a day on which circumstances occurred destined to close Benjamin Bailey's brief career as a detective. On that day he sent the following letter to the collector, in secret cypher. This letter shows that he had not been idle among the smugglers:

"CHIPPEWA, ——— ———, 1864.

"To —— ——, Collector, etc. :

"*Dear Sir*—I crossed the river last night with the same two men who thought I saved them from being arrested by Bedan's party a few nights ago. I am, however, detecting something in these men worse than mere smuggling. They are none too good for highway robbers! I admit I do not fancy crossing Niagara River with them. To be in danger of *accident* so near the rapids, from whence no human power could save one, is bad enough in good company; but it is a little worse when added to this danger I find myself crossing at night, alone with men I believe fit for murderers!

"I have just learned of a new plan in operation for smuggling whisky. It is a sub-marine fixture, carried

11*

under boats—large or small boats—and can be secretly detached and sunk at a moment's warning to avoid detection.

"This whisky is conveyed into this sub-fixture on the Canada side, and taken out and carried away on the American side in a manner so ingenious that officers have closely inspected everything seen to be moved from the boat, without the slightest suspicion. And yet an enormous quantity of liquor has been smuggled in that way in open day, with officers standing by the boat, and even taking passage in it!

"The sub-fixture has a short piece of strong, stiff, ribbed hose attached to it, and on the shore there is from two to six rods of pipe or tubing concealed under the ground, or under lumber, or whatever may be most convenient reaching from the boat landing to the cellar of some building, from which loads of anything are taken in wagons. This building having no apparent connection with the boat is not suspected. The short hose is adroitly attached to the pipe while the boat is waiting for passengers or loading; and thus a connection of tubing is formed from the boat to the building, and the sub-fixture is filled or emptied. I will explain other particulars when I see you.

"In the mean time would it not be well to have the underside of boats looked after? also buildings or docks where such a thing can be practiced?

"I have the honor to be, sir,

"Very respectfully,

"Your obedient servant,

"BENJAMIN BAILEY."

"P. S. I go to St. Catharines to-day, and if I get back in time shall make another visit to that Figsley this evening.   B. B."

Early in the morning of the same day on which the above letter was written, Figsley crossed the ferry to see Vroman.

"Meet me at Bergman's shanty to-night, at dusk," said Figsley to Vroman. "Bergman and I lost our bottom dollar at the St. Catharines races yesterday; and, you say you lost all you can spare; very well, it is coming on winter, and a man must have money. I say, Vroman, a man must have money; at any rate, Vroman, I must have money, because I must have food, drink and rai-ment—especially drink!"

"Mr. Figsley, any man is a fool that drinks or gambles enough to distress himself! But you are a strange talker, Mr. Figsley. Sometimes you say you've got gold in a secret place, or papers that will scare gold, all you need, out of Jared Bailey!"

"No matter, Vroman, you know what is up! No cow-ardice; you want more money, and so do I. Now will you be on hand, I say? It wants nerve, but we are bad enough to be bold."

"But Figsley, what can Bergman do to-night? You say his house-keeper died of consumption an hour ago, and will not be buried till to-morrow."

"Well, that is Bergman's business, not ours. He says come, he may as well be out an hour or two to-night as to stay home and get drunk! He says Hardstriker is bound to have us help take a little of the root of all evil from a rich old cattle dealer expected to pass Bergman's this evening. He wants you and Dick Slyboy to be at his house so that you and he could swear him clear—prove an *alibi* you know—in case of necessity. You see, don't you? As to Bergman, swear he was with us all the evening, in his own house. The plan is well laid, Vroman, well laid!"

"Mr. Figsley, you and Mr. Bergman both are getting too bold; but I'll think of it. If I conclude it is not too risky, I'll be there."

The plan was further discussed, but John Vroman gave no decided answer, and James Figsley returned, muttering to himself as he started, that he knew Vroman hadn't *heart* enough to hinder him from little acts of this kind, and the only *conscience* he had, was his fear of detection! "Plague take the scoundrel," spoke Figsley, to himself, "if I'd never seen him, nor Jared Bailey, either, I'd have been a better man, and I presume that would have been *better* for me. And yet *they* seem to have succeeded with even less of heart or soul than I have, which, I vow, is no boasting for myself, for did I not aid them at first to injure Eleanor? and will I not yet forget my own oath to her, and neglect to expose the evidence which would avenge the wrong plotted against her innocence? and all this, when my own room is haunted with her presence!" But we leave Figsley with his reflections, and till we meet him at Bergman's.

But there was a web of circumstances which Providence had begun for that day, which, in spite of plans or caution, was now to wind around these guilty ones and their earthly career, to bind them over to that great day, when all must render an account for deeds done here in the body.

Soon after James Figsley and John Vroman separated, the latter went to the post-office, where he received the following letter:

"FALLINGTON, N. Y., ———, 1864.

"*Dear John*—Yours is just received. Perhaps I ought to go and see you instead of writing, but, as all my letters have reached you safely, I hope there is no risk.

"It is astonishing how Figsley continues to make larger and larger demands on me. You say he is again dissatisfied—talks too much—threatens to tell the truth, etc., etc.—pretends again that he kept the true will and my two letters about them! Now, this is what he talked once before when he threatened to show who Jared Grimbold was, and is, and that if I 'lived long enough vengeance would reach me from the grave of Eleanor Grace!' Now this must be stopped or there must be another mysterious disappearance!

"You say this year he demands six hundred dollars instead of four hundred, and he will not take it in our paper money. Why, in that case, it would cost me to buy the gold thirteen hundred and fifty dollars these war times. Now, John, I am not in favor of paying him that sum, and thus encouraging him to ask more. You had better have a private talk with him just as soon as you get this letter; and don't fail to remind him that

you and Adeline and myself can be just as desperate
witnesses to get him into trouble as he can be against us."

"One thing more: you and he had better be on your
guard! for one of the heirs, Benjamin Bailey, is a *United
States custom-house detective* on the Niagara frontier! Besides this, I have special reasons not to have him get on
friendly terms with William Sommers. If you will prevent all intercourse between him and them, by reporting
that he has hinted things against the character of Miss
Laura Sommers, and if you will also get hold of those
secret papers in possession of Figsley which I wrote
about in my last letter, I will give you a deed of the fifty
acres Western land you wanted; and I will alter my will
so Jerusha shall have double what I first promised.

"Yours, as ever,

"JARED BAILEY."

The same morning on which the above letter was
received, black Jim stopped with his fish-wagon in the
road before Deacon Sommers' mansion. Now it'happened
that John Vroman on his way home from the post-office
just at this moment came up, stopped his buggy, got out
and bought some fish; and in taking some papers from
his coat pocket, when he paid for the fish, the letter from
Jared Bailey, which he had read and replaced in the
envelop, was accidentally pulled out of his pocket and
dropped upon the ground, unobserved. John Vroman
drove away, and the fish-peddler tooted his horn.

For Deacon Sommers' family always patronized black
Jim; partly because he was Dinah's step-father, and

partly because he was an honest, pious, old man, and because the old fish-peddler was no small convenience to the public.

"Why didn't my ma come wid ye?" inquired Dinah, as she came running toward the fish-wagon.

"Well, Dinah, dat so; she mout a come; an' I doesn't know why she didn't, 'less 'twas kase she didn't get started! You know dat berry often de reason, Dinah, wid folks."

"But if dey haint got no better reason, dat's an awful poor one," said Dinah.

"Ha, ha! dat's so; but I's got some awful good white fish here, Dinah."

"O! de lord ob lub! I's found a letter here in de road! May be it's from somebody's beau or suffin," said Dinah, as she picked it up. Then removing the letter from the torn envelop, her eye struck upon the last paragraph, which she managed to make out a few words of, and finally read "Benjamin Bailey!"

"De lord of lub!" repeated Dinah; and just at that moment Deacon Sommers with Laura in his carriage drove out of the yard towards them. "My sakes alive!" said Dinah, running toward Laura and handing the letter to her, "here be de berry spook ob dat letter, Miss Laura, dat ye cried so 'bout when de dark closet wor ha'nted! Now, Miss Laura, don't ye hab nobody else but Benjamin Bailey! Dat what ye said, ye know!"

Laura took the letter, wondering what Dinah could possibly have found in somebody's lost letter to put such thoughts into her head.

As Dinah went back to the fish-wagon she muttered: "Dey start off as ef dey goin' to hab der berry necks broke!" And then directing her talk to the fish-peddler she said: "Ye see dey got to hurry or dey aren't goin' to get back till dark. I reckon Massa Sommers goin' to get de money for his Canada farm."

Laura, of course, looked on the outside of the envelop of the lost letter. She saw it was post-marked Fallington, N. Y. Curiosity prompted her to know the centents of the letter; and she read it, and read it to the utter astonishment of Deacon Sommers as well as herself. Deacon Sommers was convinced as well as confounded. And Laura cried over the mistaken confidence that had been placed in Jared Bailey. She wanted to fly to Benjamin, she said, and beg his forgiveness. " They have tried, like criminals, to make us believe falsehoods, but I love him, and now I *will* love him, and I will tell him so !"

Mr. Sommers made no reply. He was too busy consulting his own thoughts; and Laura again ran her eyes over the letter as the tears ran down her cheeks. And for the next mile's drive neither of them spoke—but they thought.

"There is the collector of customs," Laura said to her father, in a low tone of voice, as they approached the street crossing, near the custom house. " Please ask him, father, if he knows a young man by the name of Benjamin Bailey."

Deacon Sommers reined in his horse and said :

" Good morning, Mr. Collector."

" Good morning, Deacon."

Then the collector and Miss Sommers spoke to each other. Deacon Sommers then said:

"As you are a man of few words, Mr. Collector, may I ask you, here, if you know a young man by name of Benjamin Bailey from Fallington?"

"I do."

"Is he a custom-house officer?"

"He is a young *gentleman* in whom I have the utmost confidence, both from what I know of him myself, and from what I am told by those who have known him from boyhood," said the collector, stretching out an indirect reply, which gave Deacon Sommers a hint that he may have been too inquisitive inquiring about a secret office!

"I beg pardon," said Deacon Sommers, "I only de- sired to know who he is!"

"Well, Deacon, he is the young man you took such a liking to on the cars this side of Rochester, at the time he gave up his seat so politely to you and me, as you may remember some months ago."

"You don't say so?" said the Deacon. "You don't say so?"

Laura smiled, but she tried not to.

"Also," continued the collector, "the same young man I heard you extolling so highly for capturing the two black-legs some weeks ago!"

"You don't say so? Well, now, I declare! And is he a fellow of good habits? temperate, and so on?"

"Temperate! he would not drink even a glass of wine to please the President of the United States."

Then Deacon Sommers thanked the collector, bid him good-day, and drove on.

Laura blushed, looked pleased, and inquired what her father thought now?

And Deacon Sommers not only admitted that he was satisfied, but astonished beyond degree.

An hour after this time Vroman missed the lost letter. He examined every pocket, even to his watch-pocket, and one coat he had not worn nor seen since the day before. Then he shook out his handkerchief; but found no letter. He retraced every step he had taken since he drove into his yard; inquired repeatedly of all in the house, and finally drove back over the road, toward the post-office, to a place where he remembered reading the letter. On returning he happened to meet the old fish-peddler, of whom he inquired whether he or anybody he knew of, had found a letter.

"Was it a letter in a yaller kiver wid de end broke open?" was the colored man's inquiring reply.

"Yes; have you found it?"

"No, I hasn't got it, but I reckon may be it be de one de girl picked up and gin to Mr. Sommers as he driv out into de road, 'bout an hour ago, or so on."

"Where did he go?"

"Why, he driv off, somewhere; de girl said to Canada to get some money on a farm dat he sole. I spect he got a heap o' land."

"Then the old villain took my letter with him, eh?"

"In course I doesn't know whose letter it was. I spect it wasn't much value; de letter had been read; for de 'velop was torn open, anyhow; an' der wasn't no money in it. Dinah, de girl, say it mout be somebody's beau."

But while the old colored man was delivering his views
to excuse the matter, Vroman was muttering to himself:
"The very worst man in the world to have that letter!
and Jared was an old fool to risk it! It may send us all
to the devil. I'll see Figsley and Bergman now; the
money and the letter both are an object; and secrecy is
an object—to *several* of us!" Then turning back to the
village he telegraphed for Jared Bailey "to come by next
train!" For he thought matters might get beyond his
control. He then went to see Figsley and Bergman.
And his interview with them resulted in a change of the
programme for the night.

It was agreed to not attack the drover, but to dress in
disguise and watch for Mr. Sommers in the mile-woods,
near Bergman's shanty; and to assault him under pretense of searching for Fenian papers against the Canadian
government; but, in reality to get possession of the lost
letter, as well as to rob him if much money was found.
In the latter case it was their intention to gag and bind
him till late enough to send him and horse and carriage
over the falls. "A mere accident, to which any of us is
liable!" Bergman had said in a wicked joke. The old
colored man had said nothing to Vroman indicating
whether Deacon Sommers was alone in his carriage; and
Vroman in his worry about the lost letter, had not even
thought to inquire; hence the company of a female in
the coming affair was not down in the programme!

CHAPTER XXV.

The Mile-Woods—How Benjamin happened at the Robber's Shanty—Concealment in the Loft—The Five Robbers—Victims to be thrown over the Falls—Benjamin resolves to die attempting their rescue.

WHEN Benjamin had returned from St. Catharines, and had taken tea at his hotel, it was dark, except the little light which the stars afforded. Having determined, however, to learn more from Figsley, to Figsley's lonesome rooms he wended his way, but only to find that he was absent. Presuming that he had gone to Bergman's shanty in the mile-woods, he then set out for Bergman's. Arriving at the shanty he entered a kind of outside passage or entry, and knocked on a partly-open inner-door, leading to the only lower room of the shanty. After waiting a short time, and hearing no person within, he pushed the door a little more open and entered the room.

There was a dim light from a kerosene lamp standing on a table in the room, but no one was present. The strong board shutters of the windows appeared tightly closed.

In a room overhead, approached by a ladder through a large open place left in the loose floor boards, there was also a dim light. In this upper room, near the opening in the floor, lay the corpse of the house-keeper, who had died that morning.

Benjamin had stood a few moments waiting for some one's appearance; when, suddenly he was startled by a half-smothered cry of murder, then followed heavy groans and low voices, and the sounds of approaching footsteps; all indicating a party of several persons close at hand. Thoughts quicker than can be repeated flashed through the mind of our secret detective. It must be that Figsley and Bergman were of the party; and if so, of course he would be safe; and he seated himself upon a short bench near the foot of the ladder which led to the loft, for escape without their observation he could not; and to attempt an escape like a witness against them, it seemed must result in certain death. He knew that Bergman and Figsley had confidence in him—confidence that he was a desperate character, and willing to become—if he was not already—as great a villain as themselves. How could they doubt it? He had told them he came upon the frontier to make money, and that he couldn't afford to be in such dangerous business unless he could make something out of it. They had seen him cautiously and alone smuggling whisky and leather and spices; had passed him on the Niagara River at night, in the very boat that Figsley had sold him for that purpose; then they had afterwards taken him in as a brother law-breaker, and he had saved them from arrest by attempting to shoot the officers—*with those blank cartridges!*

As our detective took his seat the approaching party seemed to pause a moment in a dispute among themselves at the outer entrance to the shanty, and Bailey soon had occasion to realize that he was in danger.

"I tell you this whole affair must and shall go over the falls—girl and all!" said one of the party outside, in a firm undertone, "the rest of you can have the money, but that letter of old Bailey's—the old fool—must never be heard of!"

"But if we get the letter that's enough!" replied a voice which Benjamin knew was Figsley's.

"But I tell you," said the first voice, "that this old deacon devil here and that young Bailey, are on the track of us all!"

There was no time to waste by listening; his real character was no doubt discovered; he could no longer expect the kind regards of either Figsley or Bergman. He could not even expect that they would now return the kindness that he had done them by shooting at custom-house officers! In an instant he now ascended the ladder, hoping to secrete himself till an opportunity presented for leaving the shanty. As he stepped from the top of the ladder he saw by the dim light that he stood by the side of a corpse. Not having heard of the death of Bergman's house-keeper, this discovery produced strange feelings of horror and suspicion; and added to what was already a sufficient cause of alarm.

The better to secrete himself he immediately extinguished the light in the loft. He then placed himself in a position to see, through an aperture between the floor boards, anything that might take place in the room below. Almost immediately four men dressed in disguise entered the house; the two foremost dragging an old man to a corner of the room, whose bare head revealed wounds by which he had been overcome. Two others soon afterwards followed, carrying a young lady to an opposite corner of the room. Both victims were bound with cords and were gagged to prevent any outcry.

Among the first who entered the room Benjamin recognized Figsley's voice, saying in a determined tone:

"No, Vroman! I'll see us both hanged first. You may send the man over the falls, but not the girl! That's not my way of making war—not my kind of chivalry. I'd sooner shoot the man who would abuse a weak and defenseless girl!"

"O, you would, eh? Then you've grown better since we all lied against Eleanor Grace for telling the truth against us!" said a voice in reply with an insinuating tone, and closing his remark with terrible curses over the idea of Figsley having any virtues to boast of over the rest of them.

"Well, Vroman," retorted Figsley, "I give you my word for it—and my honor—as one villain to another, that *this* girl shall not be harmed!"

"And I say she shall never live to tell what this night knows of, nor what's in Jared Bailey's letter!"

"She lives, if I do!" said Figsley.

"Then none of us would be safe," said Vroman, "and getting rid of her is a necessity we are not to blame for. None of us knew the girl was in the carriage; and she may from the very first have identified some of us by our voices."

"Vices? ha! ha! Did you say vices? What vices have *we?*" chuckled Hardstriker, making a peculiar shrug with his shoulders.

"Stop your quarrel," interrupted Bergman, with an oath, "till you have time to come to a sensible conclusion!" and saying this he unrolled a pocket book which he had extracted from Deacon Sommer's side pocket.

"Thank the devil, here is a little matter I will take charge of," said Vroman, producing the lost letter from Deacon Sommers' pocket, "and now the only way to keep its contents from sending two or three of us to the bottomless pit, is to send old Sommers and his daughter over the falls. Of course they've both read it; and, as I told you, if that young Bailey around here is really a detective, he would hear of the letter, make me all the trouble he could, and the old suspicions would start up again."

At length the money had been counted, and the letter had also been read, and was considered a matter which so far as smuggling was concerned, concerned them all. And from what was overheard by the individual under such peculiar circumstances in the loft, he had an abiding sense that things present and things to come, in a strange combination of ways, were also matters of infinite concern to *him!* Things rushed into his mind as they only can when the mind is under some extraordinary excitement like a panoramic view of one's life when some sudden death is approaching. His blood quickened its course over the wrongs which Judge Bailey had done him. The fraud of the will the falsehoods to Deacon Sommers and Laura the letter just injuring him as a detective the present imminent danger of his own life; and more than all this, an innocent and a beautiful girl was in the power of ruffians, and that girl the one he loved! All this nerved him to a desperate resolve to attempt the rescue of Laura and her father.

The cold sweat stood upon his forehead while he looked with wide open eyes on the scene below, and prayed silently for Almighty God to aid him now to deliver the innocent out of the hands of the guilty!

But his own heart responded that the day of miracles was past. The only weapon, too, which he had taken with him that day, was a small, single barrel pistol. And he was even without ammunition to load it after the first fire! And yet again and again he mentally prayed that God would show him the means of deliverance; and as his hopes sank he prayed for 'faith' in prayer!

"Well," said Bergman, "what is to be done must be done now. For the storm is getting over and three of you have some ways to go. Besides that, it's near a mile to the rapids to get this job off our hands."

"Your heartless cowardice," said Ripley to Vroman, "which leads you to call for the destruction of this girl, gains nothing by reminding me of Eleanor Grace, and how, years ago, when we sold ourselves to Jared Bailey, that damnable work led me on and on to what I am! You remember how like a mean and degraded coward to defend himself, he tempted us with money to rob Eleanor of her friends, because he could not bribe her to false hood! You and I know *how* her heart was broken and *why* she disappeared. I shall not add another such vic tim to my memory! And when I am out of Jared Bailey's pay and power and yours, too vengeance shall

12

rise for him out of the grave of Eleanor Grace. And now I swear by her memory, I will defend this girl from harm by my life if need be. So fit your plans to that!"

"Figsley, you do but mock yourself. There lies the girl before you, bound in cords; and you know her tongue *must* be silenced or all our necks be stretched."

"Then free them both," said Figsley; "restore the money, and there's no robbery; our excuse in these times is fair, *if we thought them Fenians!*"

"The money is too much to restore!" said Hardstriker, "quite too much!"

"And the money we keep!" added Slyboy.

"And the man goes over the falls!" said Bergman, "and the girl—why, perhaps we might send her away."

"No, I'll not risk it," said Vroman, half beside himself, with fear and rage. "The only safe plan is the 'accident over the falls,' for them both."

"Vroman!" said Figsley, "you and I are villains, at best, but, by my soul! (though lost it is) I'm a man yet, and so long as blood runs in my veins, and I have eyes to behold beauty, weakness and innocence, I'll defend woman as I would a child; and I'll see not the strong arm of man lifted against the life of any woman! nor to degrade her—against her will! And this I swear upon my honor, as one villain to another!"

"Coward!" said Vroman, with the look of a demon, "I'll despatch the girl myself to save ourselves, and end this quarrel at once." But as he said this and drew forth his pistol for the hellish deed, he still kept his eye on Figsley, in whose look he seemed to read danger!

It was now high time for the individual in the loft to close his prayer and come to the rescue.

And in that very instant Benjamin Bailey saw the answer to his prayer. The solemn means of rescue was at his side. It was an instant for life or death. He seized the corpse of Bergman's once abused house-keeper and threw it down among the robbers as if it had jumped among them; Benjamin uttering at the same time in a slow, monotonous voice:

"Sinners! your days are numbered!"

But the same moment that he seized hold of the corpse and threw it from him, he heard the discharge of two pistols. Figsley had shot Vroman dead, and received himself a mortal wound from Vroman's revolver! The other four, shocked at the result of the quarrel and frightened at the descent of a ghost among them, for an instant could not move. Bergman cried, "O, my God! forgive me!" and then flew from his shanty, followed by Hardstriker and Slyboy, and another whom Benjamin had not recognized. Figsley raised up, rolled his eyes towards the corpse in its winding-sheet and groaned: "O, God! is this the day of judgment? or, is this a spirit from the grave of Eleanor Grace?"

Benjamin hastened down the ladder in time to hear the receding footsteps of the robbers and note the direction of their flight. And then with a heart too full of emotions for utterance he tenderly unbound and ungagged Laura and her father.

"O, kind sir, who are you? who are you?" said Laura, when she realized that she was in the presence of

a friend, and was assured that her father was not danger-
ously injured; for in the dim light and her almost uncon-
scious state from fright, she had not yet recognized their
rescuer.

Deacon Sommers spoke at the same time: "Tell me,"
he said, "my dear sir, what is the meaning of all this,
and are you a friend or foe?"

To both questions Benjamin now replied: "I am a
detective officer, and by the blessing of God your lives
are saved." Saying this he opened the light of a dark
lantern which sat near them so that he could be plainly
seen, and then he said only as a faithful lover could have
said it: "My dear Laura, do you know me?"

"O, my dear Benjamin!" she said, with emotions that
no words can describe, and grasping his hand, "My dear
Benjamin, is it you? is it you? O, father, it is Benjamin Bailey! it is Benjamin Bailey!"

But it is impossible to picture the feelings of Deacon
Sommers and his daughter and Benjamin, as they looked
upon each other and on the scene before them! which
scene we leave to the imagination of the reader, except
to relate that as they were about to leave the solemn and
frightful place, Benjamin took possession of two revolvers
which the robbers had lain upon the table while counting
the money, all of which, together with the lost letter,
were left by the frightened criminals in their hasty flight.
The money and the letter Benjamin placed with his own
hands back into the pocket of Deacon Sommers.

"Mr. Figsley," said Benjamin, before leaving him,
"you cannot live, probably, many hours. I cannot move

you now, but will have a surgeon sent to care for you soon as possible. But as you are about to die it can do you no harm, Mr. Figsley, to tell me the truth. For I am Benjamin Bailey! and you know something about the will of my grandfather, Mortimer Bailey, which you and John Vroman signed as witnesses, twenty years ago. Is there any evidence to prove the truth against Jared Bailey?"

Figsley seemed to realize that his life's end had come; and as Benjamin put him in an easier position he replied:

"Jared Bailey was no relation of your family—he was a foundling—born in Canada. But it hurts me so to talk."

He rested a moment and then added in a weak voice:

"You will find some secret papers—under the floor—of my room—which tells the truth. They are—in the grave—of Eleanor—Grace!"

These were Figsley's last words.

The storm had now cleared away, and by the light of the lantern, a little way from the roadside, Benjamin found Deacon Sommers' horse tied to a tree. Leading it into the road Benjamin assisted Laura and her father into the carriage, and then getting into the carriage himself he drove to the house of a friend in Chippewa, where they remained awhile in consequence of Deacon Sommers' condition from the wounds he had received.

CHAPTER XXVI.

An Embarrassing Invitation—A Manly Reply—A Short and Affecting Explanation—
More Disclosures — The Fate of Eleanor Grace — The Will — Death of Judge
Bailey—Justice, Truth and Happiness.

AN hour after Deacon Sommers had washed the blood
from his face, at the house of his friend, he had apparently recovered almost as much from the effects of his
wounds as from his fright.

In the mean time the police were apprised of matters
that had taken place, and the proper authorities left to
look after the affairs at Bergman's shanty.

A carriage was procured, and one or two friends
escorted Deacon Sommers and his daughter home;

> And as straws show which way the wind does blow,
> Or a chip show the stillest river's flow,
> Or as some kindly act, howe'er so small,
> Will tell the state of feelings in us all,

so it need not be recorded here all that was said by
Deacon Sommers to Benjamin Bailey. Even the fact
that Deacon Sommers offered him no reward in money,
as might have been natural for an expression of gratitude, or to balance obligations, was noticed favorably by
Benjamin; while the manner in which Laura and her
father urged that he would accompany them home, greatly
encouraged him.

He longed to know Laura's feelings towards him; but he said at last, to Deacon Sommers:

"How can I, Mr. Sommers, how *can* I accept your invitation, to be one moment in your house, where I must see the one I love, only because your gratitude, and not your *respect*, invites me there?"

"O, Benjamin," said Laura, bursting into tears at his reference to herself and his constancy to her, "don't blame my father. How could he think they would tell *such falsehoods?* But he found it all out at last, and wanted to see you so much!"

"Mr. Bailey," said Deacon Sommers, "I feel deeply the just rebuke of your words, and the manly nature they indicate. But this occasion of my gratitude has not come before I learned to respect you! And I urge you now to go home with us that I may apologize, and explain, before expressing my gratitude. I was too confiding where there was an interest to injure you! I should have taken more pains to have learned the truth."

A few moments later and it happened somehow as natural as if it had been decreed to be so, that Benjamin Bailey was seated by the side of Laura Sommers; and this in the same carriage with her father.

Mr. Sommers and his daughter had been expected home before dark; and Mrs. Sommers had become uneasy about them. Even the showers of rain which had descended that afternoon, she thought would not have delayed them to so late an hour in the evening. The covered carriage and high oil-cloth boot in front, must have made them prefer a drive in daylight rain, than to risk the weather after dark. But if darkness had overtaken them on the road, some accident it seemed must have happened to them. Or it might be that some evil person had found out that he was going after money, though she was certain they had taken pains not even to let the servants know of it.

Perhaps she never knew how innocently Dinah had been the means of conveying that information to John Vroman by way of the fish-peddler.

Mr. Sommers and his escort at last reached his mansion. Mrs. Sommers met them at the door. From the light of the hall lamp in an instant she discovered, or fancied she discovered, that something unusual had happened. And her anxiety over their non-arrival was now almost changed to alarm at their appearance. But Deacon Sommers immediately informed her that they were all safe and little harmed; and though they had met with a little danger among some desperate bad men, it was all over now.

"We've had an awful time! mother. We came near being murdered!" said Laura, with less of caution in her announcement.

The next instant Mrs. Sommers' excitement and retrospective alarm was equaled by her confusion and surprise as she noticed the presence of Mr. Benjamin Bailey among them; whose name Laura then announced with what seemed to her mother, a singular emotion of excitement and satisfaction, as she rushed, weeping, to her mother's arms.

For a few moments Mrs. Sommers could scarcely deter-

mine what ideas in her own mind were uppermost—
safety, and danger, and murder, and what it all had to do
with Benjamin Bailey!

Explanations, of course, followed. And on that evening Benjamin Bailey was a welcome guest in the family
of Deacon Sommers!

The lost letter which Figsley had read while Benjamin
listened in the loft at Bergman's shanty, and which Laura
and Deacon Sommers had previously read, made explanations easy respecting Benjamin, but it pointed to a mysterious field of inquiry on the morrow—into the character
and secret history of Jared Bailey.

Laura's transition from so much fright to so much joy
at being restored to confidence in the integrity, honor and
manly worth of her well-tried and faithful lover, was
almost more than she could bear.

How Deacon Sommers explained his giving so little
attention to the account of Mrs. Hartley exposing Judge
Bailey, and how he was so deceived as to doubt her
veracity, we need not repeat events to record.

"It needs not my gratitude," said Deacon Sommers to
Benjamin, "as any part of my reasons now for believing
as I do, that you are worthy of my daughter. I have
been deceived by Jared Bailey and through those who
have been deceived by him, or who were, and perhaps
still are, dependent upon him. And that letter found
to-day, shows that there is still more to be developed
against him."

"To-morrow morning," replied Benjamin, "I must
know what will be found below the floor of Mr. Figsley's
12*

room. If I find secret papers there, I hope I may learn
what he meant by saying that Jared Bailey was no relation of mine."

Yes, on the morrow Benjamin Bailey was there to
witness a scene nearly as exciting as that through which
he had just passed. For Judge Bailey had received the
telegram from Vroman, and would arrive on the morning train.

At nine o'clock the next morning Benjamin with several citizens and an officer was in Figsley's room.

They proceeded to remove the stove and then a large
piece of zinc, which had been so firmly nailed to the
floor that one of the party, a superstitious old man, who
knew that they expected to find a mysterious grave there,
suggested that the zinc itself appeared to have been fastened down by some guilty hand to help hide what had
been buried beneath! The floor boards under the zinc,
it was noticed, were so nailed and matched that it seemed
as if they might have been sometime taken up and
replaced; and, yet like the nails in the zinc, it needed
first to have a suspicion awakened before it would have
been noticeable.

As they made an opening through the floor, they saw
below it, only such rubbish as old plaster, and fragments
of brick from some old fire-place or chimney, and this
covered the ground. The space between the rubbish and
the floor was narrow, and tightly enclosed by a stone
wall under the sills of the building, which, together with
the nature of the rubbish, prevented any appearance that
could give indication as to whether it had long remained
there undisturbed.

Moving aside the rubbish they excavated the ground to the depth of some three feet, when they came to a layer of flat stones; underneath which they found a straight-sided coffin, whose state of decay rendered the cover easily removed; when there was exposed to view the skeleton of a woman. The position in which the bones lay, indicated that the body had been respectfully cared for. But why was the burial in this secret place?

Nothing which might contain the secret papers to which Figsley had referred was visible. With solemnity and respect Benjamin and all present uncovered their heads and stood a few moments in silence around this mysterious grave!

While in this attitude a stranger, accompanied by Figsley's tenant, entered the room; and Benjamin fastened his eyes upon the large and burly form of Jared Bailey! Neither of them spoke. The Judge approached and looked into the grave. The color went from his face; he looked upon the persons present, and then around the room. He knew nothing of what had passed except what the sudden scene before him was revealing, and that Vroman had gone to Figsley's the night before concerned about the lost letter! Learning this at Vroman's house on his arrival, he had immediately hastened to Figsley's. And now there were awakening memories torturing his very soul with fear, as if all his secrets were about to rise up against him from the grave before him! He remembered Figsley's threats and his allusions to the grave of Eleanor Grace, and how he had wronged that innocent girl to cover up his own crimes—he trembled, as if he believed that Figsley's dark allusions and vague threats had foretold his destruction here. And yet he strove as if for dear life to meet everything in his usual manner—to appear the embodiment of innocence! and to stand upon dignity.

But from Benjamin Bailey who now possessed the key to his heartless soul and secret crimes, his usually bold and brazen face did not now conceal his alarm.

After a few moments' pause Benjamin suggested that the ground be loosened around the coffin; which being done, an earthen jar with a tightly sealed cover was found close to the head of the coffin! Benjamin opened the jar. It contained a letter and two packages.

"From the writing on the outside of these papers," said he, "it appears they are intended for the heirs of my father. The superscription reads:

"To John and Benjamin and Matilda Bailey, heirs interested in the property of Mortimer Bailey, deceased."

Then opening a paper tied on the wrapper of the larger package, he read aloud, as follows:

"This is to certify that I, Miss Eleanor Grace, do declare that this writing contains my dying statement, to be exposed when it can harm no one but Jared Bailey—a man, who, to contradict the truth I was obliged to utter against him, has succeeded by falsehood and the aid of those interested, or bribed, or entangled with him, to turn every earthly friend against me, till, without honorable means of support, I have returned thus far, to take vengeance on my slanderer! But I am too weak to go further, and now here, I will die, begging this rough man to take vengeance for me; which he has sworn to do when he can with safety to himself—— "

Had Benjamin read the remaining lines upon this paper, he would have seen upon the bottom the signature of Eleanor Grace. But a groan from Jared Bailey, as he sank into a chair, caused Benjamin to put the papers into his pocket and aid the others present in attempting to resuscitate his greatest enemy—the man who had defrauded him of a fortune, and by falsehood had broken up the happy prospects of his marriage.

But all efforts at resuscitation were useless. Five minutes later and Jared Bailey had ceased to breathe. His agitation over the evident certainty of being exposed in what he had so long hidden from the public, was more than the state of his diseased heart could endure. A fatal rupture was produced, and thus his death was strangely connected with the last criminal attempt of Vroman and Figsley! And, stranger still, it seemed that he had been sent there, after so many years, by the mysterious ways of Providence, to meet the vengeance of Eleanor at her grave, for his punishment. And from the relation which it all bore to the course which Jared Bailey had begun years and years before, it furnishes a remarkable illustration of the distance to which moral causes will reach results to bring just retribution upon those who forsake the paths of honor, and who attempt to entangle the innocent to cover their own guilt.

The grave under Figsley's floor was now covered over for the present. The papers were examined and left with the Canadian authorities, to await such action as they might deem necessary.

Benjamin now returned to Deacon Sommers', where, as soon as he entered the house, he was received with renewed manifestations of gratitude and respect. Mrs. Sommers took him by the hand, saying:

"Bless the Lord for what you have done for us, Benjamin!" And she kissed him as a mother would have kissed a grown-up son, and then she added: "We have talked of you all the morning."

But before she had begun the last remark, Laura had gained possession of Benjamin's hand, and she declared she "would kiss him too, if she never did again!" And she doubled her mother's example; while Benjamin returned Laura's affectionate grasp of the hand and innocent kisses with a fervor that each understood — an engagement renewed.

Deacon Sommers at the same time, slowly arose from a sofa, upon which he was reclining, at the opposite side of the room, and advanced towards them, holding a saturated cloth to his forehead with one hand, while he extended the other to Benjamin Bailey, and, in turn gave him sincere welcome.

At length Benjamin proceeded to give them an account of the sad and singular scene which he had just witnessed in Figsley's room; and also of the discovered papers! One of the papers found, and which was in Figsley's handwriting, read substantially as follows:

"To all whom it may concern:

"The grave in which these papers will be found, contains the remains of Miss Eleanor Grace.

"Her dead body has been thrown upon my hands to punish and haunt me for a cruelty that Jared Bailey and his family are more guilty of than I am. Her story about the will was true. Ours against her character was only told to defend ourselves! It was cruel as murder itself; and for this poor, innocent creature's sake, I would give the world could I restore her now to life, and take back the injury we did her.

"She came back here to make Jared Bailey retract what he had said to the young man she loved. She got as far as here, and said she was too weak to go further; called for pen and paper, and wrote what is herewith enclosed; then in a fit of despair swallowed a dose of strychnine and died!

" Finding that no one knew that she had come here, I feared that it might be suspected that I had poisoned her, from some motive perhaps about the will, or something else, and so I buried her secretly with these papers. Jared Bailey knows that I have buried her with these papers, but does not know where. So long as I keep his secrets he must pay me well!

"One package here contains some of his own letters about the will affair; also the true will, which Mortimer Bailey read and signed; also a second, unsigned will, which he thought he signed, but Jared Bailey had slipped it away and put the one in its place which had been prepared privately for that purpose.

"There is another little bit of correspondence here, which I propose to keep, in order to hold Jared Bailey and his lady to their agreements. For, when men are

hired to do as mean a thing as Vroman and I have done,
I'm in favor of getting my pay by keeping things in my
own power as much as possible. He talks of leaving
this section, but if I choose he will find facts can reach
him wherever he goes. The little narrative of Eleanor
Grace, herewith enclosed for safe keeping, with some
other papers, he and his aristocratic wife would not care
to have made public! Two of his own letters to Vroman—no matter how I came by them—and one of Mrs.
Bailey's, will rather tend to keep us all on a level, I think.

"The heirs will see by papers inclosed, that Jared
Bailey is no relative of the Baileys. Mortimer Bailey,
while living in Canada with his first wife, took him out
of pity when an infant. His real father was Jerry Grimbold, a tavern-keeper in St. Catharines, who at last died
in Welland jail. His principal virtues were deviltry,
tobacco and whisky. The worst thing about John Vroman is, that he is a half brother of Jared Grimbold.
And the worst thing about me, up to this date at least,
is, that after selling myself as their witness in the fraud
against the Bailey heirs, I was obliged to help them
wrong Eleanor Grace, who was too good to marry me.
And now I am cursed with her frightful presence! Poor
Eleanor; on my part I only intended to frighten her from
exposing the crime. But Jared Bailey intended more
than I dreamed of! Good heavens! if I am a bad man,
read what she has written of Jared Bailey. Read what
Jared Bailey did in his vain attempts to degrade and to
subdue Eleanor and Adeline. When they would have
married happily, husbands of wealth, education and influ-

ence, he laid plans to defeat them, blasting their hopes to accomplish his own; but baffled by their virtue in every attempt to degrade them—even by promises which, as a libertine, he never intended to fulfill—he stooped at last to bold abuse and shameful advantage.

"Failing in all, at last he attempted to degrade them by entangling them with us in a sanction and conceal-ment of the fraud in the will by offering them a bribe; and then it was that I, too, was interested in degrading them, for *they knew of the part I had taken in the fraud!* Then it was they both left the house of Jared Bailey forever—Adeline, paid and frightened into silence, but Eleanor destroyed in saving her innocence!

"O, heavens! had I foreseen it all, I would have been happier to have lived an honest slave and deserved the gratitude of those poor girls, rather than bear the remorse of having aided these brother-villains thus to have per-secuted their innocent lives, though I had gained the whole of Mortimer Bailey's property!

"But it's done now; and time must tell its story; but when, or what, or how, I can but wonder in this strange work to-night! For now I scarcely know my own pur-pose; though I would to God that this night's job were done—this corpse were out of sight—and I could know the end of the undersigned.

"JAMES FIGSLEY."

The limits designed for this volume, as well as the events now connected with its principal characters, are about to bring it to a close.

CHAPTER XXVII

Of the Events which force our story to its conclusion—And what became of the principal characters.

JARED BAILEY was buried in Fallington cemetery. The Rev. Mr. Smoothwell preached the funeral sermon. And the several instances where Mr. Bailey had given a few dollars to some distressed family, and the fact that he had contributed to the usual popular benevolent causes, and paid the largest rent for the most prominent pew in the most wealthy church, and had been the most liberal in gifts to the pastor—all this, together with other influences with which the reader has been made acquainted, seemed in the opinion of society to have struck a balance to his credit, and to have stigmatized all rumor against him, as the base and revengeful work of his enemies; when in fact the late developments connected with the letter which Vroman had lost, and the papers found in the grave, and all that directly implicated Jared Bailey in a criminal and disgraceful course, had, out of kindness to his alarmed and bereaved family and friends, for the present, been concealed from the public, at the suggestion of Mr. Sommers, and consented to by Benjamin himself. Therefore, in spite of old or recent rumors, the Rev. Mr. Smoothwell knowing little of the facts, and

remembering only his own sermons on charity and forgiveness, said an eulogy to the good deeds of Judge
Bailey, making a respectable reference to his life and
character.

"The immediate cause of Mr. Bailey's death," said
Mr. Smoothwell, with perhaps innocent feeling, "showed
but too plainly how easily he was affected over the misfortunes of others. It is true that he had been afflicted with a
disease of the heart. But the immediate cause of the rupture which produced death, was the shock given him on
suddenly learning the fate of a beloved adopted daughter, who, many years ago, had mysteriously disappeared
and met an early grave, under circumstances too painful
to relate, and which, coming to light, was the occasion of
Mr. Bailey's late visit to Niagara, the scene of his death."

Here, again, was the character of poor Eleanor, so
long since dead, slandered by unjust insinuation, which
Mrs. Judge Bailey in her secret alarm had thought necessary to convey to Mr. Smoothwell, and insist that he
should refer to the matter, "to prevent," as she said,
"any chance for false rumors!" In Mrs. Bailey's alarm
Mr. Smoothwell, however, saw only regret, affection and
bereavement!

Immediately after the funeral services the will of the
late Judge Bailey was read, when behold not one cent
of the property promised Adeline for her silence, was
willed to her; the wish, however, was expressed that
Mrs. Bailey would continue to be kind and generous
towards her *as they always had been!* To Mrs. Bailey
one-third of the property was willed, and to Jerusha, in

an indirect way, there was willed an amount nearly equal to one-third; and the remainder about equally divided among the rest of the family.

A few days after the reading of the will Benjamin Bailey and Hon. Mr. Baldwin, as his attorney, accompanied by Deacon Sommers, waited upon Mrs. Jared Bailey, and David, and Jerusha. Mr. Baldwin immediately proceeded to explain the nature of the disclosures found in the grave of Eleanor Grace, and certain other evidence which papers there found had furnished the means of tracing out. "Mrs. Hartley's letter as to your own private conversation on certain matters," said Mr. Baldwin to Mrs. Bailey, "has been fully sustained. The story of poor Eleanor Grace, whom you sacrificed by falsehood to cover the truth she could not conceal against your husband for you, is fully corroborated."

He was then proceeding to explain what Mrs. Bailey knew too well was truth as to how the will-fraud was managed, when Mrs. Bailey fainted. After a little time, however, she was restored. They were then informed that Adeline had fully corroborated the other disclosures about the will, and that unless she and her family and Jerusha saw fit to accept some offer which the rightful heirs of the property might see fit to make them, the whole property would be recovered from Mrs. Jared Bailey and her family, and they would be disgraced in court!

"And will I lose all dear Mr. Bailey promised father and me that I should have?" asked Jerusha, bursting into tears.

"From what we have lately learned, Miss Vroman, we think you certainly will!" said Mr. Baldwin.

"Give us time to think!" implored Mrs. Bailey, as the three gentlemen arose to leave the house.

"O, yes, give us time to think and say nothing!" repeated Jerusha, "say nothing!"

Not long after this interview a settlement was agreed upon by which at last nearly all the property was obtained by the rightful heirs.

To those who possessed the opportunity of learning the facts which had disclosed the real character of the late Jared Bailey, the little of other matters which also came to light, made it clear why Jerusha, the daughter of John Vroman, had been willed so large a share of the property, while it stood to Adeline's credit that she expected so little.

Adeline had been intimidated to sign the will as a witness, and then made to believe she was thereby in law as guilty as those whose plans she had happened to discover. But, soon after Eleanor's disappearance, Adeline herself had quietly arranged to leave Jared Bailey's family, ostensibly to learn the trade of a dress-maker, but her reasons for learning the trade itself were the private reasons why she left her adopted home. The fate of poor Eleanor for having uttered so much of the truth as to turn Jared Bailey and his wife into merciless enemies, warned Adeline not to appear on unfriendly terms with them. Hence it was that she received the aid she did from Jared Bailey and his wife.

In consideration of all the circumstances Benjamin, in

the settlement, allowed Adeline the sum of two thousand dollars, which it appeared to have been the intention of his grandfather to have willed her.

Of course it was not long after these events when Benjamin and Laura were married. For a time they lived in the old home near Fallington. But it was scarcely one year before Mrs. Benjamin Bailey had the satisfaction to receive their many friends, both from the village and the country, in a splendid mansion which Benjamin erected near his old homestead.

About this time Dinah's step-father, the old fish-peddler, died, and Dinah's mother then went to live with Laura as a servant. Occasionally poor old Tom—whom the reader will remember in the front yard denouncing Judge Bailey and extolling Benjamin as "de finest young man *he* ebber seed"—spent an evening talking with Dinah's mother about "de hard ole times in slavery," and often his eyes would grow dim with tears in recalling to mind "little Tilly," "aunt Polly," and years agone.

Matilda, Benjamin's sister, at the time of closing this book, was not married, but it was expected that she would be soon, to a son of Hon. Mr. Baldwin; for Mrs. Bailey, Matilda's mother, had been heard to say:

"Mercy on me! I hope young Baldwin and Matilda won't have any such trouble about courtin' as Benjamin and Laura had to have!" And then she had repeated her exclamation declaring Benjamin's wife to be the best hearted person that they had ever known "for such a handsome woman!"

Poor Col. Le Grange! his fate was a sad one. He

went into the Army of the Potomac, fought reckless of his own life—which induced his commander to report as "great gallantry"—in the battles of the Wilderness, and was finally at the taking of Richmond and the surrender of Gen. Lee to Gen. Grant. As he had said in his letter to Miss Laura Sommers, that he would do, so he had sought "the front of battle to lay down his life," etc. But fate failing to accept the sacrifice, he returned home, fell into despondency, and finally became a monomaniac, and seemed to court exposure and danger by constantly venturing along the banks of Niagara, as if in search of something, he knew not what.

Finally, on the Canada side of the Niagara Whirlpool, in one of the colonel's wild ramblings, he selected a spot beneath the overhanging rocks of the high, precipitous bank, and there building himself what is now pointed out to visitors as the Hermit's House in the Cave, he spent the rest of his days. For nearly two years he lived there a crazy recluse, seldom speaking to any one, except to inform them that he "wanted no spies around these head-quarters of the Potomac!" For hours together, with none but a faithful dog for his company, he would sit, playing an old violin, at the same time gazing on the singular, circuitous movement of the water at that roman-tic place in the Niagara River—which the visitor now approaches by a winding stairway.

At last he obtained a small row-boat, and, conceiving the idea of risking himself and dog in boat-rides close along the Whirlpool shore, he was one day carried into the terrible vortex.

Guides will continue to point out to the traveler the place of the hermit's descent down the bank, and the relics of his home in the cave.   Poor Col. Le Grange!

But we have one more incident to record.

At Benjamin Bailey's old homestead, not long after his marriage, he one day brought a small package into the house for his wife, which he informed her he had just received by express from Niagara Falls.

"O, it is some present from home; I know it is!" said Laura, with a cheerful smile, as she thought of her ever-thoughtful parents.

"No, my dear, I shall claim this as a special present for you from myself"—and then he added with a smile and manner as if the package contained some mysterious surprise—"and I am sure that you will be delighted with it for it is just what you wanted sometime ago!   And then, too, it will be such an interesting souvenir of Niagara!   I think a great deal of it, and I know you will, too."

"Do, please, open the package, my dear, I am so eager to see what kind of a present you have ordered."

"O, I know it will suit you; it's just your taste; I don't think anybody on the frontier could choose a nicer piece of merino in Canada!"

"Why! Benjamin, what makes you smile so queerly about it?   Where was it bought?"

He was now removing the wrapper, and his smile had increased to a laugh as he said:

"I bought this at an auction, Laura!   I might have sent for it before this, but somehow I left it with a friend, on the frontier, there, awhile, by name of Mr. Dobbins!"

The package was now open, and Laura joined in the laugh, as she recognized her Canada dress pattern—and the *mysterious bidder!*

"Why, Benjamin! O, mother Bailey! just look here! I'm surprised out of my senses!" said Laura.

But when mother Bailey had looked at the goods and felt the fineness of its texture, she said in a lower tone than usual:

"Why, mercy on me, darling! It's only some merino dress goods!"

"Yes, mother," said Laura, as she and Benjamin both laughed till mother Bailey was astonished. "Yes, mother, but it is a dress pattern that I tried to smuggle out of Canada across the suspension bridge!"

"Mercy on me! Laura," said Mrs. Bailey, "does everybody smuggle at Niagara Falls?"

THE END—TILL MY NEXT VOLUME.

13

REMINISCENCES OF A CUSTOM-HOUSE OFFICER.

CHAPTER I.

Custom-house Regulations at the Niagara Suspension Bridge—Strangers crossing the Bridge unmindful of Custom-house Laws—The Consequences—Amusing Incidents—A Senator—Duties on Indian Bead Work. etc.—Blaming General Scott—Inspecting a Strange Wagon by Lamplight:—Affecting Incident—How Custom-house Officers are sometimes deceived.

REACHING across the chasm of the Niagara River, two miles below the great cataract, is one of the most noted as well as most beautiful bridges in the world. It was built by a company of Americans and Canadians, and is the first suspension railroad bridge ever constructed. Its ingenious workmanship was constructed under the direction of John A. Roebling, a German engineer, and was completed in 1855, having been three years in building, and costing half a million dollars. It is a single span, eight hundred feet in length, twenty-four feet in width, and supported by four immense wire cables hanging over stone towers. The most heavily loaded railroad trains cross upon its upper floor, and carriages and footmen on a floor beneath. Deep down in the chasm, two hundred and fifty feet below, rushes the mighty rapids of Niagara! The boundary line between the Dominion of Canada and

the United States is along the center of the deepest part
of the river; hence the west end or half of the bridge is
in British territory, and the east half in the United States.
Large amounts of freight pass here as traffic between the
two countries; and still larger amounts pass over this
bridge and through a portion of Canada as traffic between
New York and Chicago. Here at the crossing of this
chasm, the United States constructed buildings for a custom house, and a number of officials were required for
duty. An account of some of the incidents at this point
which came under my own observation while a custom-
house official, a portion of the time between 1860 and
1870, will be interesting and amusing, as well as bring
out some desirable information respecting custom-house
regulations—strangers at Niagara—and life on the Niagara frontier.

From May until November the large hotels at the
Falls of Niagara were open to receive the thousands who
came to visit this romantic locality. Here, *then*, was fashion, beauty, wealth, aristocracy—and all the varieties of
travel which the scenery here annually brought together.
Of these visitors almost entirely were the passengers who,
in more than a hundred splendid hacks daily crossed the
suspension bridge, and proceeded to the various points of
interest upon the Canadian bank of the river, and after a
few hours returned to the American side; when, according to the custom of all nations, they were required to
satisfy the custom-house officer that they were not smuggling any goods into the United States. It was not the
duty of a custom-house officer, in every instance to in-

spect the vehicles of persons who were accustomed to cross the bridge. We had become acquainted with the business of nearly all, for miles on either side of the river, who were in the habit of crossing the bridge with their teams, and knowing the persons, and that they themselves knew the penalties for smuggling, an occasional inspection of their vehicles was sufficient. By law the penalties for smuggling were imprisonment, fines and confiscation of the property smuggled, and also the loss of the team and vehicle, or vessel or boat in which the goods were smuggled. Even in cases where the property brought into the country was intended to be returned in a few hours, the person was liable to forfeit the goods unless the same were properly reported to the custom house.

When visitors of Niagara Falls had made any purchases upon the Canada side—even though the articles were only presents to take home from the Falls—they were required to report them. The drivers and owners of the hacks were also liable if the same were not reported. When no purchases were made the drivers, as they passed my office, cried out: "*Nothing aboard, sir!*" And, excepting when I thought best to examine the matter further, I usually replied: "*All right, sir.*" By this it was understood that there was no baggage on board for inspection, and no dutiable articles, and that I recognized the vehicle and team as belonging to parties upon the American side, or, to persons who would soon return the same to Canada.

It was a requirement, however, of the custom-house

department, that proper judgment should be used in all discretionary matters. All baggage and goods were to be inspected; and if the officer had any grounds to suspect any person had smuggled goods *concealed upon their persons*, he could, by law, require them to be examined; and for this purpose women were frequently required to report to a lady officer.

The laws relating to customs in the United States, as well as in some other countries, were numerous and complicated; so that many of the best informed people who came to visit the wonders at Niagara Falls, were often surprised to find that they had lain themselves liable to unexpected expenses and delays, which, had they read these reminiscences, they would have avoided.

The driver of a fine hack returning from the Canada side once halted his valuable establishment before my office to allow the stranger in his carriage to make a report of some Canadian purchases.

" Drive on, sir," said the statesmanly looking passenger.

" I suppose," said I to the dignified looking gentleman, " that your driver fears to pass the custom house, if he or his passenger has any dutiable articles in his carriage."

" O, you are an officer of customs ? "

" Yes, sir. Endeavoring to collect what is legal, to aid in paying our national debt !" said I.

" Glad to find you are so loyal, sir ; but I have only a few Indian curiosities and some 'Table Rock specimens'— just to take home from Niagara Falls—only about thirty dollars worth."

" Fifty per cent. duties, sir, on the Indian bead work,

and thirty-five per cent. on the little, ornamental, bark baskets," I informed him.

"Is it possible?" said he, with a smile. "I wonder if I ever aided in making *that* law?"

When he had paid the duties and had signed his name, James Lane, to the oath upon the entry papers, I remembered that I had seen him once in Washington, and the next moment I knew that it was senator Lane of Kansas.

I have seen a carriage load of fashionable and richly dressed ladies pretend, with mechanical stares, great indignation or surprise, that their extravagant outfit of dry goods and millinery, waterfalls and jewelry, should be held in such cheap account that the driver could boldly report *"Nothing aboard!"* to an admiring official, who would then reply to the professor of hacks, *"All right,"* as if he believed it.

This common report, "nothing aboard," was frequently made the text for joking comments by carriage loads of health, wealth, comfort and pleasure; but to me it was often the source of suggesting a strange variety of reflections. The rich man passes with fine linen and costly clothing, with bonds and greenbacks, and perhaps a box of cigars and a bottle of brandy as a part of his traveling luxuries; and all this is reported *"nothing aboard!"* And now comes a poor man, with a bundle of old clothes, and perhaps a piece of new but coarse cloth—enough for coat and pants—which he thought he could afford, because a little cheaper in Canada, and this he must not report as *"nothing aboard,"* and finds the duty fifty cents a pound and thirty-five per cent. ad valorem!

One dark and rainy evening in 1866, there came from the Canada side into the United States, across this great, international bridge, a young woman and a little lad, in an old, rickety wagon, drawn by an aged horse, whose comfortable days seemed long gone past. The gate-keeper called out for their ticket, which passengers pur-chased at either end of the bridge before entering upon it, and the girl gave up the ticket as they halted.

It was next my duty, as an officer of customs, to deter-mine if this horse and wagon, or other property, if any, were liable to duty. For they must pay duty upon their conveyance, poor as it was, or poor as they were them-selves, or turn back to Canada, no matter how urgent their business, unless they had evidence that the property belonged in the States, or they could satisfy me that it would be soon returned to Canada. Observing that they were about to proceed without reporting any facts in the case to the office of customs, I said:

"Young lady, on account of the rules of the custom house, I shall have to inquire if your horse and wagon belong in the United States?"

"We belong in Buffalo, sir," the girl replied, "and we are trying to get home to-night, sir; or, as far as we can, sir."

"What!" thought I, "a young girl and a small lad, in an open wagon, going to Buffalo such a dismal night as this, and that city twenty-four miles distant!"

"At what place was this horse and wagon taken into Canada?" I inquired, and when informed that the prop-erty had been taken across the Niagara River on the steam ferry-boat, near Buffalo, I asked "if they had taken any export certificate from any custom-house officer so that they could take the property into Canada and return it to the States free of duty?"

"No, sir, we didn't know any officers at the ferry, sir," replied the girl. And then in a tremulous voice and in words that I could not regard with suspicion, she added: "We haven't done anybody any harm, sir. It's our horse and wagon, sir."

I then inquired if they were acquainted with any one near us whom they would name, to give me some reference, so that I might be justified in case I took the risk of allowing them to pass.

"No, sir," replied the girl, "we are acquainted with nobody here, sir."

"Then," said I, "I am sorry to have to tell you that unless you can give me some evidence, or at least some reference, that would justify me in letting you proceed without paying the duty, the custom-house rules require you to go back to the Canada side."

"O, sir," said she, bursting into tears, "we cannot go back that way to-night. We live in Buffalo. We are poor people, and we did not know what we had to do. We cannot get across the ferry at night if we go back that way."

"It will be morning before you can reach the ferry," said I. But she only answered this by weeping. Though I had found a flaw in her answers, and had, as an officer, become generally sensitive to suspicion, my feelings told me that I must let her pass. Innocent embarrassment

13*

might easily be a cause of an inconsistent remark. Was
it among the possibilities, thought I, that this lad and
this girl had been sent across from Canada with a story
to deceive the custom-house officer, and thus smuggle
this horse and wagon? Was I to be deceived by some
shrewd trick of a smuggler? Perhaps I was over-suspi-
cious; but it was not a pleasant reflection among custom-
house officials on the Niagara frontier to find themselves
occasionally outwitted by smugglers. Nor had I forgotten the successful trick by which a party had once
smuggled a valuable lot of silks and laces across this
bridge before the eye of one of the strictest officers, when
these goods were concealed in a coffin, carried past him
in a slow, solemn hearse, followed by the *smugglers in
mourning!*

Hence I *was particular!* And in answer to my questions the girl in broken sentences told her pitiful story.
Their father had gone to St. Catharines in Canada, one
week before, and not returning when expected, and his
family hearing that a man had been drowned in the Welland Canal, answering the decription of the father, this
son and daughter had gone there prepared for the worst.
While the daughter spoke of her father and sobbed as if
her heart would break, I felt that her story must be true.
But I had not yet examined the contents of the wagon,
and just at this moment I saw, by the light from the
bridge lamp, that there was a dark colored bundle in
their wagon, partly covered by straw which from the
light shining but dimly upon it, I could not clearly dis-
cern. I took hold of the dark-colored object more from

a habit of inspecting than from any suspicion of smuggling. I had also been in office long enough to know that even an apparent omission of duty—no matter about the combination of little circumstances which satisfied the good sense of an officer—must have some *tangible* explanation,

To make others see ourselves as we do see us!

So it was partly this feeling of caution which caused me to lift up from the bottom of the wagon what proved to be an article of clothing. At the same time I inquired what they had aboard.

The girl was now too much affected to reply, and I was myself shocked by the evident truth of the lad's mournful answer:

"It is the coat which father had on him when he was drowned!"

And indeed I *was inspecting the clothing, damp yet, with the water which had caused the dying struggles of their father.* Is it wonder that they now sobbed aloud, not well understanding the cause of such cruel suspicion! for it was no covering of smuggled goods that in the dim light I had moved aside in their wagon and lifted up before them. And as the lad in broken accents told me what it was, and with my hands and eyes upon it I saw at a glance how the coat was ruffled and torn by the hooks with which strangers had searched for the dead body! I dropped the garment; I believed their story; I let them pass; and as they went I reflected—they have "*nothing aboard*"—but grief! That night the body passed over the upper floor of the bridge by railroad; and the coffin passed, I have no doubt, the suspicious gaze of other custom-house officers.

As in many other noted localities of the world, so at Niagara the traveler finds bazaars, in which are kept for sale appropriate, curious and interesting mementoes, consisting in part of Indian curiosities, geological specimens, stereoscopic views of the various points of interesting scenery about the Falls and along the Niagara chasm.

Beautiful specimens of bead work, and of bark work curiously ornamented with colored porcupine quills, are brought here for sale not only from Indian tribes near the Falls, but I have seen some of these articles, brought across the bridge and reported to the custom house, which were made by Indian women in tribes living in the British possessions a thousand miles west of Niagara.

The beautiful feather fans, however, now sold at Niagara Falls and at Saratoga Springs and in the city of Washington, were first invented about the year 1840, by Miss Handcock, a lady of taste and education, who at the time I am writing, still resides within a few rods of the railroad suspension bridge, upon the American side, living in poverty and alone.

Nearly all of the bazaars where these mementoes of Niagara were kept for sale, were upon the American side of the Falls. There were, however, three or four buildings upon the Canada side where Indian curiosities and other mementoes of this locality were kept for sale. And in the carriages which were almost constantly crossing to and from the Canada side were passengers, who purchased considerable amounts of these articles. But on being required to pay a duty of thirty-five to fifty per cent. to the United States custom house, they began to realize that they were returning from a foreign country. If the party were in good spirits and the officer had the tact to keep them so while he performed the unpleasant duty of searching their baggage, and requiring them to report all articles purchased, the ladies sometimes smilingly announced that they had "purchased a feather fan to *fan* with; or a small, bark canoe,

'To sail the wide seas over,'

or an Indian baby's moccasin, covered all over with pretty beads; beads white and beads blue, and do you really believe the Tuscarora Indians made it? The man told us so." By this time, or more probably while the other lady was talking, another lady of the party would remind her that they had "also purchased their dinners in Canada!"

CHAPTER II.

Law against bringing Bottles of Liquor from Canada into the States—Women Smugglers—Wit of an Irish Washer-woman caught Smuggling—The Western Drover and his Tobacco, in Three Acts—The Angry Scene—Polite Kindness—Reconciliation.

AMONG those who made short visits into Canada, across the suspension bridge, were sometimes citizens as well as strangers, who were evidently not in the habit of restricting their use of intoxicating drinks to

"A dthrap of the cr'athur ev'ry morn,"

and were accustomed to raise their spirits *up* by turning
spirits *down.* As these persons passed the custom-house
office, sometimes their burlesque reports, *"Nothing aboard,
but Canada whisky,"* were *manifestly* correct!

People residing upon the frontier, knew, generally, that
the United States laws prohibited the importation of
whisky in quantities less than thirty gallons; and other
liquors also in less than wholesale quantities. There
were few strangers, however, who knew that such a law
existed.

A bottle or two of any kind of liquors could be legally
seized, if brought from the Canada side, even if the person offered to pay duty. Although I do not affirm that
I always seized such small quantities; I did sometimes
obey the law to the letter; especially when it appeared
that a quart bottle stowed away under a vest, or in a side
pocket, was more than the man could carry, or an inten-
tional disregard of custom-house laws. I have seized a
toper's bottle of whisky from under the ragged coat of a
little boy, hoping that the father would never send him
on such an errand again.

I recall an instance, too, when I examined a carpet-bag
of a woman in which I found a little food and a bottle
of milk for her children. But something made me suspect that the contents of the satchel, so willingly offered
me to examine, might be a decoy to lead me from suspicion. So I conducted her to the house of the lady examiner, near by. When I returned to my office, the toll
receiver, who had the name of being strict and watchful
in his own business, met me with a hearty laugh, and

volunteered a very confident "*guess*" that I had caught no smuggler *that* time. A by-stander also joined in the same opinion, and added that officers might as well suspect everybody else as that woman!

I then informed them of the fact that the *innocent looking* lady had just been examined by the inspectress, who found concealed among her clothing, a jug of whisky! The duty on whisky at this time was two dollars per gallon; hence people who crossed the bridge several times a day could make it profitable to smuggle even small quantities at a time.

I once tried to talk temperance to a washer-woman whom I detected smuggling whisky in flat bottles, and who was "half seas over," but she insisted that when she had to work so hard a quart of whisky made her stronger!

"Stronger!" said I, "I should think not, you can hardly walk straight now! It makes you weaker!"

"An' faith, now! Is it that ye's sayin'? An' doesn't it make my *breath sthronger?* An' mus'n't ye brathe strong if ye's workin' at all, at all?"

"But it will kill you to drink so much whisky," I replied.

"An' if it does, then I shan't have to kill meself a workin' to get me livin'! Ye see I ain't much valye meself, any way."

"But, madam, it is against the law for any one to bring whisky from Canada in this way, as I've told you before this!"

"An' sure it's not that, now, you'll make me be afther

belavin'! fur hasn't meself the right to bring me own clothing, and whatever is in me own pocket, for me own use, without bein' stopped by a dacent man like yourself, now?"

"Well, madam, I have taken you to the lady examiner and found you smuggling bottles of whisky too many times to overlook it much longer."

"Indade it's your own fault that you have found it! an' it's no counthry *at all*, at all, if we haven't the liberty of our own pockets!"

Where admonition was disregarded a few seizures in such cases was generally an effectual discouragement.

One pleasant morning a drover came across the bridge on foot, carrying a well-filled traveling-bag, and was proceeding to pass the custom-house office without reporting whether his baggage contained dutiable goods, when I informed him, as politely as I could, that it was a rule of the custom house to inspect baggage passing here. He turned with an angry reply:

"What's the use of bothering us every time we come through here, to open our traveling-bags? You know well enough we never have anything but our clothing!"

"I have no doubt, sir," I replied, "that you are as honest as any stranger that passes my office; and though I may believe that no stranger's baggage contains smuggled goods, the government requires me to *know* it by actual inspection."

"Well, I guess!" retorted the angry man, "I rather *guess* my *word* is good, and when I tell you I have nothing dutiable, that's *enough!*"

"I have no reason to doubt your word, sir."

"Then why don't you *take* it, sir?"   .

"Simply because it is my duty not to do so. I see no more reason to pass *your* baggage without *knowing* what is in it than to pass that of other strangers. You will have to open your baggage, sir!"

The enraged drover then set down his traveling-bag, and threw a bunch of keys upon the floor, swearing that if I was so particular as *that* I should open it myself, for *he wouldn't!*"

"Stranger," said I, forcing a smile, "I have plenty of time this morning, but is it extremely polite, sir, for a man of your evident good sense to throw your keys upon the floor and expect me to pick them up, and then waste time to pick out the right key?" The drover seemed scarcely more annoyed than surprised at the manner I assumed; but he replied:

"Well, if you arn't going to examine my traveling-bag I shall take it and go on!"

"My friend," said I, looking him earnestly in the eye, "I have come across a great many kinds of people while here in the custom house, and I can generally manage to do everything pleasantly. And I do not intend to be drawn into a quarrel. Your baggage, however, will be detained here till you pick up your keys and open it!"

"You have no right to bother me about my baggage at all; for all there is in it came from Detroit, and I haven't stopped in Canada nor bought anything there."

To this I said nothing. He hesitated a moment, and then picked up the keys and proceeded to open his

traveling-bag; and, to swear that I was no gentleman for
doubting ·his word; that he would report me as an
unreasonable officer if he could find out where to do so!

By this time he had opened his baggage, and on examining it I found a quantity of tobacco—not so much that
I need to have seized it—and yet enough considering his
disregard of duty in not reporting it, to have justified
me in seizing it.   So I said:

"Stranger, if I were disposed to do so the course you
have taken in neglecting to report this tobacco, would
justify me in seizing it, no matter where you bought it;
but I have so much pity for your ungovernable temper
and your evident ignorance of custom-house laws, that I
shall permit you to go, and I will pass the tobacco just
the same as I might have done had you treated me
politely; and I do not even expect your thanks for doing
you the favor which is in my discretion."

My utter astonishment was completed when, without
seeming to notice what I had said, he asked "*if I didn't
intend to pack his baggage as nicely as I found it?*   Kase,"
said he with an oath and a curse, "you've disarranged it."

The idea of my having disarranged a pair of old pants
and a dirty shirt, etc., which I had found crammed into
a traveling-bag to hide his tobacco, was so ridiculous
that I smiled as I replied:

"No, sir!"

But he seemed to preserve a remarkable *evenness* of
temper as he started off, swearing that I had detained
him when he was in a hurry! and hadn't believed him
like a gentleman, when he had *told* me he wasn't bringing

things out of Canada! and that I had treated him like a thief! and that I ought to be reported to Washington or some place, he wished to God he knew where!

I considered, at the time, that I had lost that battle; it seemed I had not even gained a moral advantage. He had completely driven me from the field of discussion— had abused me before and after I had granted him a favor, and, in all probability, would boast of out-witting me with his Canada tobacco, and exaggerate the quantity in order to make out some charge against me in the neglect of duty as an officer!

I tried to think of some passage in the Scripture, from which I could derive consolation; but memory only upbraided me with the passage in Proverbs, which advises us to "answer a fool according to his folly." And then I regretted that I had not tried some profound explanation like Sambo's, when he explained to a colored individual, why " de moon ware ob more immense importance dan de sun; kase," said he, "de moon gib light in de *night time* when we *need* light, but de sun only in de day time, when *we don't need none!*" For ludicrous sophistry is more potent with some people than fairness and good sense.

But this incident of the drover who had that morning no doubt taken a dose of Canada whisky, has a sequel.

A few months after I had written the account of the above incident, which I wrote soon after it occurred, I got on board a train of cars in company with my wife. The car was being crowded with passengers. Observing two seats near each other, occupied by only one gentleman each, I asked one of the men if he would be so kind as to take a seat with the other gentleman, so that myself and lady could have a seat together. He coolly replied:

"I presume, sir, that you can find a seat in the next car!"

Just at this moment a rough looking man, a half dozen seats in front of us, arose and said to us:

"Here is a seat the gentleman and lady can have, and I'll find another for myself somewhere."

We took the seat, thanked him for his kindness, and he found another. I remarked to my wife that that stranger had a good heart in his jacket, if he did look a little rough externally. The circumstance, however, was soon forgotten, or stowed away in the rubbish of memory, where human foresight sees not, whether it will ever be called up again.

A few weeks passed. I was again in my office. A drover having crossed from the Canada side called at my office door, and reported his traveling-bag for inspection. He proceeded to open it, as if he had passed an office of customs before. After a moment or two, I had a faint impression that I had seen this stranger before. A few words in a friendly way passed between us. At last, as the recognition flashed upon me, I said:

"My friend, are you not the man whose tobacco I passed, about six months ago?" When I made this inquiry I had not the faintest idea that he and I had ever met before or since the tobacco affair. But imagine my surprise when he replied:

"Yes, sir, and I am the man who gave you and your lady a seat in the cars the other day!"

He said this in a manner so friendly of the two incidents, so strangely contrasted, that I cannot describe the effect which it had upon my feelings! I remembered the scene with the drover and his tobacco only as plainly now, as I did the incident of his kindness in the cars. I took him by the hand, and we were immediately friends. And, when at last he left my office, he *did not swear* that he "would report me to some place, he wished to God he knew where!" but he did urge me, if ever I came West, to come and spend a week in his prairie home. With pleasure I assured him that I should be glad to do so.

The victory was won; the manner in which I had treated his hasty and passionate course in our first interview, gave me a friend, when an angry course on my part would have given me an enemy.

After the above incident, I saw more than ever before, the wisdom and beauty of that Scripture injunction, "*charity!*" And that they who can govern themselves best, can after all, govern others most. Forbearance and kindness towards others in the wrong, when we are in the right, is *not* cowardice, but moral bravery and power to reason rightly. It stands above considerations of petty selfishness, and is high philosophy, as well as the truest Christianity.

CHAPTER III.

Appearances often Deceiving—The Beggar's Bundle—The " Intelligent Gentleman " —" A Reliable Source "—A Little Reflection—The Sulphur Springs—Suspension Bridge Tolls—A Midnight Office—The Devil and his Wife.

WHILE in my office one day, there came across the bridge a stranger, whose whole appearance indicated poverty. The pack which he carried looked like poverty's bundle! Such instances had been frequent. I had often permitted them to pass with a slight scrutiny. In this case I saw fit to have the man show me what his burden did really consist of. As I had expected, I found nothing smuggled. The toll receiver smiled as he saw me inspect the bundle of this man, so apparently a pauper; and he also informed me that "of course the man could have nothing dutiable for he had crossed the bridge by begging a free passage!" An intelligent and influential gentleman who happened to be in the ticket office saw me put this poor man to the trouble of showing what was in his bundle—a trouble of *ten seconds*. A few minutes before that he had seen a well-dressed man pass my office with a well-filled satchel, in the same direction, and I had simply looked at him, and allowed him to pass without an inquiry; and yet the latter was an entire stranger, and I knew nothing of the contents of his satchel.

In a few days after this, it was reported by a politician who desired my situation, that I used no judgment in the discharge of my duty as a custom-house officer; and the above circumstances were cited in proof of the above allegation. A friend came and told me that somebody was finding fault about my course as an officer; but he hoped that there was no just occasion for it.

"Anything in particular complained of?" I inquired.

"Something about your examining the bundle of a pauper, last week, and paying no attention to the baggage of well-dressed strangers."

"Any other case talked of?"

"Well, I've heard of your putting some of our influential citizens to the trouble of opening their baggage!"

"How do they tell the beggar story?" I inquired.

My friend related what the "intelligent and reliable gentleman" in the toll office had noticed. I heard him through, and then said: "Major, I'm surpised; I'm perfectly astonished at the account you have given!"

"There!" said my friend, "I told them that I did not believe you were either so indiscreet or so careless in your official duties."

"But wait, Major, you don't understand my surprise! I am astonished only, to find that the 'intelligent and reliable gentleman's' account of what he saw was so accurately told!"

"True? Is it true?"

"Yes, true!"

"Then in the name of common sense can you explain it to your advantage?"

"Easy enough, sir. The well-dressed man, whose traveling-bag I did *not* examine, had not been in Canada at all. I remembered him as having only a little while before gone on the bridge—saw him standing on the bridge to look at the falls and the rapids, and noticed he did not cross into Canada. This part the 'intelligent gentleman' had not seen. Now, as to the pauper. Do you suppose, Major, that I can afford to have smugglers find out that every man can pass me with a bundle, if he be only disguised as a pauper?"

The Major laughed, and changed the subject.

When he left me I could not suppress a few reflections. Was it not possible, after all, that an "intelligent gentleman," perhaps, too, an "influential gentleman," or a "*reliable source*," sitting down a moment to observe other people's business, might see very simple facts which he couldn't see through? And, as a general rule, is it not fair to presume that there are *reasons* for some things if people's conclusions could only get sight of them? while sometimes it is "la! me! why, Mrs. *Jones* heard so, and of *course* Nathaniel was to blame!"

> Well, it's a fact that isn't a wonder,
> That people are liable to blunder;
> And hence the best that any one can do
> Is just to reflect—a moment or two.

I am here reminded of an amusing incident in the school-days of Gerrit Smith, when he once preferred reflection even to explanation.

A few of the students were in a room at a play or game which had been forbidden. Suddenly it became known that the professor was coming. It was doubtful whether the students would have time to escape at one door before the dreaded professor would enter at another. Gerrit hid himself flat upon the floor behind a bench and under a writing-desk. The others barely managed to escape from the room before the old professor entered. But the man of discipline had heard the confusion; and, glancing his eyes around the room, he spied a human form under the desk; when, coolly addressing himself to the object, he inquired: "*Who is that under the desk?*" The individual under the desk, without the slightest change of position, slowly and deliberately answered:

"Gerrit Smith, sir."

"What are you doing *there?*" sternly demanded the professor.

To which interrogatory, Gerrit, with the air of one not wishing to be disturbed, replied:

"*I am reflecting, sir!*"

The professor smiled, and left the room, remarking that "it was *well* if Gerrit had been driven to reflection!"

The duties on all merchandise prevented much intercourse between the inhabitants of the Canadian and American sides of the river. The toll received by the owners of the bridge for foot and carriage passengers, however, in the summer season, averaged over one hundred dollars per day, besides forty-five thousand dollars per year paid by the Great Western Railway Company for their cars passing over the upper story of the bridge. The toll of one hundred dollars a day was principally received from visitors who came to see the falls and the surrounding scenery, taking their pleasure rides in carriages to visit the Canada side and to see and to cross this

14

noted bridge. Not more than one-fifth of the amount of tolls was received from Canadian travel.

The building for the office of customs which I occupied, was so situated that when the toll office and the bridge gates were closed, no footman could pass to or from the bridge except by passing through the customs office. The gates were closed about ten o'clock in the evening, after which there was very little crossing. The watchman of the bridge on the Canada side, John or Michael, collected the tolls from the few passengers which passed during the night. But the customs officer at the American end held the United States keys of the door and the gate, which made it necessary to disturb him before any one could pass at that end of the bridge.

Such was the locality of my office building, situated so close to the roar of Niagara, and at the mouth of so beautiful and wonderful a work of art; and this together with the night scenery and the straggling characters which darted through my office, interrupting my writing or my slumbers, created—shall I say—*occasions of surpassing interest!*

For a number of miles either way, this was the only place of exit from one country to the other, for stragglers, thieves and robbers, as well as belated citizens and strangers.

In my own house, when at home, of course I fastened the doors and windows for night, as everybody does; but what was the use of having such whimsical notions, or being disturbed by such trifling events, in a room on the brink of such a romantic river, where I had no one to defend but myself? What if four or five robbers and house-breakers, with false keys and genuine pistols *should* demand the silver watch I carried? Had I not a perfect *right* in such case, as an officer, to pitch them headlong, all five of them, twenty feet from my office, over the bank, two hundred and fifty feet down into the Niagara rapids, and gaze on them as they were falling into such a river by moonlight? And then had I not a right to go out on the bridge free of toll to wait for another similar edition? or, to compose myself and poetry, under the inspiration of such moonlight scenery, and such events! Or had I not the right to start another slumber upon my office lounge, with the United States keys in my pocket, while the river and its everlasting serenade kept on!

It is a mistake, if any one think he could not learn to be studious or occasionally take an hour's repose, in *such* an office, on *such* a river, with a bridge of such "immense grace," and with so *little* to disturb or make afraid, and so much to make meditations and sleeping time interesting! In an office so full of incidents by day, and where dreams were made of little realities by night, why could not any one stay there occasionally o'nights to study and write, and serve their country, and draw their pay?

Among the specimens of criminal-looking outcasts, which one could hardly fancy might be found in prison or out—or frightened across any frontier—was a pair of human beings, male and female, who came through my office from Canada, two hours after midnight, in the spring of 1867. You could not imagine a bad quality nor any mixture of sin, poverty and ignorance and misfortune which had not, to all appearance, overtaken them, even to the misfortune of the man having found a woman that "matched" him! Whisky had given them the same red eyes, and continued dissipation the same shade of complexion over the same ground-work of tan and exposure. They looked alike, were each of medium size, and evidently had fought alike, and drank alike, for I declare to you, without exaggeration, that the face and eyes of each appeared to be, as nearly as possible, marked *alike* by blows and scratches! Besides all this, there was an expression of face which told me more than I could repeat in words—a look of nothing good and a mixture of everything bad; all of which corresponded with the time and place of their serious flight and their sudden appearance before me. The pair, representing both sexes as they did, suggested some lower order of human beings, or else a return-sample from perdition; for the moment they had passed through my office, I said to myself, with a smile I could not suppress: "There goes the devil and his wife, sure!" They were, evidently, too desirous of escaping from Canada to have any present object but safety to themselves.

CHAPTER IV.

The Preacher's Brandy—Strange Companions—Mr. O'Flinigan—Astonishing Figures—The Unfortunate Widow—Custom-House Laws—Two Puzzling Questions—
When are Household Goods and Tools of Trade free of duty.

"WE have to inspect baggage, here, sir, on account of
customs," said I to a well-dressed man, who walked by
my office evidently with no thought of noticing custom-
house regulations.

" Well," he replied, "I am in something of a hurry;
do you have to require us to open such little things as a
satchel which travelers carry just a change of clothing
in ? "

" Yes, sir, that is the rule here, but we give as little
trouble as possible in doing our duty."

He began opening his satchel, but manifested his hurry
in such a polite and civil way, and asking about the
departure of trains that I felt reluctant to delay him;
but I had lost so much faith in appearances that I preferred positive evidence when convenient. Whether his
hurry was genuine, or simply to give me an opportunity
to be so obliging that I would only examine the top of
his traveling-bag as he opened it, was a question which
appearances did not positively decide. In such a case
the remedy was evident—I must examine a little below
the surface, which I did, and felt a large package half
filling the satchel. " What is this?" said I.

" Why, you don't charge duty on just one book—a
Bible—even if it is a large, nice book, do you?"

"But what is this, in these two bottles below the Bible, sir?"

"O, yes; I forgot to report them. My family are a little out of health; and I was told that the Canada brandy is a purer article than I could find upon our side of the river. But if there be any duty to pay on that or the book either, of course I'm willing to pay it."

"As to the brandy, sir, it is against the law to bring it into the country, even if you did report it, except you had a full case to pay duty on."

"Possible, sir? I did not know it."

"Then it seems a little queer that you did not report these odd companions—a new Bible and two bottles of brandy—before I reached the stage which I have in searching your baggage."

"Really, Mr. Officer, I was not aware of the importance of my doing so. I did not know that *nations* took notice of such small matters. Had I known it, I certainly would have been more mindful."

"We are expected to be very particular at this point, sir, I admit; but, from your manner, stranger, I presume you intended nothing wrong; yet, to an officer of customs here, where deception is so variously attempted, you will see that innocent circumstances sometimes appear very suspicious, and sometimes, as in this case, a little mixed. This Bible, for instance—an expensive one, too—*indicates* that you are a man of good intentions — perhaps a preacher, and yet two bottles of brandy, and your neglecting to report, do tend to confuse the question! and, besides, very good people on the frontier here, *will* smuggle 'for their own use,' or some other excuse."

"Mr. Officer, this seems stranger than it really is. I am a clergyman, it is true, but other men buy Bibles also. And, as for the brandy, why, we are all liable to sickness!"

And now for the particular information of a certain government officer who used to call around as a kind of detective to watch other officers, and local matters which he did not, and of course could not understand, as well as officers living in the locality, and consequently who used to criticise the discretionary little acts which officers did or did not do, I will here most positively state that *perhaps* I passed that new Bible and the bottles! At any rate the preacher departed in due time for the cars and in good humor.

I had scarcely taken a seat at my writing-desk when a man whom I barely recognized as a resident of the town approached me with that peculiar privilege which some men take. If you were busy with accounts they would approach you, and leaning one hand upon your shoulder and the other upon your desk, would go into a low, confidential whisper, as if *your* time was worthless and their business a friendship to eat you up; and, as if you certainly must know them because they had seen you before. If you fail to recognize them they will tell you who they are, where they saw you, and proceed to make your acquaintance, by telling that which has no interest to any one but themselves, and when you finally find out the single question they wanted to ask, you have heard also a history of their grandmother!

Well, the instant this man approached me as aforesaid,

one hand on my shoulder, the other on my desk, he
placed his face so near my own that his disagreeable
breath forced me to move backward, first simply moving
my head; but this he did not notice, and continued to
whisper something about "hams and bacon and a little
whisky for his own use," when I made another retreating
move of my face, which he seemed to take as another
attitude for listening; and his disagreeable tobacco breath
still reached my olfactories. By the time he had reached
the subject of duties, his breath, a slight mixture of
whisky with a strong scent of tobacco, compelled me to
make a third retreat by hitching my *chair* backward.
Finally I was driven to beg his pardon for being obliged
to tell him to stand back like a gentleman and tell me
what he wanted. My olfactories were too good and my
politeness too little to endure longer such a mixture of
whisky, tobacco and impudence.

The hints of my retreating movements had made no
impression on him; and the severity of my last rebuke
was only sufficient to make him stand up at a proper
distance for conversation. He neither apologized nor
took offense. He did seem a little "confused," but none
too much "set back!"

He continued to talk of smoked hams and bacon—
how he had been "wondering" for some time if he
hadn't better come down and see me, and see if he
couldn't make some "*arrangement*" so I would not charge
him so much duty; and to see what I knew about the
prices in Canada, and if I didn't think it would pay better
than to buy hams at the groceries on our side of the
river, etc., etc.

"Is it the *duty* on hams and bacon you wish me to inform you about, sir?"

"Yes, sir, that is it, exactly! I thought, your honor, if I knew the duties you would ax me I could tell if it would be cheaper for me to buy them on the other side."

And without waiting for me to tell him the duties, he branched off again about the grocerymen here, that "wouldn't trust a man till Saturday night! an' it's niver a cint that Pat O'Flinigan ever chated thim yet, ather," said he.

"Mr. O'Flinigan, if you are ready to hear it, sir, the duty on smoked ham and bacon is two cents per pound, and all duties over five dollars are to be paid in gold; if under five, they may be paid in silver."

"Yes, I see," said Mr. O'Flinigan, reflectively, "but may be I shall not buy any. I thought I'd ax you to see about it. Couldn't you let me bring over a small keg of whisky and a few hams without any duty? Come, now, and I can give you a dollar for your own pocket!"

"I guess you don't know me, Mr. O'Flinigan."

"O, indade I do, Mr. Officer, and I'm the man that intends to vote for you."

"Mr. O'Flinigan, I cannot give you any opportunity to smuggle!"

"O, well, now, niver mind a little joking! Of course you know I wouldn't chate the governmint out of a cint. An' I wouldn't smuggle the laste of anything *without your permission!* But I tuk a thought that may be you would think it an act of charity to a poor man like meself to get over a small load of sich things for meself

14*

and a few others; an' I always tuk you to be a charitable man, Mr. Officer, indade I did. What do you *say*
now? It's just as I tell you; everything is too dear on
this side of the river, an' I've got a large family to
support."

"I'm sorry for your misfortunes, Mr. O'Flinigan, but I
cannot aid you in breaking the laws!"

"But it's not for meself I'd ask it; an' what's a poor
man to do in this counthry if he can't get enough for his
family to ate?"

"Mr. O'Flinigan, will you take it kindly if I will tell
you of a better speculation than for you to smuggle?
and tell how you have lost a comfortable house and lot,
and can get it back again?"

"I'm sure you can't tell me *that*, now, for I niver had
a house and lot to lose!"

"Well, sir, how much a day do you waste for grog
and tobacco? Be honest now and we'll figure up."

"O, it's *that* you mane! Of course, now, your honor,
I wouldn't be irriverant, but I wish ye'd let the timperance question alone, and jest do me the favor I'm askin',
if ye plase! Indade it's jokin' to talk about the thrifle
I've iver spint for whisky, or tobacco, ather! An' ye
sees I've had the good on't for the thrifle its cost me."

"Mr. O'Flinigan, you must be about fifty, and you
would be astonished should I show that you have spent
two thousand dollars that way."

"Indade I should, for I niver had the half of that in
all me life!"

"Well, now, Mr. O'Flinigan, has it cost you three cents
a day since you were twenty years of age, for tobacco?"

"May be it has, now, that little!"

"That, sir, is just $10.95 a year, $109.05 for ten years, and $327.15 for thirty years."

"Indade, now, that is more than I thought it was for tobacco—it *is*, now."

"But, wait, Mr. O'Flinigan; we have not reckoned the yearly interest on what you have spent, which, at seven per cent. for thirty years, would make $327 amount to a little over $1200 for your tobacco, and if you have also spent on an average three cents a day for whisky, that is $1200 more, and altogether $2400!"

"Faith, now, an' its 'asier to pr'ache than to practice! an' even if your figures are right, it's too late to save it *now!* I always riveranced Father Mathew an' the timperance question, but it's not asy to foller the best o' pr'achin'."

"If you once get rid of the habits you will find it easier than being a slave to them! besides the comforts saved to yourself and family!"

"Indade, now, Mr. Officer, you are a strange man for a *politician*, to talk as if ye niver take a '*social* glass,' nor *trate the friends that vote ye into office!*"

Here my conversation with Mr. O'Flinigan was interrupted by other duties. A woman called to inquire if she could move with her household goods into the States from Canada without being required to pay duty.

I informed her that the law allowed household goods and tools of trade to be brought into the country free of duty, if they had been in use one year, and were not intended for sale.

"Nearly everything we had," said she, "has been burned up, as well as the house we lived in; and, in trying to save our only child from the flames, my poor husband lost his life. And I am trying to get back home. It is not quite a year since we bought these household goods in Canada. Will I have to pay duty if it is not quite a year?"

"Madam, what is the value of the goods you wish to bring?"

"Not more than fifty dollars' worth. That is all there was saved from the fire, except the carpenter's tools my husband worked with. I have no money to pay duty on goods nor on the tools."

Both questions puzzled me. The law, strictly to the letter, required that duty should be paid on the household goods, because they had not been in use *one year;* and, yet it seemed I ought to take a liberal view of this case, under the circumstances. Then as to the "tools of trade" which the law allowed a person to bring into the country "for use" and "not for sale," what was I to say about that? It was not likely that a *woman* was bringing *carpenter's* tools into the country with the intention of using them, but more likely with the intention of disposing of them at some future favorable opportunity. And yet, ought I to charge duty upon the effects of this poor, unfortunate woman, when I could have passed the same "tools of trade" *free of duty for her husband,* in case he had lived to have moved here with her?

Well, reader, what would you have decided on these points? If you could have construed the law, or "the spirit of the law" in favor of such poverty, misfortune and grief, you would have done so. Perhaps *I* did. Perhaps I believed that my superiors in office were sensible enough not to censure my course in any case till they gave me opportunity to show all the particulars.

CHAPTER V.

Excursion Parties crossing the Bridge — Amusing Incidents — More Information about Custom-house matters—Qualities requisite for an Officer—How to please the Public and still inspect their Baggage—The Stove-pipe Hat—The man who said "by Mighty"—Emigrants crossing the Bridge—Other Incidents.

EVERY few days there crossed this frontier a company of hardy-looking foreigners, bound for the Western lands of the United States. Most of them crossed the bridge in the cars, but it happened very often that as many as twenty-five to fifty families, with all the hand-baggage of bundles, babies and boxes which they could carry, passed on foot, having gotten off the cars to see the place, and to buy bread, supplies of which were kept for sale by Germans of the village. I noticed that these foreigners looked economical, but never ragged or shiftless. They were dressed comfortably well, but plain; the women all seemed to despise the folly of fashion's extravagance. In warm weather, unlike American women, they seemed to have no troublesome fears about "tanning," no anxiety about complexion. Many were entirely bareheaded; and the twenty-five cent head-fixtures which some of them wore it was impossible for even a Yankee to invent or discover a reason for. Whenever these cheap head fixtures, however, were thick enough to warrant the conclusion, I took my Yankee privilege of "guessing" that their use was a protection against burdens which they might find it convenient to carry upon their heads after the fashion of the Swiss; and then I conjectured that the light fixtures were a mere style which had descended from the useful to the unornamental and useless. An American lady frequently wears what is equally useless and just as unbecoming, but takes good care to have it cost a little extravagantly, so that her servant girl cannot afford the same.

Although these hardy German women seemed able to endure hardships and inconveniences, I saw nothing in their costumes of such useless bulk as a lady's waterfall of 1866. Either from pride or some other reason, they were traveling without that mysterious material bound to the back of their heads! Although emigrants who have traveled three thousand miles are not always noted for their tidy appearance, yet I never saw one of these women wearing a street dress of such length as to drag the dust around her feet. It seemed as if the dress of a German woman was made to wear. They seemed also to have adopted the principle of "woman's rights." They acted like men; took the right to carry their own baggage like the men, and so far as I could observe, they seemed to expect and receive no more attention or favors from the men than the men bestowed upon each other. It was a singular fact that of the numerous crowds of emigrants crossing this bridge and pressing their way Westward, nearly all were Germans.

But here now is an exciting day at Niagara Falls. An excursion party of hundreds of Canadians have arrived, and another of Americans. They have just left the cars and are crossing the bridge on foot in long, crowded lines. And in order to view the bridge, the falls and the rapids to advantage, they pass one way upon the lower floor and return on the upper floor, on either side of the rail-road track, and ascend or descend by the winding stairs at either end of the bridge.

As these crowds leave the bridge they are talkative, but as they approach it they are silent with wonder and admiration. If the excursion is an intelligent picnic party, it is safe to declare that while they first gaze on the scene before them none are thinking of sponge-cake or pickles and sandwiches. But here they are coming from Canada, and I must inspect their baggage. Stop a moment. You are laughing at my inconsistency, and perhaps you are saying, *verily* the author of these remin-iscences *must* be writing under difficulties to talk about inspecting the luggage of a picnic party!

But, dear critic, I assure you upon my honor, that of all the baggage from trunk to bandbox or basket that passed my office, that of a picnic party was the most delicious for inspection. And by the proper tact at turning my duty into a humorous examination, I found offense was seldom taken; and often I was invited to know by actual inspection whether the contents would bear the praises I had bestowed upon their delicious

appearance. For of course I always lavished on them
the usual compliment that the fruit, which I suspected
had grown in their own orchards, or the frosted cake
made in their own kitchens, was the *"nicest I ever saw."*
I confess I met with poor success in convincing some
people crossing with the picnickers of my authority for,
or the propriety of inspecting the contents of huge baskets or hand-satchels, when *they* knew so well that their
luggage contained only fruit, and frosted cake. But generally I succeeded in convincing the most obtuse individual that no customs officer with ordinary human eyes
by only looking on the outside of an opake bundle, basket or traveling-bag, could see the contents of the same;
and if a custom-house officer was bound to prevent smuggling by inspecting *any* baggage, it was his duty to prevent any smuggler from taking such an opportunity to
bring a huge basket full of kid gloves into the United
States, instead of sandwiches. A silk dress pattern that
might be carried in a satchel would have cost at that
time (1866) fifty dollars in gold, and was liable to a duty
of sixty per cent.; hence it was not too small a matter
to save thirty dollars in gold for the government, whose
war to put down the rebellion had left our country in
debt twenty-five hundred millions of dollars!

But there were times when there was no time to reply
to the angry comments of now and then a person in a
crowd of footmen and carriages who had never before
passed a custom-house office. At such a time and with
those who neither understood nor admired the inquisitive
duty of a customs officer. the only remedy to prevent

contention and yet dispatch business, was to assume the authority of an officer in a manner that implied duty and business! but discriminating, of course, according to the apparent intelligence of the person addressed, that he might not mistake duty and dispatch to go away and report that the officer's manner was worse than his duty.

The few frontier residents who crossed this bridge in carriages, generally intended to return the same day; sometimes not until two or three days; and it would have been a very great inconvenience to the people living near the line of the two countries if the officers of customs for both countries were not permitted to use their discretion in allowing people to drive into the country without payment of duty for a few hours or longer, on a visit, or on business, in cases where the officer had reason to believe the parties were honest and would return their conveyances. This to some extent was done; in which cases the name and a description of the horses and vehicles were recorded in a book kept for such purposes by the officer, and the parties were required to return and report the same at some specified time. They were informed that if they did not report within the required time that their conveyance would be liable to seizure.

In cases where the officer did not feel satisfied to trust persons, as in the case of entire strangers, who could give no satisfactory references, they were sometimes permitted to deposit the amount of duties as security, and on their returning the dutiable property to Canada the money was refunded. Persons driving through Canada, from "the States," especially, had to make this arrangement with the Canadian custom-house officers. They drew back the amount left as security, at the port where they went out of Canada. But all this would not clear them from other difficulties unless before entering Canada they had taken an "export certificate" of their dutiable property from the United States custom house, to show to the United States officer at the port where they again entered the States.

Well, here comes a horse and buggy from the Canada side. There are two persons in the old, open buggy. One is a surly, thin-visaged, cross-looking old gentleman; his face is red, and with other indications, it is evident he has a habit of drinking too much whisky; his hat belongs to the stove-pipe style, and was probably once new. If this should become a matter of any importance to know in evidence, I have no doubt but our old custom-house detective or the chief of the Niagara police, could determine the probable time when he purchased it by a calculation based on facts and supposition. As near as I can myself make out the date, without making a drawing of the hat and consulting a professional hatter, I should say the style was one in vogue seven years prior to the time now under consideration, and that the miserly appearing old man, looking his red eyes from under its brim, had bought it one year out of date that he might be able to spend the amount saved thereby in whisky. The width of his coat collar indicates also that it was about that time that he treated himself to a new suit of clothes; but since that time he had probably treated himself to other "treats" which he much preferred, and of a kind suggested by his strawberry nose. His whiskers are so gray that they are almost white, except where some late stains of tobacco-juice have asserted claims over other hair dyes for superior hue and neatness! His shirt-collar, though not of the most approved pattern, is clean and well ironed, as if the neat, plain, care-worn woman by his side, frail as she is, is the faithful wife, *struggling to keep alive the last spark of her husband's self-respect.*

He is evidently sober now, but it is more evident that he prefers to be otherwise. He is restless, disagreeable and unreasonable, and all this and more you read at a glance as he stops and hands his ticket for crossing the bridge to the gate-keeper, and swears at the weather for its prospect of rain.

There is a crowd of ladies and gentlemen waiting for him to pass the toll office. And as he is a stranger, I am waiting his report to the customs office. His wife, in a low whisper, seems to have gently attempted to check him from swearing "before all these people," and then in a savage undertone I hear him *curse her!* and the *crowd,* too!

But now he is starting up his horse with another curse and a blow from his cudgel. And it is time for me to inquire *if he wishes to make any report to the custom house,* for he evidently has no intention of making any report. But it is in this way I prefer to call this crabbed, old man's attention. This will only seem to suggest that as he has fully passed my office door he is probably mistaking *where* to make his intended report. Of course a man of his morbid sensitiveness, which, I have already discovered, will not well bear to have me speak in any manner which he can construe as implying ignorance of custom-house rules! In fact, such men don't like the use of *any* terms that can possibly remind them of any of their numerous faults.

So I said (for while in my office room I was in easy talking distance,) "here, sir, is where you report to the custom house."

He halted, as if half-surprised, and in a coarse, angry voice replied:

"Well, what of it, if it is? *I* don't have to make any report."

"You are a stranger to me, sir, but I suppose your horse and wagon belongs on the Canada side?"

"Of course it does," he replied, "and what odds does that make, when I'm only coming over here on a visit, and am going to take it back again when I get ready! Or, do you take me for a cussed *smuggler?*"

"My friend," said I, "I suppose you must be aware that I ought not to allow *entire strangers* to pass the customs office with dutiable property, without knowing who they are, and when the property is to be returned to Canada."

"Well, sir, my *word* is all you need!"

"But, perhaps," said I, "you can refer me to some person here who knows you."

"I don't ask anybody to back my word, sir—*not no man, sir!*"

"Are you going to return to Canada to-day?"

"Well, *by mighty!* you custom-house officers are getting cussed particular over here in the States. But I know what your duties are as well as you!"

"Then, of course, my dear sir, you will give me some reference, or state where you wish to go, or when you wish to return this horse and buggy to Canada."

"Well, by mighty! I've lived within ten miles of this frontier for years, and the United States is getting cussed impudent if we can't come over here without all this fuss!"

Then while he went on to swear about things in general, his wife told me where they were going; that they were only intending to call an hour or two on a friend, and then go back. "It will be all right," said she, mildly.

"Yes, it's all right, of course," chimed in the old grumbler, "but it's *cussed* impudent to bother an old man like me! Does he think I'm a smuggler?"

"Never mind, husband, the man must do his duty."

"Well, what in *cuss* has that got to do with *me?* I'm no *smuggler.* I wouldn't even *sell* as good a horse as this is, to any such cussed country! for none o' their abolition greenbacks. Of *course* I wouldn't."

On the word of his lady I decided to pass them; and addressing her I said:

"Madam, if you are only going to see Mr. A——B——, at the —— hotel, and are to return so soon, I will register this gentleman's name, if you please, and you will please report when you return."

"What is the use," said the voice from under the stovepipe hat, "of such cussed foolishness as *that?*"

"And the box, there," said I, "in your buggy, it is my duty to inspect that."

"There, by mighty!" exclaimed the mouth under the strawberry nose as the stove-pipe hat magnified an angry shake of the old man's head, "do you want to examine a box of horse-feed because there is two or three dozen eggs in it?"

"Why, husband, do let the man look into the box," said his wife, removing the cover, "how can the officer know what may be in boxes without a chance to see inside of them?"

Then, speaking to me, she said:

"We know we've no right to smuggle, but we thought custom houses don't notice two or three shillings' worth of anything, so I put into this box just three dozen eggs for a present. That's all right, isn't it?"

"Say, Mr. Officer," interrupted the old man, "are you going to let us pass or not? or, are you going to keep us here a whole cussed _hour_, by mighty!"

"I beg your pardon, sir, but is it I, or you, who are causing so many unnecessary words?"

"It's you, sir, by being so cussed particular. _I_ know what your duty is. You've no business to inspect things and bother people this way, when you know they are not smugglers."

"Stranger," said I, with forced calmness, "you are an older man than myself, but allow me to inquire what business you follow?"

"Me? I've kept tavern thirty years within ten miles of here, and you've no business to question me as if I were a smuggler."

"Do you trust your liquor to every stranger who swears he knows your business better than you know it yourself? and would such course recommend him to *your* favor?"

"Not by a mighty sight!"

"Why, then, should your course recommend you to my favor? But you may pass and return to-day, sir. What is your name?"

"Smith, sir, Smith!"

"Any other name besides Smith, sir?"

"Yes, sir, John Smith—John Smith's my name, sir!"

So I registered John Smith, at last, realizing that that name meant almost anybody, but thought I could safely rely on *his description!*

Toward night John Smith, the aforesaid, of the stove-pipe hat and strawberry nose, tavern keeper, went back with same horse and buggy. John Smith nearer the point of being intoxicated, but better natured; from which it would appear that being drunk was his most normal habit!

Let us hope that John Smith finally reformed, and that whatever was unseemly in his manner, even so far as recorded here, will lead some reader to consider his own doings or his own sayings. Let us hope, too, that life among all classes will become at last so correct that no rough things need be pictured to lead any to avoid in themselves what they criticise in others.